HIT LIST

Maggie Black Thriller #2

JACK MCSPORRAN

inked entertainment

ISBN: 978-1-912382-12-5

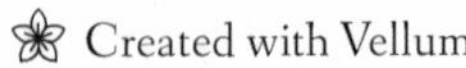

Series Guide

The main Maggie Black Series consists of full-length novels featuring secret agent Maggie Black.

The Maggie Black Case Files is a prequel series of self-contained missions which Maggie completed prior to the events of the main Maggie Black Series.

Both series can be read before, after, or in conjunction with the other.

Maggie Black Case Files

Book 1: Vendetta

Book 2: The Witness

Book 3: The Defector

Maggie Black Series

Book 1: Kill Order

Book 2: Hit List

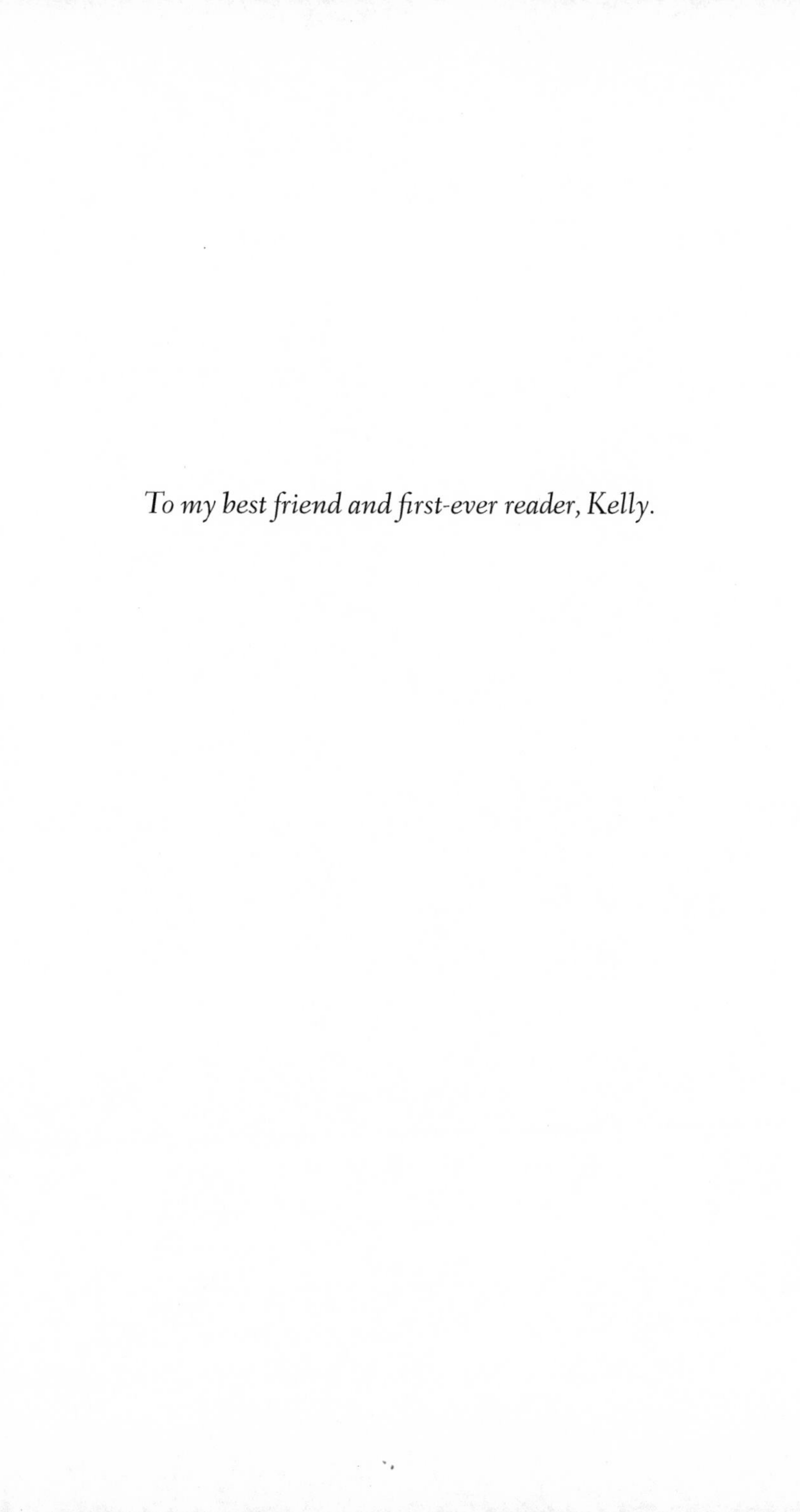

To my best friend and first-ever reader, Kelly.

Chapter 1

Beijing, China
9 July

Secret Agent Jim Hunter was homesick.

He'd been in Beijing for over a week now and was glad his mission there would soon come to an end. Hit jobs were easier. In and out. Leave as soon as the target was dead, and head back home to Susan and the kids.

It was Becca's birthday soon, and he made a mental note to hunt the airport stores before his flight for something she might like. John was more straightforward, being only eight. Teenage girls were a whole different experience, and one Jim often stumbled through with badly timed dad jokes and dodging the odd, unexpected meltdown over some trivial thing or other.

Becca was a good girl all the same. Almost a young woman now, though never in his eyes. No matter how old she got or where her life took her, she'd always be his little princess.

One thing Becca would not be getting for her birthday was a new phone. Not because it was too expensive, or the fact she'd just gotten one less than a year before, the model already out of date, or so he was told. No, she wasn't getting one for her own safety.

It was the same reason he found himself in Beijing, so many miles from the comfort of home. He longed for the frantic mornings where everyone rushed to get ready for work and school, munching on the toast and jam he always made sure they ate before leaving. Longed for the movie nights they enjoyed each Friday, snuggling on the couch and eating popcorn.

This was his last factory visit today, and he'd seen more than enough over the last week to seal the deal on the case against Mark Islington.

"Mr. Rundell?" asked a pock-faced man waiting outside for him, yawning under the rising sun.

"Please, call me Andrew," Jim replied, shaking the local's hand and bowing. "It's nice to meet you, Fu Peng."

Andrew Rundell was one of many names Jim had adopted during his time at the Unit. Sometimes it was difficult to keep track of them, each cover profile blending into the next. Thankfully, deep work with aliases wasn't a common exercise for him, other than using his fake passports during his fleeting visits around the world. As one of the Unit's go-to cleaners, most of his work was done behind a sniper rifle or involved sneaking up unannounced to quickly euthanize whomever his employers dictated. A snap of the neck. A slit of the throat. Easy, effective, and efficient.

In this case, he'd been sent on the undercover mission due to another tool in his skill set. Being one of the few agents fluent in a host of East Asian languages, he was sent to China's capital to gather intelligence.

Jim, a.k.a. Andrew, flashed his security ID pass.

"Where is Mr. Xiao?" Peng asked, checking over Jim's shoulder like he expected him to round the corner any moment.

"He couldn't make it, unfortunately. Took ill last night and hasn't been able to leave his hotel room since."

The extra-strength powdered laxative Jim mixed into the broth of Mr. Xiao's soup during dinner the night before had done the trick and left his assigned escort incapacitated. Xiao had a habit of sneaking up behind him, and Jim wanted him out of the way for his last day of snooping around Mark Islington's factories.

"He's not coming?" Peng asked, scratching his head and looking back at the factory doors.

"It's just me today. For the inspection."

Peng froze. "Mr. Xiao never mentioned anything about an inspection."

"That's because he didn't want you to know," Jim replied in fluent Mandarin.

While he spoke Pekingese, the prestige dialect of Beijing, Peng, like most of the factory workers, had been brought in from small villages far beyond the city. The further into the sticks you traveled, the cheaper labor you'd find. Not that any of the locals Islington employed had it much better, but the villagers were more desperate and less streetwise than their city folk counterparts.

"Shall we?" Jim asked, walking past Peng and letting himself in. Peng may be in charge of this particular factory, one of many Islington owned in Beijing and the surrounding areas, but so far as the Unit could gather, no Brits had ventured out to them since Islington first opened the doors, relying on less than legitimate Chinese business partners to keep things in order. The fact Andrew Rundell was here did not bode well for Peng, or anyone else.

Or so they'd think.

Peng mopped a layer of sweat forming across his top lip that had little to do with the sauna-like humidity. The possibility of failing this supposed surprise inspection would be enough to distract the man while Jim collected the final pieces of evidence required to put Mark Islington's business ventures to a stop and, hopefully, the man himself behind bars.

Given the sweltering heat outside, Jim didn't think it was possible to get any hotter, but an intense wave of stuffy, human-stewed air swept over him when he opened the rusted metal door. Sweat and oil overpowered his senses, and Jim shrugged off his linen suit jacket, his only reason for wearing it to instill an official air about himself.

"What is it you're inspecting? If you don't mind me asking?" Peng hurriedly added.

In truth, it was the standards, or lack thereof, of Mark Islington's manufacturing company. In the last six months, four Brits had died due to his faulty products, which he had made in China and exported around the world. The batteries inside certain brands of mobile phones were the culprits of the fires that had sparked in the victims' houses, malfunctioning when plugged in to charge. Being burned alive was some way to go, and Jim was glad to help in taking down Islington, who refused to accept fault and continued producing the dangerous and defective goods.

"Overall production," Jim replied instead. Production and costs would be all Islington cared about, and any mention of standards would likely raise suspicion. From the exposed pipes and electrical wires in the uncovered ceiling, to the leaking taps in the corner that sat near huge production line machines, Jim doubted the words *health and safety* had ever been muttered in any of Islington's factories. Every one he'd visited before this had been the same, and he was unsurprised to learn one of them had caught fire and burned to the ground with some of the workers trapped inside.

"We've never come up short on a quota, and all our orders and shipments go out on time."

"Mr. Islington thinks you're capable of doing more. It's my job to discern if that is indeed the case. Now, please show me around."

Peng complied, keeping his opinions about an increased workload to himself. From the pale, drawn expressions on the workers' faces they passed on the shop floor, everyone was pushed to the brink already. Jim even had to step over some hastily made beds shoved in nooks and crannies behind machinery and under tables. Unlike in Britain, work-life balance was not a concern for management and the very notion of an HR department appeared unthinkable.

Like he had done in all the others, Jim made a show of pressuring Peng with a slew of rapid questions as he typed away on his phone. He even pretended to take a couple of calls along the way as he inspected the damp, rat-infested stock room and gave the excuse of a cafeteria a wide berth. The smell alone was informative enough.

Along the way, Jim kept his phone recording the audio while snapping a deluge of photos to deliver to the Unit when he got back to his hotel room. Leon Frost, his new boss after the debacle with Bishop, would be pleased with his work. He'd collated enough evidence to ensure not even Mark Islington's best and most expensive lawyers could defend him in court.

Peng never noticed, too busy stumbling over the answers to his questions and wringing his hands each time Jim stopped to pretend to inspect something or to snap a quick photograph under the man's nose.

After thirty minutes of procuring photos and recording Peng's incriminating answers to his many questions about the factory, the workers, and how things were managed, Jim was just about satisfied with the inspection.

"What's through there?" he asked, spotting a door down a narrow corridor.

Peng instantly startled and almost jumped on the spot. "Nothing. It's just a back office. That's all. Nothing to concern yourself over."

"Is that so?" Jim asked, stepping toward it.

"Wait," Peng cried, catching up with him. "Don't go in there."

Ignoring Peng, Jim ventured down the hallway and turned the door handle, stepping inside before Peng tried more than words to stop him. Whatever lay inside, Jim was willing to bet it was something he should know about.

"Ah," said Jim, taking stock of the room as the door slammed behind him and Peng sauntered off back down the hall. Two armed men stepped in front of the door he'd just entered through and shoved him in front of the man waiting behind a large desk.

It was indeed just an office, as Peng had said. It was who sat inside that was the problem.

"Jim Hunter," Mark Islington said, motioning to the empty seat in front of his desk. "Sit down, please."

It seemed Peng's nerves hadn't come from his lies about the inspection. It was over getting Jim to this point without giving Islington's plan away.

Touché. Perhaps Peng would get a bonus for pulling it off. Or at least avoid the beating he would have received had he failed.

Jim scanned the room for an alternative exit, the two brutes by the door too risky to try to break through given their pistols aimed at his head.

"I think it only fair I know your name if you know mine," Islington said when Jim didn't try to run past his men or drop to his knees to beg forgiveness. His accent spoke of old money and an Oxford education, surprisingly not too far off Jim's background. Though, he was a Cambridge man through and through.

Jim sat down, not showing the slightest sign of fear, but it was most definitely there as he noted the lack of escape routes. Not even a window.

Islington appeared just like the pictures Jim had been supplied with, as if he'd just walked off a yacht on the Jamaican coast and sauntered into his seat. His thinning hair was slicked back with too much product, his tan not altogether genuine, just like his porcelain teeth that winked at Jim through smiling lips.

"Nothing to say?" he probed.

"What were you expecting?" Jim asked, turning over every option in his mind. He hadn't come armed, worried about being searched before being allowed entry to the factory—an omission he was sincerely regretting now.

"Oh, I don't know. I would have at least liked you to appear shocked at the mention of your true name."

"Sorry to disappoint," Jim quipped. He would need to apprehend a weapon from one of them. Maybe get around Islington before his men had time to react and hold him hostage to garner safe passage out of the factory. Even as he reviewed it in his head, Jim knew it was a long shot.

He shifted his weight on the seat, ready to pounce at an opportune moment.

"Who do you work for?" Islington demanded.

Jim cocked his head and leaned forward, resulting in the movement of the men behind him, their feet creaking on the bare floorboards. "Now, that is one conversation we are not going to have." Giving up the Unit wasn't an option. Never had been and never would be.

Gripping the armrests of the rickety chair, Jim tensed on the balls of his feet and prepared to attack first. The element of surprise would be his best bet.

"Very well, then," Islington said, appearing almost pleased with Jim's refusal.

Before Jim had time to get up from his chair, Islington revealed a gun of his own and pulled the trigger.

The last thing Jim Hunter thought of was his family, of Susan, Becca, and young John, as the blast of a single gunshot rattled through the room and a bullet buried itself between his eyes.

Chapter 2

Alicante, Spain
10 July

Ex-secret agent Maggie Black sprawled out on the lounger with a contented sigh. The scorching sun hung directly above the penthouse apartment she'd been staying in for the last week, the sloshing of waves below the perfect soundtrack to her rest and relaxation.

The private top floor of the apartment was a little slice of paradise, high up and secluded from the busy stretch of coastline below. An outdoor seating area took up one side, surrounded by lush plants and flowers where Maggie had curled up on the comfy couches and devoured five books. It had been a while since she'd been afforded such luxury. Working for the Unit didn't leave much time for reading anything other than classified files.

Her phone buzzed, and Maggie reached to answer.

"Chaírete," said a familiar Scottish voice in her ear.

"It's 'hola' now. I came to Spain." Greece had been wonderful, but Maggie wasn't used to spending so much time in one place. Old habits die hard, and after two weeks in Santorini, she began to grow uncomfortable.

"Madrid again?" Ashton asked.

Maggie shuddered. "No, I headed south this time. Alicante." After what happened a little over a month ago, Madrid didn't hold the happiest memories.

"Nice," Ashton said. "I'm supposed to go and see my parents, but it's bloody freezing up in the Highlands right now. Want me to come visit you instead?"

"I'm not in the mood for clubbing." Maggie got up from her lounger and padded across the warm wooden floor to the balcony. She leaned on the railing and looked out at the glittering ocean. The water was a brilliant aqua blue, the sand of the beach almost white and dotted with people who seemed no bigger than her thumbnail from this high up.

"That's fine," Ashton said. "We can just chill by a pool and get drunk on sangria."

"Now that I can get on board with." Maggie turned away from the picturesque view and walked around her little haven.

She dipped her toe into the swimming pool, which filled up most of the outdoor space. The sun had warmed the water to the perfect temperature, and she sat along the edge and submerged her legs.

"How did you get on at the doctor?"

"A clean bill of health," said her best friend.

"Liar." Maggie knew from experience a broken rib took at least six weeks to heal, and Ashton had multiple fractures to deal with.

"Well, the prescription the doc gave me makes it feel that way. Have you heard from Leon?"

"No." Maggie hadn't spoken to him since Bishop's funeral. He understood her reasons for needing to get away from it all for a while and be by herself. After being framed for murder by her boss and leaving the Unit, she needed space to think and recharge.

Any discussion of her and Leon's relationship, if there even was a chance of a relationship at all, could wait until she got back.

"I tried calling him yesterday," Ashton said, "but it went straight to voicemail."

Maggie leaned back, the heat relaxing her muscles as it washed over her sun-kissed skin. "He'll be busy with his new job."

With Bishop dead and the covert intelligence agency in disarray, it only made sense to promote Leon to fill the vacant position of chief.

"Think the new boss man will want to spend some

time in the sun?" Ashton's tone was meddlesome, his stance on Leon having done a complete turnaround since their reunion—a reunion made necessary so they could help Maggie clear her name.

Maggie sighed and stared at her feet in the water. "I don't know, Ash. Things are complicated."

"They always are with you two. Has it settled in yet? Being a free agent," he asked, knowing she wanted to change the subject.

"It doesn't feel real," Maggie admitted. "I keep expecting the phone to ring with an assignment."

Having been with the Unit since she was sixteen, trained from a teenager to live a dangerous life of espionage, it was taking a while to come to terms with no longer being an agent. It was all she'd known for twelve years, and now she wasn't quite sure what to do with herself.

Ashton laughed. "You'll get used to it. Life is far more fun on this side of the Unit. Believe me."

A sound came from behind her and made Maggie's ears prick. A creak of wood.

Footsteps, she was sure. At least two sets, both trying to be silent in their ascent, coming up the stairs from the living space below.

Maggie pulled her legs up from the pool and got to her feet. "I've got to go."

"Everything okay?" Ashton asked, hearing the switch in her voice.

"Yeah, just some unexpected visitors," Maggie said, adding a third person to her tally. She grabbed her towel and dried off so as not to leave a trail of water. "I'll call you later."

"*Adiós, amigo.*"

Ashton hung up, and as the approaching footsteps grew louder, Maggie ducked behind the wall of the outdoor shower. Her hand instinctively reached for her gun, but it wasn't there. She wore a bikini and sunscreen as opposed to a holster with her Glock 19.

Maggie watched from her position and stuck her head out just enough to catch a glimpse of the intruders. Three people dressed in suits sneaked out from the top of the stairs. One woman, two men, all of them trained professionals judging by their rigid postures and watchful eyes.

Not one for sitting back and hiding, Maggie stepped out into the open. "I wasn't expecting company."

Each of them snapped their heads toward her, their expressions a mix of surprise and annoyance. Clearly, Maggie was better at sneaking around unheard than they were.

Maggie crossed her arms and regarded them through her tinted sunglasses. "You know, it's rude to enter someone's apartment without so much as a knock."

And dangerous.

Maggie felt severely underdressed in the company of these strangers, their shirts buttoned to the neck, matching ties and reluctance to shed their jackets giving Maggie the whiff of a superiority complex.

"We need you to come with us," ordered the woman, her hair cropped short and face stern. A wire hung visibly from her ear, and a bead of sweat trickled down her neck.

Maggie shook her head. "That's not going to happen."

"She wasn't asking," said the bald man to the woman's right, a full head taller than his colleague.

Both speakers were British, which didn't surprise Maggie. She was beginning to suspect *who* they were, but still, it was far from clear *why* they were here barking commands.

"Watch that tongue of yours, baldy, or I might have to cut it out."

Baldy strode forward, but the second man blocked him with a warning hand.

Maggie grinned. "Yeah, best stay back. I wouldn't want to mess that nice suit of yours."

"One way or another, you're coming with us," said the second man, politer than the other two but just as serious. "Please choose the easy option and kindly get your things. There's a car waiting outside."

Maggie wasn't one for following the orders of strangers. Especially strangers who were all carrying concealed firearms. She cocked her head to the side and stepped toward them.

"I'm not an easy-option kind of girl. Whoever sent you should have told you that."

The sun must have gotten to Baldy's head because he shoved his partner away and lunged at Maggie, grabbing for her shoulder.

While she may no longer be an agent, she still had all the years of training and experience. Already leaning her weight on the balls of her feet, Maggie dashed to the side and avoided Baldy's grasp. Lashing out with a kick, she smacked her foot across the man's jaw and sent him crashing to the floor.

The woman jumped into the fray at the sight of her fallen partner and came at Maggie with a swinging fist. Maggie ducked and swiped the legs from under her opponent, who fell flat on her back and sucked in a winded breath on impact. Maggie caught her square in the face with a jab that left her stunned, ensuring the woman wouldn't get up while she dealt with the last one standing.

"Stop!" yelled the third suit, marching toward them all. Maggie was back on her feet now, the familiar surge of adrenaline pumping through her veins, her body falling into old habits and seeming glad to be put to use again after weeks of inaction.

The man reached inside his jacket where his weapon lay, and Maggie moved. Yanking his arm back, she caught hold of his hand and gave it a sharp, efficient twist.

He hissed in pain as Maggie used the advantage to

lock his whole arm in a hold behind him, sending him helplessly to his knees.

The ringing came from somewhere on the man's person. Maggie followed the sound and reached inside his jacket, taking both his gun and mobile phone. "Now, who could that be?"

"Have you made contact?" asked a voice when Maggie answered.

"He has," Maggie said, using her shoulder to hold the phone to her ear. "It's not going too well, though."

"Ms. Black?"

Maggie held the man with one hand and admired the standard issue gun with the other. The weapon confirmed her suspicions. "The one and only."

"It's Director General Helmsley," announced the voice.

Maggie groaned and twisted the man's arm further in frustration, resulting in a pained yelp. "Grace, do you mind telling me why you're so rudely interrupting my holiday?"

The director was silent for a moment, clearly not liking Maggie's use of her given name. She cleared her throat. "I need you to come in."

Maggie almost laughed. "I left, in case you've forgotten."

When Maggie had requested to leave the Unit for good, Grace Helmsley hadn't exactly been pleased with her decision. Nevertheless, she was efficient—almost clinical—in making sure all the paperwork was signed, and that Maggie's access to headquarters was revoked.

"We have an ... ongoing incident."

Maggie didn't miss the strain in the director's words but found herself detached. She was done following orders and dropping everything at the last minute at the Unit's request.

"Not my problem."

"Actually, it is," Helmsley countered.

Maggie narrowed her eyes. "What's going on?"

Was this some kind of trick? A way to lure her back?

"I won't say over the phone. A seat is waiting for you on the next flight back to London."

No, the Director General wasn't the type to pull any stunts to get Maggie back. She was too blunt and to the point for that. Whatever was going on, Maggie didn't like it. The slight shake in the unwavering woman's voice sent sparks of unease through her.

"And if I don't get on it?" Maggie asked, still holding the third man by his arm.

The director huffed. "The matter is time sensitive," she snapped, "and I can't waste any more of that time having this conversation. Believe me when I say you most definitely want to be on that plane."

Maggie released the man from her hold, and he scurried out of her reach to cradle his arm. "Pleasure as always, Director General." She made to hang up but stopped when Helmsley spoke again.

"Get on that plane, Black. Please."

That did it. In all her years working under the woman, Maggie couldn't recall Grace Helmsley ever pleading to anyone. Something was wrong. Very wrong.

Maggie craned her neck back and sighed. She knew it was too good to be true. Walking away had been too easy.

"Fine. I'm on my way." Maggie stepped over the squirming intruders and took one last look at the tranquil view. "And by the way, next time you need to reach me, try calling instead of sending a bunch of stiffs from MI6 to play chaperone. I could have killed them."

"Duly noted," Helmsley said. "I'll see you soon."

Maggie hung up and moved to pack her things.

She was getting bored anyway.

Chapter 3

London, Great Britain

Rain poured from the heavens over London in usual English summer fashion. Maggie pressed the buzzer at the front entrance to Inked International, the front for Unit headquarters, and waited. Drops of water dripped over her leather jacket from the edge of her umbrella in the same pitter-patter that washed over the streets.

It was a far cry from the Spanish penthouse.

"State your name," said a voice through the intercom.

Maggie kicked the door with the toe of her boot. "Queen bloody Elizabeth."

The lock clicked open, and Maggie pushed her way

inside, shaking her umbrella out over the tiled floor, much to the front-desk receptionist's chagrin.

"Ms. Black, you need a visitor's pass," he said in alarm, fumbling for a name tag.

Maggie shot him a glare, and he sat back down. "Don't worry. I'm not staying long."

The Director General didn't have an office in the building. The Unit didn't technically exist so it wouldn't do to have the head of the Secret Intelligence Service take up residence here. Her office was at Vauxhall Cross with the rest of MI6.

Taking the elevator to the fourth floor, Maggie made her way to Bishop's old office and knocked. Helmsley opened a moment later seeming like she'd been by the door awaiting Maggie's arrival.

She ushered Maggie in and closed the door behind her. "Thank you for coming."

Niceties? Maggie's initial dread intensified. She sat down at the conference table where she'd been briefed for many assignments during her career. "It didn't seem like you wanted to leave me much choice."

Helmsley took a seat across from Maggie and fiddled with her tablet. "I sent them for your protection."

Maggie shook her head in exasperation and looked around. Bishop's office had been spartan during his tenure, but he'd allowed himself some small items. His usual mug adorned with the British flag was gone, as was the photo of his twin daughters. Any trace of the man had been removed. Maggie forced away the twang of sadness the vacant room stirred within her. Bishop had been a liar and a traitor.

"I can look after myself, Grace. Now, what's up?"

Helmsley pushed aside her tablet and laced her hands together in front of her. "Shit has well and truly hit the fan."

The Director General wasn't one for dramatics. If she said things had taken a turn for the worse, she meant it. Maggie sat up straight. "How bad?"

"We've been hacked." Helmsley almost spat the words, furious outrage flaming behind her sharp eyes.

Maggie balked. "Hacked?" The Unit were the ones who did the hacking, not the other way around. The staff of analysts and computer techs were the best of the best, headhunted from all over for their brilliance behind a keyboard. Maggie had relied on them for all sorts of issues during her time as an agent.

"Yes." Helmsley straightened her suit jacket, her feathers well and truly ruffled. "I don't know how they managed it, but they did."

Hackers wouldn't break their way through the supposedly impenetrable firewalls of the Unit just to prove they could. It was a significant risk to take, and Maggie was willing to bet Helmsley had the entire strength of the Unit working to track down the ones behind it. Whatever the hackers wanted, they wanted it bad. "What did they take?"

Helmsley swallowed and met Maggie's eyes. "The list."

Maggie frowned. "What list?"

"The list," Helmsley repeated irritably. She turned back to her tablet and linked it with the projector screen on the wall. A video began to play, giving Maggie flashbacks to a mission in Paris at the end of last year. Only it wasn't a young man speaking about blowing up the city this time.

A young girl sat in an empty room, her fear palpable even through the screen. Her entire body tremored, and she watched someone from behind the lens with nervous distrust as they filmed her. She couldn't be older than eighteen.

A man's voice yelled at her from offscreen, and the girl recoiled, flinching as if she expected to be hit. Maggie didn't recognize the language the man spoke, but he barked at the girl again in broken English. "You read. Now."

The girl nodded emphatically, and her bottom lip quivered. "I'm speaking on behalf of those loyal to Ivan Dalca," she began. The lilt to her words told Maggie that although she spoke it very well, English wasn't her first language.

Dark, natural curls fell down her back and matched the deep brown of her eyes. Her cheeks weren't as filled as Maggie suspected they usually were, the slenderness of her body indicating she'd been underfed. She was

Middle Eastern in appearance, and beautiful in an innocent sort of way. A tear slipped down her cheek, and the man gave her a clear warning to continue.

"We demand that Ivan be released with immediate effect and allowed to leave the country unharmed. We have broken through your stronghold and know who each and every one of you are."

An arm came into view and handed the girl a photograph. Maggie gripped the side of the table, recognizing the face.

"This is Secret Agent Jim Hunter. He is currently stationed in Beijing, posing as an employee to factory owner Mark Islington. Under the name Andrew Rundell, he is gathering intel on the inhumane working conditions inside the factories to bring down Mr. Islington's illegal operation."

The girl's voice shook as she spoke, the severity of the situation and the harsh wording odd coming from her.

"To prove that we are serious in our demands, we have released this information to Mr. Islington and his known associates. The longer you take to release Ivan Dalca, the more of your agents we will expose. Their lives are in your hands."

The image of the girl blinked out as the video ended.

"Agent Hunter is dead," Helmsley stated. "We received the video yesterday, and they did as they said. They blew his cover before we could reach him."

Maggie slumped in her chair and ran a hand through

her blond locks. She'd stood outside in the hallway chatting to Jim Hunter barely two months before, laughing at his usual jokes and friendly taunts. "Have you told Jim's family?"

"We informed his wife, Susan, earlier today." Helmsley shifted in her seat, her obvious discomfort unsettling. Maggie was used to her no-nonsense attitude and cool demeanor. Even her bob of gray hair was slightly out of place, her uniform power suit creased like she hadn't gone home since receiving the video.

"And your other agents in the field. Have you withdrawn them?"

"Those we could contact."

Maggie knew the drill. Contact wasn't always possible in the field, especially for deep undercover jobs. It was far too risky, both to the success of the mission and to the agent's cover. News wouldn't reach agents on those types of assignments until they themselves made contact.

"Who's Ivan Dalca?"

"A Romanian sex trafficker, among other things," Helmsley informed. "Selling young girls is where he makes most of his money. He was charged with trafficking offenses and has been at Her Majesty's Pleasure for the last six months."

Prison. Maggie thought as much. She nodded her head toward the screen. "And these people?"

"Members of his criminal syndicate, we believe. Dalca's reach across Europe is vast. A considerable amount of those trafficked here from the continent each year have passed through his hands at some point in the process."

Which explained why his people would resort to blackmail. There was too much money involved to leave him behind bars. Too many opportunistic rivals who would be eyeing the syndicate's weak spot as a way to take over Dalca's operations.

"Are you letting him go?" Maggie asked. It wouldn't be the first time such a trade had been made behind closed doors.

Helmsley slammed a fist on the table. "We don't negotiate with criminals."

"Even if it means the lives of your agents?" Letting one poor excuse for a human being go in exchange for the lives of her old colleagues seemed like an easy decision to Maggie.

"Dalca's imprisonment was an international headline," Helmsley said. "I can't bloody well let him waltz out of prison a free man."

Maggie understood. The Unit didn't exist, and it had to stay that way. If Ivan Dalca were suddenly let go, the media would be on it in a heartbeat. With no good reason for letting him out that could be explained to the public, Helmsley's hands were tied. Even if she did find a way to slip him out unnoticed, there was no guarantee Dalca's people wouldn't release the information they'd stolen anyway. Or sell it.

No, letting Dalca go wasn't an option. Which left Helmsley with quite the predicament.

"So why am I here?" Maggie asked, getting to the point of their little meeting.

Helmsley leaned forward. "These people need to be stopped before they can do any more damage."

Maggie knew where this was going. She kicked her chair back and headed for the door. Leaving the Unit was one of the hardest decisions of her life, but she'd made up her mind, and nothing was going to drag her back in.

She opened the door and stopped at the threshold. "I'm sorry about Jim and what's happened, but it's no longer my problem."

Helmsley spun her chair around to face Maggie. "Unfortunately, it is."

Maggie squeezed the handle in her grip and took a deep breath, trying to keep the rising nausea at bay. "What do you mean?"

"It's not just active agents on that list."

Maggie slammed the door closed so hard, it almost broke the glass. "You have got to be kidding me."

"I wish I were," Helmsley said, her face grim.

Rage bubbled inside Maggie. She shoved out the chair next to Helmsley and sat down, getting in the older woman's face. "Talk."

If Helmsley was afraid of her, she didn't show it. Instead, she merely faced Maggie and told her what she knew.

"Everyone who has worked for us, past, present, active, or inactive, is on that list. We're still not sure what else the Romanians took, but they have enough to expose any one of us at any given time."

Which meant Maggie. Leon and Ashton, too.

Not only that but if the Romanians had access to the missions each of them had carried out, it wasn't just the agents at risk. It was everything. The entire workings of the Unit could be exposed, and the people within it.

Helmsley nodded, seeing the cogs turn in Maggie's mind. "If they managed to obtain even a fraction of the sensitive information on our database, the results of it going public could be catastrophic."

"Not exactly ideal for international relations." Or for that matter, Maggie and her friends. All three of them had lied, stolen, double-crossed, and assassinated for Queen and country. Most of which had been done under the guise of someone else, aliases being a particular specialty of Maggie's. Those aliases would be exposed, airing out everything she had done.

"Everyone spies on each other," Helmsley said. "We all know that, but we can't come out and admit it. It's another thing entirely for any given country to learn the details of our efforts, allies or otherwise."

Maggie had been on many of those assignments. While things may appear rosy between countries on the outside, it was another thing entirely beneath the surface. Supposed allies were actually rivals, rivals turned to allies. It was a continually evolving series of relationships, and even the slightest thing could tip the scale for the worse.

"They didn't release Jim's name to the public, though." Maggie had checked every available news outlet she could on the way home, trying to figure out what had caused the Director General to send for her. There was nothing about her former colleague anywhere.

"We believe the Romanians are keeping it between them and us for the time being. They know the impact a public release could have and are using it to force our hand."

Had they immediately gone public and exposed the Unit, they would have no more leverage, nothing to hang over the Unit's head to get Ivan Dalca released from prison. Better to keep the information to themselves and leak it to those select people on the receiving end of the Unit's spying.

"You never really leave this kind of life once you decide to live it," Helmsley said, seeing the struggle in Maggie's eyes. "It has a tendency to follow you whether you like it or not."

Maggie pinched the bridge of her nose. "Why me? You've got other agents at your disposal. Ones who actually still work here."

Helmsley met her eyes, too proud to beg. "You were my best. If anyone can stop this before it gets any worse, it's you."

A couple months ago, Helmsley's words would have stirred a sense of pride in Maggie. Compliments were never part of Helmsley's management philosophy, preferring to stick to the facts. And the fact was Maggie had the best record among her peers.

It was also a fact that she was no longer an agent.

Maggie's eyes drew to Bishop's desk where an unpacked box of files and other office items sat. Had Bishop still been alive, he would have been present at this meeting. His predecessor wasn't. "And Leon? Where's he?"

"He's tied up right now on another issue."

Maggie was about to pry into what that issue was, but the director pursed her lips. She may want Maggie's help, but it was clear Maggie was still very much out of the Unit.

Not that it would stop her name from being released to the people she'd fucked over during her time as an agent. That list of names alone was longer than all the agents who have worked for the secret agency.

"I'll need to think about it."

"Don't take too long. The people on that list don't have much time."

Maggie heard the implied threat within: *Neither do you.*

Chapter 4

Ashton sat back on the sofa in Maggie's riverside apartment and finished the rest of his whisky in one gulp. "Well, shit."

Maggie paced the floor in front of him, nursing her own drink in her hand. Willow, the stray cat who seemed determined to be a constant guest, danced between her legs, evidently happy to see Maggie back from her travels. "A succinct way of putting it, but yes. Shit."

She'd filled him in on everything she'd learned from the Director General. Usually, when Maggie told her best friend about Unit business, she was breaking the rules of her employment. Now that she'd left, all those rules went out the window. Aside from the fact she'd signed and agreed to the Official Secrets Act, of course, but it had never stopped her from discussing work with Ashton.

Besides, the Unit had bigger things to worry about than Maggie spilling classified information now that the Romanians had their list of agents.

Ashton poured himself a refill and topped up Maggie's glass. "What are you going to do?"

Maggie sipped the amber liquid and relished the warmth as it burned down her throat. "I don't know yet," she admitted.

Rain continued to spatter her window like blood. It dripped down the glass in globs, distorting her view of the illuminated city skyline and the rushing Thames below.

"You always have a choice, you know," Ashton said, as if reading her thoughts. "If you don't want to take this on, then don't. You're not an agent anymore. Helmsley and her little minions can deal with it."

Maggie pressed her forehead against the window and let the glass cool her aching head. Taking a back seat and letting others do the work was never one of Maggie's strong points.

Could she trust the Unit to handle this? Helmsley didn't seem to think so. Otherwise she wouldn't have called Maggie. The dent in her pride alone must have been a tough pill to swallow.

"What about you?" Maggie turned to her best friend. "Your name is on that list, too."

Hard as he might try to hide it, Ashton was just as shaken by Maggie's revelation as she'd been. If any of his nefarious business contacts learned of his past deeds as an agent, he'd be in just as much danger as everyone else at the Unit. Maybe more so, given the kind of people he did business with.

Ashton finished his drink, not meeting her eyes. "I'll send my parents off on holiday until this all blows over."

A pang of hurt echoed through Maggie. While it was a relief she didn't have more than Leon and Ashton to worry about in all this, the thought of family stirred the void not having one brought. It was a part of her life she didn't like to dwell on.

"What about Declan?" Maggie asked, shoving the poisonous concoction of loneliness and jealousy back down the hole and sealing it away.

Ashton shifted in his seat. "He's in rehab, again."

"I'm sorry." Ashton didn't speak about his older brother much. Over the years, he'd tried and failed to get him sober and back on his feet. It killed a little piece of Ashton every time Declan relapsed, but even after all these years, he never gave up on his brother.

"Best place for him," Ashton replied with a light tone that didn't match the pain behind his deep-blue eyes. "I just hope he stays there this time."

Maggie knew Ashton well enough to know Declan wouldn't be admitted into the rehab facility under his real name. Even if Ivan Dalca's people did leak Ashton's name, they'd be hard-pressed to find his brother. For someone who played his life like a dangerous game of chess, Ashton always made sure his family was safe and secure.

Maggie slumped down next to him on the couch, curled up her legs, and leaned on his shoulder. "And you?"

"Business as usual. I have a few ongoing ... projects to tie up."

Maggie didn't like the sound of that. "Be careful," she warned.

Ashton shot her a wicked, dimpled grin. "I'm always careful."

"I've heard that before." Maggie had lost count of the number of times she needed to help get him out of a sticky situation. "I don't need to remind you of our last 'vacation,' do I?"

Where most would shrink at the mention of the time they almost got their friend killed, Ashton simply laughed. "Now that was a fun holiday."

Maggie sipped her drink to hide her smirk.

"What did Leon have to say about all this?" Ashton continued in a not-so-subtle shift of topic.

"He wasn't there. Helmsley said he was dealing with another issue."

Maggie bit at her bottom lip. Did Leon know Grace had interrupted her vacation and dragged her back to London for a meeting? Was he on board with Maggie coming out of retirement so soon? He was shocked when she'd left, but he had respected her decision to follow a different path. If he knew the Director General's intentions, surely he would have called Maggie first to warn her.

Ashton's face turned sour. "Helmsley wants you to do her dirty work for her, again, but won't even tell you where your man is or what he's doing that's so important not to be dealing with the hack?"

"He's not my man," Maggie said automatically.

Ashton rolled his eyes. "Aye, he is. The sooner you realize that, the sooner you both can get on with your lives. But that's beside the point. How do you know this isn't some ploy to get you back into the fold?"

"You're saying Helmsley had Jim killed as part of some elaborate scheme? Come on, Ash." Ashton's distrust of the Unit and their dealings ran deep, but even he knew they wouldn't resort to killing one of their best remaining agents to get her back.

Ashton arched his eyebrow, knowing exactly what the Unit was capable of. "I'm just concerned, that's all. You finally made it out, and now suddenly you're ready to dive back in. Can't you do something else?"

"Like what? Stay home and knit?"

Ashton scooped up Willow, who sat by his feet, and scratched under her chin, her fur the same color as his styled, dark hair. "Well, you're two more of these away from being a cat lady already."

Willow let out a deep, satisfied purr in agreement.

Maggie sighed. "I'm about as happy with all this as

you are, but how can I even think about moving on and starting my new life with my past threatening to ruin it before it even starts?"

"They can't come running to you every time they can't deal with their own problems, Mags."

But it wasn't just their problem. It was Maggie's and Ashton's, too.

"It's the fact they've asked me for my help that concerns me. For Helmsley to do that means it must be bad. They've already lost Jim, and it's just a matter of time before the Romanians release the name of another agent."

Maggie let her unspoken point settle into the silence. That next name could very well be one of them.

Ashton downed what was left of his drink and smacked his lips. "Well, I've got to get going." He stood and stretched his tattoo-covered arms into the air, his fingertips brushing her ceiling, and then shrugged on his expensive designer coat. "I'll have our friend Gillian fix us all up some new identities, just in case. In the meantime, keep me posted. I'll ask around and see if I can learn anything about these hackers."

"Thanks, Ash."

He leaned down and kissed her cheek, giving Willow one last chin scratch before leaving. His phone was at his ear before he was out of her apartment. "Hi, Dad, it's me. Listen, how do you and Mum feel about a wee trip to Mexico?"

The door closed behind him, leaving Maggie alone with her thoughts.

A shiver ran through her. She wrapped a throw around her shoulders and stared out the large window to the sounds of windswept rain that promised stormy times ahead.

The penthouse in Alicante seemed like a whole other world now, one that she had only been allowed to visit before being dragged back into reality. The Director General's words replayed in her mind.

You never really leave this kind of life once you decide to live it.

As much as Maggie hated to admit it, Helmsley was right. No matter where she had gone over the last six weeks, no matter how many miles away from London and her old life she ventured, her past came along with her like an unwelcomed guest.

No matter how hard she tried, her grief over Brice Bishop had taken its toll. Both for the man he once was, and for the man she thought she'd known before his secrets spilled out and altered everything for her.

It wasn't just the loss of her mentor, and the only person close to resembling a parental figure she'd had since losing her mother at the tender age of six. It was the loss of justification for everything she had done as part of the Unit. Every slice of a knife, every bullet she let loose from her gun. Every lie she'd told, and every life she'd taken. All of it she could cope with, knowing what she did was for the greater good. That those she took down had destroyed innocent lives and threatened many more to come. It was the one thing that allowed her to sleep at night, no matter the nightmares that plagued her slumber. As long as she was on the right side, a soldier on the front line of justice, she could continue to do what others could not.

All of that shattered with Bishop and his unofficial missions.

Maggie didn't know how many of her assignments over the years had come from Bishop's side gig. A part of her didn't want to know.

Bishop had used her and the other agents as pawns, pimping them out to anyone who could afford the high fee of his services. He had made Maggie one of the very people she believed she was fighting against. He had guided her hand countless times to carry out the nasty work of criminals to benefit from their shady dealings. Adam Richmond, the reporter, the final innocent Maggie had killed on Bishop's orders, was the last, but he was by no means the first.

While she was vacationing in paradise, her mind was in hell. Night after night she lay awake, thinking of the countless missions she'd completed, of each and every face she'd taken out with vicious efficiency, wondering which of them hadn't deserved it.

Now that she was back home, all of it wore on her even more. Bishop had made her a monster, and she didn't know how she was ever going to restore what he had taken. Didn't know if it was even possible.

Maggie spent the next few hours in silence, weighing her options. Her own demons aside, there were more imminent threats to contend with. When it came down to it, people's lives were at stake, including her own and those of the people she cared for most.

Her hands had dialed the number before she even realized it. Straight to voicemail.

"Hey, it's Leon. I can't take your call right now but leave a message after the beep."

Maggie made to speak but ended the call instead and dialed a new number.

Grace Helmsley answered straight away.

"Fine, I'll help you."

Maggie didn't know how she could even begin to make amends for the things she had done under Bishop's command, but one thing she did know how to do was to protect the people she loved. Right now, they were in danger, and she would do all she could to save them. Even if it meant returning to the very life she'd just walked away from.

"Good," Helmsley replied. "I'll pick you up tomorrow morning at seven o'clock." Without another word, the director hung up.

"You're welcome," Maggie muttered and tossed her phone on the table.

Willow came and curled up on her lap, staring up at her with those big, bright eyes.

"I'm only going back this once," Maggie told her. "As soon as the mess is settled, I'm out for good."

Willow considered her for a moment, then closed her eyes, decidedly unimpressed. Maggie sat up late into the night, vowing with each sip of her drink that her return was only temporary. Only it wasn't the cat she was trying to convince.

Chapter 5

11 July

At precisely seven in the morning, a black SUV pulled up outside Maggie's building. Though she couldn't see through the tinted windows, she knew it was her old boss. The thick bulletproof glass and armored wheels were a dead giveaway.

The rain hadn't let up from yesterday and poured from the heavens. It plummeted to the pavement and splashed back up upon impact, ensuring those who ventured outside got well and truly drenched.

Maggie put the hood of her jacket over her head and tucked her long blond ponytail out of the way. The front passenger side door opened as she ventured out into the summer rain and recognized a familiar face.

"Hello, Baldy," Maggie said, as he opened the door for her with one hand and held an umbrella over her head with the other. His face sported a nasty bruise that was almost as dark as the scowl he gave her. Not a word came from him, though, the big man on his best behavior in front of his boss.

Maggie got into the back of the car where the Director General sat waiting, impeccable as always in a fine woolen coat and power suit.

"Maggie."

"Grace."

Baldy returned to his seat up front, and the driver, who Maggie noted was the female agent she'd also met at the penthouse, took off into the busy London traffic.

"I'm glad you decided to come."

The certainty in Grace's voice, like she knew all along Maggie would agree to her request, irked her more than she cared to admit. "I'm only doing this because my name is on that list. I'm not back."

Helmsley arched an eyebrow. "Who said anything about wanting you back?"

The MI6 agent driving sniggered, but Maggie smiled, too. Grace's notorious reputation for cutting remarks wasn't exaggerated. She was sharper than any knife Maggie had come across, and she liked the older woman all the more for it.

"Where are we going?"

"Belmarsh."

"Ah," Maggie said. They were going to meet Ivan Dalca.

It took thirty minutes to reach Her Majesty's Prison Belmarsh. The category A men's prison was situated in London's southeast, over the river in Thamesmead, adjacent to the Woolwich Crown Court. Maggie eyed the facility—a fortress of brick buildings encompassed by thick gray walls. Inside, the prison housed some of the most high-profile criminals in the country, some of which were in residence thanks to Maggie's own hands.

Serial killers, terrorists, pedophiles, major drug traffickers. Belmarsh had them all and more within its walls and was known for containing those who posed a considerable threat to national security. Including Ivan Dalca.

"What can you tell me before going in?" Maggie asked as they pulled close to the barrier up front and announced their arrival through the intercom. Security must have been warned they were coming as they were allowed straight through to the carpark.

"He's a raving lunatic," Helmsley spat. "Completely bonkers, thinking he could ever stand a chance of getting out."

"Noted, though I was thinking more along the lines of things we can use to learn as much as we can from him." Men like Dalca liked to brag. It was the Achilles' heel to his kind, the need to crow about their achievements like little school boys looking for a gold star. Or, to instill fear and dominance. It was all one big pissing match.

Female criminals weren't as stupid. They tended to revel in the secrecy of their accomplishments with nothing but a victorious gleam in their eyes and the tug of a grin at their lips.

"He's a chauvinist pig, for one."

"I figured as much." Maggie had met his kind before. Pimps and sex traffickers tended to have a warped view on women, even the ones who supplied men and children. They viewed them like a farmer would his cattle, like a piece of meat to sell for a price. Over and over again until they eventually broke. They weren't humans to people like Ivan. They were stock.

"Smart, too. Unfortunately," Grace continued as they parked and got out of the SUV, the two agents trailing close behind in vigilant silence. "The only reason we apprehended him was through sheer coincidence. He was visiting a drug dealer friend right as we raided the house on a bust. Quite the catch that day, let me tell you."

"And now he's causing just as much trouble from his cell." Maybe even more, at least as far as the Unit was concerned.

Grace's heels clicked along the concrete to the front door. "Bastard."

Maggie stopped before they went inside. "Have his people released any more names?"

"Not yet, but I fear it's only a matter of time. We need to end this quickly, and by any means necessary."

Maggie opened the door and held it open for the Director General, more out of habit than politeness. Helmsley was no longer her superior. Not that she didn't respect the woman. Like Maggie, she too would do anything she could to protect her country. Even if it meant torture tactics toward a threat.

A man, Maggie guessed the prison governor, stood by the front desk awaiting their arrival. His ill-fitting suit clashed with his loosely knotted tie. Graying hair crowned a stern face with a strong jaw and thick neck.

"How long has he held out?" Helmsley asked him, forgoing introductions. She marched right past him and headed for the secured doors, forcing him into a jog to catch up.

"The whole night, ma'am." His meaty hands turned a key in the lock, and the door whined open, echoing off the cold, bare walls. The beginnings of bruises surrounded his knuckles, the skin red and slightly swollen. Though he may be the one in charge at Belmarsh, it was clear he liked to get his hands dirty.

Helmsley's mood darkened at the news. "Has he said anything?"

"Nothing of importance." The governor led them through a labyrinth of narrow halls and steel-barred doors, avoiding the signs for the general population areas where most of the inmates were kept.

Whistling and catcalling met them when they passed through solitary confinement, prisoners pressing their faces to the small glass windows of their cell doors. Maggie and the others were likely the only people they'd seen for a long time, other than the guards. Their eyes held a glazed, defeated stare like wild lions confined to the small, domestic enclosures of a zoo.

Humans weren't meant to live in such conditions. Maggie shuddered, glad she wasn't on the other side of those doors, a fate that would have been her own had Bishop not saved her all those years ago. She balled her fists at the thought of Brice and avoided the prisoners' faces. Some people were monsters and deserved the cages they were in.

The next door led them down to the depths of Belmarsh's basement. It was damp, and an aged scent lingered through the stale air. A guard stood sentry by an enclosed room, and the governor welcomed him with a firm nod.

"I warn you, ma'am, he's violent," he said.

Grace patted Maggie's shoulder. "I'm sure we'll be quite safe, Harold."

Harold sized Maggie up with resignation, all five feet six of her curved, feminine body. To most, she hardly radiated danger, but that was just the way she liked it.

Being underestimated had a wealth of advantages, and Maggie exploited them all to the fullest when needed.

"Ready?" Helmsley asked her.

"What if his people find out?" Given the lengths Ivan's people had gone to in order to try and secure his release, torture seemed a rash move to Maggie. Not that she was worried about Ivan's well-being. It was his people's reaction to the news that concerned her.

"We've cut all of his communication," Helmsley assured. "Including his snake of a lawyer."

While it was clear Grace refused to negotiate with Ivan and his people, it seemed she was not beyond bending the rules on the man's rights as a prisoner.

"What if the lawyer tells them he's not allowed to see Ivan?" Anything that could infuriate Dalca's people could result in more names being released in punishment. Given the power they held over the government, Grace was playing a dangerous game by antagonizing them.

"He's no longer a problem."

Maggie knew what that meant. Grace was nothing if not efficient. "Let's get this over with, then."

The guard stepped aside, and Maggie and Grace entered the dark room. The sharp smells of sweat, blood, and piss assaulted her senses as soon as Maggie passed the threshold.

They'd seated Ivan Dalca on a cold, straight-backed metal chair to ensure optimum discomfort. His bare back was to them, his body positioned to face nothing but a blank wall. Even in the dim light, Maggie could see the welts and trickles of blood across his shoulders and upper arms.

The governor had kept on Ivan's underwear, most likely to protect their delicate feminine sensibilities. Not that Maggie was complaining. The trafficker's arms and legs were bound with thick rope around the chair legs, coiling tight around his weathered skin.

"Ivan," Helmsley practically growled.

The man spat out a glob of blood at their feet and raised a defiant chin at their presence. "You again."

His dark, thinning hair was damp, and not just from sweat. A bucket and rag lay off to the side, causing Maggie to relive her training days when she and the rest of the candidates were subjected to torture methods. Waterboarding had been particularly traumatizing.

Ivan's gaze moved to Maggie, and his sneer changed to something more predatory. "Changed tactics, have you?" he asked Helmsley, licking his lips while he surveyed Maggie up and down. "Is this a peace offering? I must admit it's been a while since I had a nice piece of ass."

Grace lurched forward and thrashed her hand across Ivan's face with a slap that echoed through the dimly lit room.

Ivan's face snapped to one side, but he released a moan in mock pleasure. "I like it when you play rough."

Maggie kept her cool and watched the Romanian closely. Whatever had been done to him over the last twenty-four hours hadn't removed the fight in him. While his body may be in pain, his mind was fully intact, the iron will behind his eyes still present, unlike the prisoners they'd passed on the way down. He had a nose that had suffered at least three breaks in his lifetime, along with a ragged scar that ran up from his chest to under his right ear. This was not a man who would break without a real fight. A fight Maggie and the Unit didn't have time for.

Helmsley brushed nonexistent dust from her suit, her temper having simmered down to normal. "This is futile, Dalca. You know as well as I do there is no way this will work. We do not negotiate with terrorists."

"Terrorist, am I?" Ivan laughed. "Well, that's too bad. For your agents, that is."

"How did you manage to infiltrate our database?"

"Me? From my cell? It doesn't have a toilet seat, never mind a computer."

Helmsley's lips thinned. "Your people."

"Perhaps your 'Unit' is not as secure as you think." Blood coating Dalca's teeth gleamed as a wide grin spread in a slash across his face. He was enjoying himself, relishing their anger and breathing it in like fresh air.

Maggie shared a look with Grace. No one ever suspected Bishop's betrayal. Was there someone else just as corrupt within the ranks? Information such as the list would fetch a handsome price on the black market. More than enough to make someone very rich indeed.

Helmsley broke Maggie's knowing gaze and cleared her throat. "Where are your people stationed?"

"How should I know?" Ivan shrugged but wasn't quick enough to mask the pain in his face the movement caused him.

"You can end all this if you give us a location," Maggie added, her limited patience running dry. Ivan was toying with them like a cat would mice.

"We move around."

"Names, then," Grace snapped, her own tolerance for the Romanian wearing thin. "Whose puppet strings are you pulling?"

"You may be prepared to allow the names of your own to leak, but I am not. I'd rather die."

"You might if you don't start talking. I can't keep an eye on your guards 24-7."

"They might lose control," added Maggie, pacing in front of him. "Take it a bit too far. Accidents happen."

Ivan gave another bloody grin. "I'll take my chances."

Maggie moved before she realized it. Lashing out with her foot, she kicked Ivan back and sent him and the chair crashing to the floor with a clang. "Listen, you piece of shit," she said, standing over him and pressing her boot down on his head so his face scraped the rough floor. "People I care about are on that list. If anything happens to them, I swear you will pay for it. All this will feel like a trip to the spa compared to what I'll do to you."

"Then arrange for my freedom," Ivan said through the pained grit of his teeth. "It's a simple trade for the lives of those you claim to hold so dear."

"Maggie," Grace said in warning.

Maggie pinned him there for a moment longer before releasing him. She then stepped back to the Director General's side.

It was no use. Ivan would hold on for as long as he could. He had too much to gain from his silence. If he even knew anything at all. If he were as conniving as Maggie suspected, he wouldn't know enough about his people's plans to ruin the operation. The more in the dark he was, the less the Unit could get out of him. He knew they wouldn't risk merely killing him, either, thanks to the list hanging over their heads. Even strapped to a chair, Ivan knew he held the power here.

"Well, I can see this conversation is at an impasse. The sooner you decide to talk, the better." Without so much as a second glance, Grace walked off and left the room like she had better things to do than deal with Ivan.

Maggie leaned down and whispered in his ear. "She might not be prepared to kill you yet, but if my friends suffer, I will gladly come back and slit your throat while you sleep. I'm going to take down your people and burn your seedy empire to ruin. I promise you that."

Ivan turned to her, his unwashed smell and sour

breath turning her stomach. "Do stop by again soon. I'll see about arranging a conjugal visit."

Maggie ignored him and turned to leave.

"Oh, and if things don't work out with the Unit, you can always come and work with me. A woman like you would look nice on my arm."

Maggie stopped at the threshold. "I'd sooner rip your arms off. Among other appendages."

Gathering herself, Maggie returned to Helmsley and the governor who waited outside. There was nothing else she could do here.

"Keep at him, Harold," Grace ordered, leaving the man and his guard to it.

Maggie walked by her side, nails digging in her palms. "He won't fold."

"I know."

Back in the car, they both sat in silence as the extremity of the situation settled in. Even if he knew anything useful, Ivan wasn't going to talk. They were at square one with very little to go on.

"What now?" Maggie asked eventually.

"We go at them, full force."

"What about what Dalca said?"

Grace shifted in her seat. "You think I have another traitor in my midst?"

"Before Bishop, I would've said not a chance. Now, I'd say just about anything goes."

Bishop had died and taken any trust Maggie had for the Unit with him. If he was capable of betraying them, anyone was. What made it so much worse was the fact she didn't see it. Not until it was far too late. For someone who had taken down so many criminals, who had grown an instinct for sniffing out vile people, she never once suspected Brice of any wrongdoing. She'd idolized him, and her blind faith in the man had cost many their lives while leaving a trail of destruction Maggie couldn't begin to think about.

How many lives had been altered by her actions? How many wrongful deaths had tallied up over the years on Bishop's orders? How many times had Maggie been the one to strike the killing blow to an innocent target that some high-paying crook wanted out of the way? And what kind of person did that make her?

All these questions and more had plagued her since Bishop's revelation on that rooftop, mere moments before he toppled to his death. It niggled at her like an itch she couldn't scratch. She had been Bishop's favorite, the one he sent out on the most classified and challenging missions. It had been a source of great pride for Maggie during her time as an agent, but now the burden that came with such an accolade was almost too much to bear.

"Not full force, then?" Helmsley asked, breaking Maggie from her troubled thoughts.

"Unless you believe you can fully trust everyone in the Unit."

"What would you suggest?"

Maggie considered this for a moment, falling back into her old ways as if she'd never left it all behind. "Agents' lives are at stake, so let them know what they need to know to stay safe. Anything else should be on a need-to-know basis. That way, if information leaks, the pool of potential double agents will be a narrow one."

Grace nodded her agreement. "And you?"

"I'll find them. A syndicate as big as Ivan's will leave a trail of breadcrumbs for me to track." Maggie would fight her way to the heart of Dalca's operation with her bare hands if she had to. While she may not deserve a second chance, she sure as hell wasn't going to let a piece of scum like Dalca ruin the only chance she had. She'd fought too long and too hard to reach that point, and nothing, not even Ivan's stolen hit list, would take it from her. She'd already given too much.

A phone rang from somewhere on Grace's person. "I have to take this," she said, slipping the device out from inside her jacket. "Helmsley," she answered.

After a moment, Grace's whole body tensed.

"Affirmative. I'll be back at HQ within the hour." She hung up and blinked.

"What is it?" Maggie asked. Whatever it was, it wasn't good.

"A new name has been leaked."

Maggie stopped dead, her heart thundering in her chest. "Who?"

Helmsley held back, not meeting Maggie's eyes.

"Who, Grace?"

"Leon."

Chapter 6

Outside of Mogadishu, Somalia

Secret Agent Leon Frost had been on a few missions to Somalia, but this was by far the most dangerous.

Despite being pushed out of the country's capital some years ago, Al-Shabab had never lost sight of regaining control of it. Countless attempts to return to their level of power in the city had failed, their influence and ideals a shadow of what they once were across the plains of the African country. Slowly but surely, and with a lot of bloodshed throughout, the splinter cell of the now-defunct Islamic Courts Union had lost the vast majority of its territorial gains established when Ethiopia stormed Mogadishu.

While dominance over land held its own source of power, the true power of such groups, Leon knew, lay in the minds of the people. It didn't take much to turn a civilian into a new recruit. Questionable foreign policy and botched air strikes did most of the work for the terrorists, allowing them to slither into the hearts and minds of the impressionable and the young, all of their new recruits no stranger to suffering. Leon couldn't help but think of himself at that age, angry and eager to belong. To be a part of something bigger than himself. In another life, in another place, he could have fallen for it all, too.

On the surface, things appeared to be more settled than any other time Leon had found himself in the country, though, compared to most Western countries, *settled* wasn't a term many would use to describe the current situation in Somalia.

Over the years, Al-Shabab had and continued to strike against the African Union's peacekeepers and their attempts to eradicate the splinter cell for good. Despite more than twenty thousand African troops and allied support from Western governments, the terrorists still carried out horrific attacks on a regular basis, sometimes killing hundreds at a time. The government called their slew of suicide bombings a clear sign of desperation, which wasn't a lie.

Yes, the weakening Al-Shabab were desperate, but if

Leon had learned one thing about terrorist groups, it was that they could be patient. Very patient.

While the government was busy trying to deal with the distraction of the constant attacks, a growing subset of militants sat and waited for their time to strike. The man in charge of said subset was Yasir Osman.

When the orders for the mission reached his new desk, Leon could have sent one of the many agents he now outranked. Taking over Bishop's role as chief hadn't been a decision he'd made lightly but, after what happened with his former boss, someone had to step up. Someone people knew and looked up to, according to Director General Grace Helmsley, who'd offered him the job. While flattered by the uncharacteristic praise from his superior, in the end, it came down to trust. Leon no longer trusted anyone around him to be in charge of the Unit. Not with Maggie gone, Bishop dead, and the turncoat Nina on the run.

Checking his watch, Leon made the final preparations for what he planned to be his last day of his long mission. It was time to end it.

The few belongings he'd amassed were already stowed away in one of the jeeps, the keys to which sat in the pocket of his cargo pants. Provisions mostly—clothes, water, some food, and all the guns he could steal without them being missed.

Leon slipped a large and freshly sharpened serrated knife into his waistband and made sure to untie the laces of his boots. He only had one shot, and nothing could go wrong.

He paced around in the small confines of his spartan room, counting down the minutes. Yasir kept to a schedule, a mistake for anyone with a target on their back, and this was the first opportunity Leon had had in the four weeks he'd been around the man. Four weeks of watching and waiting for the right time to act. It was now or never.

It wasn't until Yasir murdered three British soldiers, here to train and help the Somalian military and their affiliates eliminate Al-Shabab, that the Unit was called upon to take the man out. He was becoming more brazen as his numbers and strength grew, ordering a tirade of attacks over the last few months, growing hungrier to prove himself. Any hope Somalia had of lasting peace couldn't be achieved with Yasir Osman alive. He posed too much of a threat, which was why Leon found himself undercover in the man's compound.

Slipping out of his room, Leon walked as casually as he could across the inner courtyard of the large estate that housed almost forty men who'd offered themselves to Yasir's call to arms. While most of Yasir's soldiers continued with the charade of their normal lives, going to work each day and biding their time until orders were sent by their leader to be his willing puppets, Yasir kept a solid detail of his closest and most trusted disciples around him.

It was quickly approaching midday, and the sun grew

blistering hot in the cloudless sky, sending trickles of sweat down Leon's back. The air was humid, and it had taken him a while to acclimatize, being used to the mild, rainy British weather. His struggles with the heat didn't compromise his cover, though. If anything, it helped it and allowed him to joke with the resident soldiers who jovially teased him about it.

Two of the men passed Leon and stopped for a quick chat before rushing to their rooms in time to pray and then sleep. Their shift in the watchtower was over while the next pair took their rotational shift. Yasir was paranoid, and rightly so. He just didn't know the enemy would come from the inside.

Penetrating Osman's inner circle hadn't been easy. In conjunction with the Somali government, who already had a man on the inside, they had developed a story to get Leon in.

It wasn't too far from the truth, which always made for the best kind of cover. The Somali's mole had told Yasir of his cousin, who immigrated with his wife to London in search of a better life years before. Having made something of themselves with a successful business, they had the available funds to help Osman's plight, as well as a willing soldier in their one and only son.

Leon's parents were Nigerian, and though they'd worked hard all their days, they were far from wealthy until he had been able to support them on his agent salary. Still, with such an offer dangled in front of Yasir, he had agreed to both the cash and the new recruit. He was happier about one of those gifts than the other and had given Leon quite the rundown in questioning before allowing him to stay in the compound.

All of his soldiers had to prove themselves. For Yasir, that could be done one of two ways: action or money. Most of Osman's soldiers had gone the first route, either eager to fight or unable to come up with enough money to satisfy him. While Leon's choice wasn't viewed as the bravest option, a terrorist cell couldn't operate without cold, hard cash, and Yasir's existing financial backer was running dry after forking out the funds to keep the compound running and the soldiers armed with weapons and explosives.

Once Yasir seemed satisfied with him, helped along by Leon's faked fanaticism and speaking both fluent Somali and Arabic, he was welcomed into the fold. Ever since then, he'd been impatiently waiting for the right moment to carry out orders.

Walking through the courtyard, Leon ducked into the private quarters afforded to Osman for being the one in charge. The Dhuhr prayer was just about to begin, and a bell sounded through the compound in reminder. During Leon's residence, Yasir had always prayed with his two bodyguards who never left his side.

Leon had heard around the compound from the other soldiers that Yasir had lost his patience with them the day before, declaring their breathing far too loud for him to concentrate on his prayers. The resulting shift in Yasir's usual schedule was the perfect chance for Leon to reach him unguarded. With his bodyguards relegated to a room down the hall during prayer times and everyone else taking part in the noon prayer, Osman was alone.

The main hallway of Yasir's private rooms was silent, the ringing of the bell the only thing accompanying Leon's drumming heartbeat in his ears. He slipped his feet out of his boots and padded down the wooden floor the rest of the way, making use of the Afghan rugs to soften any noise his large and muscled frame might make.

The element of surprise was vital for a job like this. Shooting his target, even with a silencer, would cause too much noise and raise the alarm too early for him to make any attempt at an escape. Having to rely on a knife meant getting up close and personal with Osman; he'd have to do it before the man could call for help.

Yasir's room was just a few feet away, and anticipation sparked inside Leon like electricity, pumping adrenaline through his veins the same way an impending hit always stirred within him.

"Assad? What are you doing here?" a voice demanded behind him, calling him by his mission alias.

Leon froze and turned on his heels to discover who had caught him in Yasir's out-of-bounds quarters.

Tahiil Osman stood with arms crossed as he waited for an answer, brows burrowed to the center of his forehead.

Bloody hell.

With a deep breath, Leon plastered on an innocent face and smiled at Yasir's younger brother. "I have a message for Yasir."

Tahiil eyed Leon's bare feet. "And this message can't wait until after Dhuhr?"

Leon sighed inwardly, glad for Wudhu, the ritualistic washing of hands, feet, arms, and legs before prayer that could explain his lack of shoes. "It's important."

"Then tell me, and I'll pass it along to my brother after prayers," Tahiil replied, doing little to hide his distaste.

Leon had tried to befriend the younger man, but he took any praise Yasir sent Leon's way as a personal slight, especially after his mess-up during their last outing to the capital.

"Yasir said all information should be taken straight to him," Leon reminded him, a strict rule that had been enforced after a miscommunication on Tahiil's part almost got Yasir assassinated two weeks into Leon's stay. Leon hadn't been present, but Yasir was furious when they returned. He beat Tahiil within an inch of his life.

Yasir had taken to mostly ignoring his brother since then, deciding to forgo the usual punishment of death that would result in such a mishap from any other soldier. Leon often wondered if Tahiil would have accepted death easier than being shunned by his brother. He idolized him in an almost religious way, having been raised by Yasir after their parents were murdered in an air strike.

Mistrust shadowed Tahiil's face, shrouding his features with an almost sinister glare. "Then, by all means, let's go see him."

All Leon could do was agree. Turning around, he knocked on Yasir's door as quietly as he could without seeming suspicious. The last thing he wanted was to raise the attention of the guards down at the opposite end of the rooms. Now he would need to take both brothers out and be quick about it.

Leon took in Tahiil's slight but athletic frame and considered the threat level. Yasir was bigger and stronger than his sibling, but Tahiil would be faster and would sacrifice himself willingly to protect his brother if it came to it. He'd take him out first before focusing on Yasir and hope the extended time wouldn't result in the bodyguards being alerted. If that happened, his already slim chances of a clean escape were ruined.

"Come in," Yasir called, frustration clear in his sharp, impatient tone.

Leon turned the handle and stepped inside, already reaching for his knife with his free hand.

Tahiil stepped in behind him and closed the door before Leon noticed the guards.

Four of them, two on top of Yasir's usual pair, pounced from all angles. Leon spotted Yasir Osman in the far corner, watching with a hard face and dangerous eyes as his men attacked.

Hands grabbed behind him, and Leon only had time to ram his head back and smash it against Tahiil's nose before four sets of fists slammed into him from all over. Tahiil swore as blood flowed like a river out of his nose, but Leon found no satisfaction in the sight.

Bringing him to his knees, the guards forced his head up to face their leader and pinned him into an unbreakable position while they disarmed him of his concealed knife.

Yasir stepped forward and stared down his nose at his captive. "Nice try, Leon Frost, but not good enough."

Chapter 7

London, Great Britain

Maggie slammed a fist on the desk and swore a diatribe of fear and frustration.

"Calm down, Agent," Helmsley ordered. They were back at Unit HQ, and Grace had just returned from being briefed by her agents, keeping Maggie waiting for her in Bishop's old office like a headmistress would a naughty child.

"I'm not an agent anymore." The urge to tear things apart coursed through her shaken nerves, growing stronger with each minute that passed. Leon was out there somewhere, and his cover was blown.

Helmsley sat down and busied herself with her

tablet, the epitome of calm and control. "Punching things won't help."

"It usually does," Maggie grumbled and slumped down on a chair. Grace was right. Smashing up Leon's unused office wouldn't help him. "Play the video."

Helmsley obliged.

Like the one shown to Maggie yesterday, the unknown girl appeared in front of a camera. She appeared much the same as she had in the other clip, though the palpable fear that emanated from her was now mixed with something else. It lay behind her eyes, just a glint of it. Defiance.

The girl held up a picture in her hand, and Maggie felt the blood drain from her face. Seeing Leon's face only made it that much more real, the weight of the situation crashing into her like a tidal wave that threatened to send her emotions over the edge. Maggie clenched her teeth and willed the tears forming in her eyes not to fall. Not in front of the Director General.

"This is Secret Agent Leon Frost. He is currently stationed in a covert operation in Somalia to gain intelligence on a splinter cell of Al-Shabab. Under the guise of the son of Somali nationals, he will attempt to insert himself into the group and report back anything that can aid in the assassination of the cell's leader, Yasir Osman."

Venom laced the girl's words, her voice shaking in anger now as well as the fear that had been there in the first video. Maggie couldn't help but wonder how long that would last before Ivan's men beat or raped it out of her. Of how they would view her strong will as a challenge, a game they would take great pleasure in winning.

"This information has been passed on to Yasir Osman's militia group. The longer you continue to ignore our demands, the more agents we will compromise. Release Ivan Dalca before another of your agents loses their life."

Helmsley closed the video as the girl repeated the demands.

Maggie worried at her nails, chipping the polish from them. "Have you made contact with him yet?" Being mid-mission in Somalia explained why she hadn't heard from Leon. For all Maggie knew, he was unaware of the hack.

"It's not that simple," Helmsley said.

"Explain."

"The parameters of the mission changed once Agent Frost got there. Initially, he was to gather intel as the video said, but he had managed to infiltrate the cell deeper than we had hoped."

Damn Leon. He always was too good at his job.

"What is the mission now?"

"He managed to work his way into the inner circle of the cell's leader, Yasir Osman. In his last report, Frost spoke of being invited to Osman's compound out in the sticks. It was an opportunity we couldn't squander."

Maggie's eyed widened. "He's going to try to take the man out? In his own compound?"

She was all for taking risks; it was part of the job description. But the risks taken should be calculated ones, and no matter how much the government wanted this Yasir Osman dead, Leon knew better than to throw himself into such confined danger. It wasn't like him.

"Leon assured me he was capable of the task."

Leon was capable. Of that, Maggie had no doubt. He'd kill his target, and efficiently, too. It was his escape plan that concerned Maggie. In her experience, compounds were fortresses—secluded, heavily guarded, and filled with the enemy.

"When was that?" she asked. If luck was on their side, Leon could have carried out his mission by now and would be making his way home imminently.

"Four weeks ago."

Maggie closed her eyes. Four weeks was a long time for a hit. By nature, they were in-and-out jobs. It didn't do to linger after assassinating someone. Once the kill was made, you got out. Complications sometimes arose. Nothing ever went strictly to plan. Perhaps Leon hadn't been able to get as close as he'd initially thought. Or maybe his attempt at ending his target had failed.

Maggie didn't allow herself to ponder that option too long. "And nothing from him since then?"

"No," Helmsley said. "Being in so deep, communication has been suspended until Agent Frost makes contact."

Maggie didn't like it, but she understood. Any attempts the Unit made to reach Leon could blow his cover. Not that it mattered now.

"Make contact now," Maggie insisted, conscious of each and every second they wasted talking. "Get him out before he's exposed."

Helmsley took a deep breath, the shake in it the only crack in her otherwise composed exterior. "We can't."

"You mean you won't," Maggie retorted, leaning over the desk.

"We don't have that kind of power over there," Helmsley snapped. "Agent Frost knew that going in."

"So, he's on his own? Just another expendable asset that can be replaced? Collateral damage?"

"I never said that."

"You don't have to."

The disaster with Bishop had helped Maggie see the Unit for what it really was. Ashton had been right all those years ago when he got out. The agency's agents weren't people. They were property, just like Ivan's trafficked girls. Assets. They targeted Maggie when she was desperate, as they had done most of the other agents. Young and impressionable, they were molded into killers who could take orders without question and sent out to risk their lives time and time again.

Helmsley rose from her chair and glared down at her.

"Don't you dare for a second think that I don't care about my agents. I chose Frost as my new chief."

"Yet you let him go on the mission," Maggie said, kicking her chair back and rising, too. "Bishop was never deployed on any jobs when he had the position."

"Frost's skill set made him perfect for the brief. You know that as much as I do. He fit the profile for the kind of man we needed. He insisted he be the one to go."

"You could have sent Yonas Ibori." Maggie couldn't recall if he spoke Somali, but she knew for a fact he could at least speak Arabic.

The Unit liked to keep more than one asset of a particular type. Whenever Maggie was tied up on a job, Nina would be sent instead of her. As they were both white women and fluent in Russian, this kept them busy. Yonas and Leon were the same. Their African heritage was used to the Unit's advantage, both men finding themselves on the continent more than the likes of Maggie.

"Ibori's on paternity leave. He and his husband adopted a little girl last month."

Maggie would need to send them a card. She almost laughed at the thought. So mundane amid the surreal conversation she was having with her old boss. Leon was in danger, and no one was there to help him.

"I'm not going to stand by while you do nothing. You might be fine with crossing him off your roster, but I will not give up on him. Ever."

Grace huffed. "I see Bishop's assurances that the two

of you were no longer romantically involved was yet one more lie."

"Whatever." Maggie had heard enough. Leon was on borrowed time, and she wasn't going to waste any more of it talking to a cold, old battle-axe.

"Where are you going?" Helmsley asked as Maggie shoved past her.

"To save him."

"You're needed here," Helmsley called behind her.

Maggie stopped and turned at the door. "Leon needs me, and that is all I care about."

"He could already be dead."

"If he's dead, then god help the people who did it."

Chapter 8

Farnborough, Great Britain

Farnborough Airport lay thirty-five miles southwest of London. It had rained the whole way there, the day nothing but a grim downpour of gray. So much for summer.

Maggie hadn't spoken much during the journey, too lost in the multitude of things that could go wrong with their plan, of what could be happening to Leon, and the danger that had arrived on their doorstep so soon after Bishop's betrayal. It was just one thing after another.

"Thank you for this," she said as she got out of the car and collected her hastily filled duffel bag from the trunk.

"Of course." Ashton took the bag from her, and they

rushed out of the rain to the check-in building of the private airport. "He's practically my brother."

"You didn't talk for years."

"Exactly."

Maggie allowed a smile and hugged her best friend's broad shoulders once they were inside. "Seriously, though, thank you."

"We'll get him home," Ashton promised into her ear and squeezed her tight. "Don't worry."

Unlike a commercial flight, checking in and going through security was a breeze. Maggie had more than one passport with her, unsure which of her aliases might be needed for what they were about to do, but no one asked her for any documentation. She gave Ashton a questioning look, to which he replied with a sly wink.

The private jet, an elegant Legacy 500, sat waiting for them at their corresponding gate. A sleek, eight-passenger plane that came with all the mod cons the social elite who could afford such luxury could want, including Wi-Fi, beds, a fancy dinner-and-drinks menu, and a cabin attendant.

"This must have cost a pretty penny," Maggie said, guilt rising within her at costing her friend so much money. Not that she refused Ashton's offer when he gave it. Guilt she could cope with. Losing Leon was a whole other beast entirely, and a possibility she would do all she could to avoid.

"Don't worry, Mags. The guy who owns the plane owes me a favor, so I got it cheap."

Maggie's and Ashton's ideas of "cheap" were two very different things.

"Hi, welcome," greeted a handsome young man at the foot of the drop-down stairs leading up into the plane. "I'm Craig, and I'll be your cabin attendant for your flight." His eyes stuck to Ashton as he spoke, giving the Scot a little more than mere professional attention. Maggie couldn't blame the man. Ashton was quite the sight, with his immaculate dark hair, muscled, tattoo-covered arms, and deep-blue eyes that promised mischief.

"Nice to meet you," Ashton said, handing over their bags.

Craig introduced them to the two pilots once inside, and they prepared for takeoff. Ashton had made it clear the flight was urgent when making the arrangements, so they prepared to leave as soon as he and Maggie sat down.

"A double whisky for me and the good lady when you get a minute, Craig," Ashton said with a knowing grin before turning his attention back to Maggie. "You look like you need one."

"Nine hours, Ash," she said, staring out the window as they left the interior loading bay and taxied out onto the runway. "A lot can happen in nine hours."

"Don't think about it that way. For all we know, Leon's made it out already. Don't forget, he's as resourceful as you, and almost as resourceful as me. And anyway, if he does need our help, that gives us nine hours to plan."

The tears she'd held back in front of Helmsley slipped down her cheeks, betraying her outer resolve. Craig arrived with their drinks and handed her a napkin without comment. Ashton didn't seem to worry about talking in front of him or the pilots, so Maggie didn't either. She was sure their discretion was well paid for.

"You really love him, don't you," Ashton said, watching her from across the table between them.

"I can't think about any of that right now." What mattered was preparing for what they must do. They didn't have much to go on, but at this point, Maggie was desperate and willing to risk anything to get Leon out of Somalia in one piece.

"You're not an agent now," Ashton pressed, not for the first time. "You can be together without the Unit sticking their noses into things."

It wasn't just the Unit, though. Not even two months had passed since she'd left the job and her old life behind, and already she'd been dragged back into it. She was beginning to think she'd never be able to escape.

"We'd never be able to have a normal life."

Ashton considered her for a moment. "With you two, I don't think things will ever be normal. You've just got to take what life throws at you and try to make it work in the process. You're both miserable without each other.

Besides, who wants a 'normal' life anyway? Whatever that is. Sounds boring, if you ask me."

Maggie stared down at her hands. "What if I do?"

"Then fight for it," Ashton said with an unusual sharpness. "You're willing to fight for so many things for other people, Mags, but when it comes to your own happiness, you shy away and give up."

Maggie blinked. "Kick me while I'm down, Ash."

"I'm giving you a kick up the arse. You're in need of one, and I love you too much to let you sit there and feel sorry for yourself. You're about to fly thousands of miles to rescue Leon, but you're still sitting here thinking of all the ways you and he won't work when it's clear that you're head over heels for the man."

Maggie sat in silence, unable to retaliate with a response. It wasn't every day she was slapped with the truth like that, especially from Ashton.

The engines ramped up behind them before the breaks were released and the jet raced down the runway for takeoff. Smaller planes always seemed more precarious to Maggie; the impact from hurtling up thousands of feet into the sky and navigating the wind felt more intense in the close confines.

Not that the classy private jet was claustrophobic. At almost thirty meters long and two wide, it was like sitting in someone's living room. The interior was decorated in beautiful maple wood and cream leather, making it appear more spacious. The seats were large and comfortable enough to sleep on without them being turned down into beds, and a long couch ran the rest of the length of the plane behind them before reaching the restroom at the back. As far as flying went, this was the way to go. Maggie only wished they were headed on vacation as opposed to diving headfirst into what could be a very dangerous shitstorm.

"Now," Ashton said, once the plane settled above the clouds and the engines calmed down, "what's the plan?"

Maggie hadn't had time to come up with anything detailed or foolproof. All she had cared about was getting to Somalia as fast as she could. Now that they were on their way, she was left with the task of scrambling together a plan that could work.

"Helmsley came through," Maggie said after what felt like a century of tense waiting. They were only a few hours away from Somalia now, and she grew more anxious and agitated with each passing minute.

Tossing her ego aside, Maggie had sucked it up and called her old boss, not bringing up their little scene from earlier when she'd walked out. Grace never mentioned their tiff either. Both women seemed to care more about getting Leon out now that it was clear Maggie was arriving there in a matter of hours, whether the Unit liked it or not.

"The Somali government has a man inside," she explained to Ashton. "He isn't at the compound, but he was the one who managed to set up a meeting with Yasir and told him about Leon."

Maggie filled her friend in on everything the Director General told her about Leon's mission and how he was masking as the son of wealthy Somalis living in Britain. Even Ash had scoffed at Leon's plans to take out Osman from inside his own compound in the middle of nowhere. This only reinforced Maggie's view that it was a dumb move, given that Ashton had a habit of throwing himself into the thick of things without thinking first. She almost smiled with chagrin at the thought. Wasn't she doing the exact same thing now?

"How can he help?" Ashton asked, tucking into a steak dinner Craig had made for him. Maggie had no idea how he could eat so close to a mission. She'd forced down what she could of the complimentary snacks earlier, knowing she'd need the energy, but they only made her churning stomach worse.

"Yasir hasn't ventured into Mogadishu after an attempt on his life a few weeks ago by Somali soldiers. He sends his younger brother now instead, and he has arranged a meeting tonight with their men stationed in the city."

"Why are they meeting?"

Maggie read the email Grace had sent and memorized the address of their meeting place; some run-down house at the edge of town in an area even the soldiers avoided. "The contact didn't know, but it's most likely to arrange another terrorist attack on the city."

"And what?" Ashton asked as he polished off the final bites of his meal with a glass of white wine. "We're going to crash the party?"

Maggie shook her head. "I'm not, but Ekaterina is."

"Ah. Doing a little business in the area, is she?"

"She is now. If I can get to that meeting and speak with Yasir's brother, we might be able to talk him into setting up another meeting with the man himself." It was a long shot, but it was more than they had before they took off. Maggie clung to it with every bit of hope she could muster. It had to work.

"And you think said meeting might be held in Yasir's compound since he's giving Mogadishu a wide berth?"

"It's the best chance we've got. Otherwise we're left with trying to break in." Though it was an alternative option, it was one Maggie would prefer to avoid.

Ashton appeared to be of a similar mind. "If this Al-Shabab cell is as legit as you say they are, breaking in undetected will be nigh impossible."

"Which is why we need to be at that meeting."

"And this is where Ekaterina comes in."

"And her bodyguard, of course. Helmsley's arranged for some weapons to be 'donated' for the meeting by our own troops stationed in the city. They don't have many to spare, but it will hopefully be enough to convince Yasir and his brother that we have a lot more where those came from."

Ekaterina Kovrova was one of the many aliases Maggie had adopted over the years, the skill of taking on a new persona one of her particular specialties. Ekaterina was the ideal one for the task that lay ahead. She was Russian, for one. Russia was hardly known for its love and close ties with Britain and the rest of the Western world, which people like Yasir vehemently despised. It would at least explain why Ekaterina was willing to do business with Yasir's militia.

The big plus for using Ekaterina was her profession. Thanks to the excellent work of Ashton's friend Gillian, an eccentric housewife turned criminal forger, the name Ekaterina Kovrova was known all across the black market. Through a network of eyes and ears, rumors, and taking responsibility for trades and deals no one could pin on anyone, her alias was well established as being one of the most elusive, discreet, and well-stocked arms dealers available.

"Weapons won't be easy to come by for their group now that they've been shafted out of all the major ports and cities." Ashton wiped his mouth with a napkin and leaned back in his seat with a satisfied full belly. "The chance to purchase new stock won't be easy for them to refuse."

"I hope you're correct," Maggie said. "Right now, that's all we have going for us."

Neither of them brought up the fact they had no plans for what they would do once they reached the compound. Aside from it being hard to predict what might arise, they were both well aware that they might not make it back out again—if they even made it that far in the first place.

Maggie got up and stretched her stiff back, thankful that she'd packed the vital necessities needed to transform herself into the Russian, along with a few other options. "I better get ready. We'll be landing soon."

Ekaterina had come in handy when Maggie was framed for murder, and she could only hope that her alias would help her out of this situation, too. She'd wormed her way out of too many sticky situations not to believe in luck, and if there was ever a time for Maggie to catch a break on a mission, it was most definitely this one. It wasn't only Leon's life that could depend on it—it was hers and Ashton's, too.

Chapter 9

Mogadishu, Somalia
12 July

Being undercover in such heat was a whole new level of irritating. Even under the cloak of night, a close, humid air hung thick in Mogadishu, like breathing in a sauna.

Maggie's head itched under her wig. Unlike her own wavy blond hair, Ekaterina's fell almost to her waist, black as raven's feathers and severely straight with a blunt fringe. At least she could forgo her contacts for this one. Maggie's forger had given the Russian alias her same ice-cold eyes.

Dressed in a sharp, fitted business suit to match

Ekaterina's ever-serious nature, it was all Maggie could do not to strip off her jacket and wave a hand over her face. It was just after midnight and Maggie wasn't looking forward to how hot it would get once the sun rose. If they lived long enough to see it, of course.

They had to make their own way to their contact's house. It was in a nicer part of town than their meeting place, but that wasn't saying much. The whole of Somalia was like the Wild West.

Dilapidated buildings lined every dusty street, most of the small businesses shuttered down for the evening. No one had any business being out on the streets at this time; most of the locals knew better than to stay out after dark. While daylight didn't guarantee safety, night was for the devious, the deceitful, and the dangerous.

Maggie kept her eyes sharp as Ashton drove the beat-up car, used in some small attempt to blend in. The city was notoriously hazardous—gun violence, robberies, murder, and kidnappings were as common as the sunrise. The British government listed Somalia as a strict no-go zone when it came to travel. Not that it was the kind of place people wanted to go for their two-week vacation from work, but anyone thinking of going to Mogadishu was strongly advised otherwise. Maggie could see why.

Craig and the two pilots remained at the Aden Adde International Airport, inside the plane and on the runway by Maggie's advice, and under strict orders to leave if they felt their lives were under any threat. Westerners weren't welcomed by most in Somalia, and though the woman and two men were aware of the dangers, their eyes had bulged when Ashton handed them a gun each and showed them the basics.

The British soldiers had met them upon landing with the promised guns, the team of men warning them not to stay long. Maggie didn't intend to. If things went her way, they would be back in the air before morning, with Leon among them.

Eleven minutes from the airport, their contact lived around the corner from the Banadir Hospital in a run-down, two-story building. Ashton parked out front and Maggie spotted a head peeking out the window behind closed curtains. A minute later, the man was outside, checking up and down the empty street before approaching their car.

Maggie and Ashton got out, armed with some of the weapons the soldiers had provided for tonight's ruse. Maggie held her hand close to where a concealed gun hung at her waist, ready and willing to use it at the slightest sign of danger.

"Ugaas Warsame?" she asked, having memorized the name Helmsley sent over.

The man nodded. "Maggie Black?"

His English was broken but clear enough, which was good considering neither Maggie nor Ashton spoke a word of Somali or Arabic. Ugaas was a tall, slender man with sharp cheekbones and hard eyes that spoke of someone who had witnessed many hideous things in his lifetime. Maggie knew the look, having seen it in the mirror often enough.

They each shook hands with their new comrade, keeping introductions short.

"Switch to my car," Ugaas said, motioning them to follow him to his beat-up truck. "Safer. Tahiil knows it."

"How long have you been undercover against Yasir?" Ashton asked.

Having both been on long jobs pretending to be someone other than themselves, Maggie and her best friend knew the effects a long-term mission could cause. Losing touch with what was real and what wasn't was a common side effect of prolonged infiltration, and Ugaas wouldn't be the first person to have switched alliances during the process.

"Eighteen months," Ugaas replied, coming over to help Maggie move the two large crates of weapons from the trunk of their car to the back of his truck. "Though not much longer. I hope."

Helmsley had assured Maggie that Ugaas was unaware of Leon's name being leaked, at least according to the Somalian's handler. A pang of regret stirred within Maggie at that, but the less the man knew, the less she had to worry about things going wrong. The success of the job already hung on a knife edge.

Ugaas drove them to the opposite end of the city, avoiding Jidka Warshaddaha, the main street that ran through its heart. While Maggie and Ashton knew Ugaas was undercover, the military and associated militia groups who fought against Al-Shabab didn't, and they would show no mercy if they believed him to be a part of the terrorist cell. Not to mention the many questions Maggie and Ashton's presence would cause. They'd already gained enough unwelcomed attention at the airport.

"Does Tahiil speak English?" Maggie asked, searching the truck for signs of working air-conditioning, only to come up short.

Ugaas shrugged. "A little. Like me."

It would have to be good enough. She was at least confident the presence of the weapons would help Tahiil understand her proposition. If he didn't see it as a threat and shoot them before Maggie could even say a word, that is.

Ashton fidgeted next to her, wearing a black T-shirt and combat trousers instead of the slick suit he'd worn during the flight. Any foreigner who found themselves in the city would be insane not to bring protection in the form of a guard, and preferably a whole crew of them. Ekaterina wouldn't be so dumb or so bold as to not come along with at least one armed man by her side.

"You know Assad?"

Maggie frowned before remembering it was Leon's false name for the mission. She managed a "yes" but nothing more. She needed to remain composed and in control going into this meeting.

"I hope he kills Yasir." Ugaas rummaged in his pocket and produced a worn, crumpled photo of a toddler. He was a cute little thing, with a big infectious smile and a whiff of black hair. "My boy," Ugaas said with pride. "He's two next month. I wish to be there for the day."

"I hope you get to see him soon," Ashton said, handing the well-loved photo back over.

Maggie avoided staring at it too long, her recent past threatening to relive itself. Of the doctor's office. Of falling apart on the floor at the news. Of not being able to tell Leon.

Ugaas slowed down outside a series of residential buildings that were little more than rubble now, the recent victims of a grenade or bomb. "This is it," the Somalian announced. "Once Tahiil arrives, I will come for you. Too dangerous before then."

Maggie nodded in agreement. Ugaas wasn't the only person meeting Tahiil. All the local members planted in the city were to be there for some announcement of Yasir's. The thought of being so close to a group of terrorists made Maggie's muscles twitch, her reflexes wanting to enter fight mode and take them all down.

"Take one of the crates," she said before Ugaas left. "We'll bring the other when we enter."

Their arrival would be more welcomed if Tahiil had time to inspect some of the merchandise before they met face-to-face. Two unknown white people walking in without an invitation would not end well. Even with Ugaas vouching for them.

"Very well." Ugaas took the crate and pointed out a hiding spot near a secluded part of the wreckage, close to the group's usual meeting point. "Good luck," he said.

"You, too," replied Maggie, taking a deep breath. They were all going to need it.

Their contact left them and went to stand at the meeting place. They'd arrived early to ensure no one saw Maggie and Ashton before they wanted them to, and as the time ticked by, more and more of those loyal to Yasir trickled in. They never arrived in groups, sticking to a maximum of two at a time, a nice tactic to stay under the radar on the journey there.

"Twelve now," Ashton whispered, sneaking a glimpse of the new arrivals. "The odds are not in our favor."

"We've taken out more than twelve before," Maggie reminded him, and herself. They'd been in worse situations, though standing there, she couldn't think of any.

Eventually, the group quieted their chatter and fell into silence. Footsteps echoed through the wasteland and off the crumbling walls.

An authoritative voice said something in greeting.

Maggie inched next to Ashton to get a good look. "That's Tahiil, all right," she murmured, getting a better visual of him now than the image on the surveillance photo Helmsley had sent over. The cluster of waiting men bowed their heads in respect.

Tahiil wasn't alone. Behind him stood three more men, all of them armed with AK-47s and belts of grenades. Sixteen against two now.

It seemed like forever standing there and waiting to be sent for, even though Ashton's watch said it was only eight minutes. Tahiil spoke for a few of those minutes before noticing the crate at Ugaas's feet. They exchanged words, heated on Tahiil's part, placating on Ugaas's. After some rushed explanations from Ugaas, Tahiil settled a bit and had his guards examine the box before looking himself.

They must have been to the man's liking, for he asked Ugaas a host of questions before their contact said something he didn't like. Tahiil's back straightened, and he barked orders to his men. Maggie didn't understand, but the circular hand gesture that came with it was universal.

Search the surroundings.

Ashton tensed beside her and Maggie battled against the urge to reach for her gun.

Tahiil was shouting at Ugaas now, but their contact continued talking, his voice growing more urgent as he appeared to try to explain himself for bringing Maggie and Ashton with him.

Fear penetrated Maggie's thoughts, but she willed them back and got into character. Ekaterina would never falter to something as weak and human as fear. Her cold, calculating nature was far too pragmatic to deal with such a base emotion.

Instead, Maggie straightened her back, told Ashton to put his hands in the air, and did the same before one of the three guards discovered their hiding spot.

The barrel of an AK-47 pointed at them soon enough, along with some choice words from the guard. When their lack of understanding grew apparent, the guard nudged over to his boss with his gun, and Maggie and Ashton stepped out and headed toward Tahiil.

Not before being shaken down and removed of all weapons, of course.

The first guard kept his gun targeted at them while the other two completed their search and tossed all the weapons found in with those already inside the other crate. The second crate was dumped at Tahiil's feet, and the guards kicked the backs of Maggie's and Ashton's knees to send them kneeling to the floor before their boss.

Tahiil regarded them with vile distaste. He wasn't a big man like his brother was supposed to be, gangly almost, with a thin neck Maggie would have liked to wrap her hands around until he stopped breathing. His freshly broken nose was evidence enough that someone else very recently indulged the urge to lay hands on him.

"English?" he inquired to Ashton, ignoring Maggie.

"Russian," Maggie said as Ekaterina with unflinching offense at her guard being thought of as the one in charge. "Though I speak English, too. He is my guard."

Tahiil frowned and stared at her for a moment like she was an animal at the zoo. "What is a woman from Russia doing here in Mogadishu?"

"Business. And believe me when I tell you said business is not done on my knees." Maggie moved her gaze to the crates.

"Weapons?"

"Yes, weapons. Now can I get up? The rubble is digging into my knees and ruining my clothes." She made sure to keep a noticeable accent while speaking English.

One of the guards checking the crates said something to Tahiil, and he nodded before turning back to Maggie. "These weapons are the ones the British use over here. Not Russian."

"Yes," Ekaterina agreed. "That's because they're stolen."

Something in Tahiil's face changed at that, but Maggie couldn't decipher what it meant.

Without being approved to do so, Maggie got up. One of the guards grabbed at her shoulder with forceful fingers to return her to her knees, but Tahiil held up his hands.

The guard let Maggie go, and Ekaterina dusted off the spot on her suit jacket where the man's fingers had been. "I'm here to sell. From what I hear, you are in the business of buying, yes?"

"We have more than enough weapons."

"No, you don't."

Tahiil's fingers twitched like he wanted to slap her, but Maggie continued talking.

"You haven't had any new shipments since losing the ports. Knowing this, I will charge you more, but I think you'll find my prices are still fair."

"We could take them," Tahiil said.

Ekaterina didn't flinch, despite the increasing unease inside Maggie. "By all means, take these samples if you want. They are just a drop in the ocean compared to the artillery I have at a secure location."

"I could force you to tell me where."

"Assuming I know, that is," Maggie retorted, thinking back to Osman down in the basement at Belmarsh. "I said they were secure, and that includes the location being secure from my knowledge to avoid such threats. If you want them, you will have to buy them. Or more correctly, your brother will have to buy them."

"How can we be certain where your loyalties lie?" Tahiil asked after a long silence.

Ekaterina gave a tight smile, unused to the feel of it across her lips. "The only thing I'm loyal to is money."

Another long silence passed.

Maggie was about to talk again when Tahiil broke the unnerving quiet and issued orders to his men. The guards moved forward while the men stationed in the city began to disperse back out home.

"A single man and a mere woman are no threat to my brother. Let's see what he thinks of your offer."

Before Maggie could reply, a guard heaved a bag over Ashton's head while the other two held his fighting arms.

Tahiil pointed to Ugaas as well who stopped dead as the others left around him. Once they'd bagged Ashton, the guards forced him into one, too.

Maggie stood her ground, making sure to display Ekaterina's displeasure but not showing any signs of resistance. While they may be arriving with covered heads and tied arms, Tahiil was taking them to see Yasir.

Which meant she was one step closer to Leon. Maggie only hoped she wasn't too late.

Chapter 10

None of them said a word.

With Tahiil speaking English, the risk of him overhearing a hushed conversation was far too risky.

Sweat trickled down Maggie's back as she struggled to breathe in the overbearing heat of the van they'd been shoved into. The rough canvas over her head stifled her air supply and rubbed against her face and neck, irritating her skin. None of it helped the nauseating bubble of anticipation that rose within her.

They rode for what must have been an hour, each of the captives bumping into each other as they traversed uneven terrain. Ugaas banged into Maggie as the car took a sharp turn in the road and he slumped at her side. His whole body tremored, and she crossed her fingers that the man was capable of remaining calm. Scared people did rash things, and rash people were dangerous. Especially in a situation like this.

The van slowed as the sound of scraped metal clattered outside. Gates being opened, from the sound of it. Once the clattering stopped, the van carried on at a snail's pace before stopping. The engine died, and the van shifted as those up front got out.

"Maggie," Ashton whispered.

"Keep to the story as long as possible," Maggie replied, making the most of the few precious moments alone. "We still need to find Leon."

The back doors opened, and strong hands grabbed at her. Maggie, retaining her persona of Ekaterina, swore in Russian and swatted at the culprit as best she could with her bound hands.

Half dragged, Maggie got out of the van and sighed deeply, welcoming the drop in temperature from the vehicle's stuffy confines. The heat still clung to the night air, but even the slightest change to her discomfort was much appreciated. Being British, Maggie operated much better in the snow than she did the blistering sun.

The Al-Shabab members conversed in their own language as Maggie was shoved forward and ushered along with the tip of a rifle at her back. Instead of panicking, she focused on getting her bearings. Underneath her feet, the ground was gritty, like sand. It changed to something more solid twenty or so paces into their walk, and the temperature dropped again. They were somewhere inside now.

"Where are we?" Ekaterina demanded.

"I told you," Tahiil said, now in front of her. "I'm taking you to see my brother, as you wanted."

"Take this bag off my head. Now." Her voice echoed off bare walls and carried down what she guessed to be a hallway.

Tahiil sighed. "Very well." He spoke to his men who grunted and went to work at untying her hands and then removing the insufferable sack.

The black hair of Maggie's wig stuck to the layer of sweat that covered her face. As the men worked at releasing Ashton and Ugaas, Maggie took the opportunity to take in her surroundings while she pretended to straighten her disheveled self.

Her suspicions had been correct. They stood in an empty stone hallway with only a rug to decorate the space. A few doors ran along the right-side wall, stopping at a fourth at the bottom. Maggie stole a glimpse out a window to her left and took in what she could of the exterior space inside the compound. Next to the van that brought them sat a row of jeeps, most of them new and expensively modified. While it was a bad sign that Yasir appeared well funded, Maggie preferred the positive outlook. At least they had their pick of getaway cars.

Assuming they even made it that far.

"This isn't the way you treat a potential business partner," she snapped, rubbing at her wrists.

"It's a safety precaution, I'm sure you understand." Tahiil's lips split into a sharp-edged grin.

Maggie folded her arms. Ekaterina had well and truly used all her reserves of patience. "As you said, I'm just a mere woman. What threat could I possibly pose to you?"

"This way, please. My brother is waiting for you."

"Good. I can speak to someone capable of talking terms. I'm through dealing with underlings."

Ashton shot Maggie a warning look. She knew she was goading the man, but there was something about Yasir's younger brother that made her skin crawl.

His grin turned to a sneer as he knocked on the final door at the end of the hall. A voice called from within, and he ventured inside, switching his dark expression to a more neutral one before passing the threshold.

One of his men made to push Maggie forward, but she shot him a warning scowl and strode inside with Ashton and Ugaas behind her. Gun or not, she would not show any of these terrorists fear. Not when they fed on it like maggots on a carcass.

The armed men followed and circled behind them, stoic soldiers in front of their leader, awaiting orders.

Like Helmsley's notes had indicated, Yasir was a much larger and more imposing man than his sibling. Though they shared the same dark features and hooked nose, his presence dominated the room whereas his brother slinked to the sidelines unnoticed.

Yasir sat behind a desk. His broad shoulders, calloused hands, and an array of battle scars across his muscled arms showed he wasn't one for sitting back and letting others do his dirty work. He was hands-on as he oversaw his terrorist operation, and Maggie was willing to bet he was a formidable threat all by himself.

The brothers exchanged words, Tahiil seeming to fill in Yasir on the happenings of his interrupted meeting in the city. Like Tahiil, Yasir didn't appear happy when Ugaas's name was mentioned, one of the only things Maggie could make out during the exchange.

Ugaas shifted on his feet and averted his gaze from Yasir. Maggie tried to catch his attention to give him some sign of encouragement that things would be okay, but his eyes were rooted to the floor in subservience.

"My brother does not speak English," Tahiil announced. "I will translate for him."

Maggie balled her fist. For all she knew, he could be telling his brother anything he bloody well wanted.

She raised her chin and spoke directly to Yasir, effectively ignoring Tahiil. "My name is Ekaterina Kovrova, and I am a Russian businesswoman. I have a cache of weapons, stolen from the British envoy here in your country. I'm here to offer you a fair deal for them."

Tahiil relayed her words to his brother who listened intently, all the while pinning his attention on Maggie.

She didn't so much as flinch under the man's scrutiny as she awaited his response.

His voice was a deep rumble that vibrated over the room. Tahiil nodded and said, "You are far from home. Why come so far to sell guns to me when you could have stayed home and sold weapons there?"

Maggie nudged Ugaas, not trusting Tahiil for a second. "Is that what he said?"

Ugaas nodded, so she answered.

"I go where the weapons are. I managed to acquire a supply here and wish to sell them in Somalia. I don't need to tell you how hard it is to smuggle anything in and out of here, thanks to the government and the number of pirates waiting for easy pickings."

"And why come to me?" Yasir asked through his brother.

"Simple supply versus demand. You're in need of weapons in your fight against the West, and I have stock to sell."

"Even if you know those weapons would be used against British soldiers?"

Maggie laughed, which was an odd thing for someone as stern as Ekaterina. It had a strange, maniacal edge to it. "I'm Russian, Mr. Osman. And I think if there is one thing we can agree on, it is that there is no love lost between them and us. Quite frankly, I don't care how you choose to use the weapons, as long as you purchase them."

"Purchase?"

Maggie crossed her arms and gave Yasir an exasperated look. "Yes, your brother and I have already had this conversation about 'taking them,' so perhaps he can fill you in."

Yasir huffed a laugh when Tahiil explained Ekaterina's fail-safe plan of not knowing the location of the weapons. He even appeared impressed. "Smart."

"Yes, I thought so. Now, can we move ahead and talk business? I have a flight waiting for me, and I don't care to miss it."

Yasir shook his head slowly, his voice dropping dangerously low as he told his brother what to say.

"No business. No weapons. No deal."

"Why not?" Maggie asked, her pulse quickening.

"We cannot trust you," Tahiil replied.

Ekaterina was nothing if not a good negotiator. If anything, their lack of trust could help Maggie and Ashton stay in the compound long enough to find Leon. So, she improvised.

"If you're worried about collecting the shipment, I can arrange for them to be brought here, or collected by your men at a location of your choosing. I'll even stay here until they arrive, if you insist. My choice of buyers is limited in this country."

Yasir stroked his long beard as his words were translated. "It is strange that you chose to come here when you did."

"Meaning?"

Ugaas froze at her side as Yasir spoke, his already worried expression turned to something close to despair.

"We found a mole within our ranks today," Tahiil relayed, "and then you show up out of the blue. It is also strange that the same man who introduced us to the mole is the same man who brought you to our meeting."

Yasir continued, standing from his chair as his voice grew close to shouting while Tahiil rapidly translated.

"In my experience, where there is one rat, there are many." Yasir stabbed a finger at Ugaas. "If you are a rat, then so is this bitch and her guard. There is only one way to deal with those who try to betray me, and it is the same way we deal with the infidel scum we fight against."

Yasir continued, but before Tahiil could translate, Ugaas dropped to his knees and pleaded with the terrorist leader. Tears spilled down his cheeks and desperation soaked into each of his words as they spewed from his mouth.

Ashton tried to pick Ugaas up, but one of the guards behind them shoved a gun in his face.

Yasir swept a hand across the air like a knife and sneered down at Ugaas. He said something with an air of finality to it.

"What did he say?" Maggie asked Ugaas.

Ugaas looked up at her with haunted eyes. "He said that—"

Maggie never got to hear what Yasir said. Before

Ugaas could finish telling her, Yasir took one of the guns from his men and shot the man clean in the head.

Blood spattered across Maggie's and Ashton's faces, pieces of Ugaas flying through the room and sticking to the walls in globs of red and black.

Tahiil laughed and gave an order to the soldiers, eyes alight as he translated for them. "Take them out back, with the other one."

Ashton moved first. He made for Yasir, but his men were on him before he could so much as take two steps in their leader's direction. A fist smacked into his jaw, followed by a brutal kick to the stomach from another as an arm wrapped around Maggie's waist and pulled her back.

She kicked out as the men continued to assault Ashton, tackling him to the floor. Her foot caught one of them with a satisfying crunch before another snatched her feet and held them together, no matter how much she tried to wriggle free from his grasp.

They were outnumbered and unarmed. Knowing it was useless, Maggie stopped struggling and fell into a dead weight as they hoisted her and Ashton up and carried them out of Yasir's room.

Instead of leaving the way they came, the men, followed by Tahiil, carried them down a second hallway and through a door that lead to the back end of the compound.

Two of the soldiers dragged Ugaas's dead body

behind them, talking jovially as they walked, like it was just any other day. Ugaas's head was obliterated, the close-range shot blowing a hole straight through the poor man's skull. Maggie bit back tears as she caught sight of the photo of his son, the corner peeking out from his jeans pocket.

A security light blasted on as the macabre band marched outside, illuminating the plot of land with a bright yellow glow.

Dark smears trailed through the sand-covered dirt. In the center of the plot, lit up like a stage, was a mound of dug-up earth. Shovels lay beside it, along with a large, human-shaped hole at least six feet deep. Surrounding the hole lay smaller mounds of recently upturned dirt that had been patted back down. Maggie was under no illusion of what lay underneath, even if the graves held no markings of memorial.

Maggie struggled to see more from the way the men carried her, but something else caught her attention as they drew nearer. Something else next to the vacant hole.

It grew clearer the closer she got to it, and her heart plummeted as realization kicked in.

It was Leon. Unmoving and lying in a pool of his own blood.

Maggie screamed. They were too late.

Chapter 11

shton must have spotted him, too, because his voice added to Maggie's cries.

Leon.

Dead.

Maggie thrashed in her captives' grasp, twisting, kicking, punching, and scratching until she broke free. Landing on the ground with a thud, she scampered across the sand to where her lover and friend of over twelve years lay, still and silent as the night around them.

The men didn't come after her. Where was she going to run off to? Not far given that they were in the middle of nowhere and she had multiple guns pointed at her. If she dared try to shoot off into the darkness beyond, she'd be dead before she reached the compound wall.

"Leon," she said, in a high-pitched wail. "Leon, wake up."

He didn't move, his face turned from her as he lay in a crumpled mess. Maggie turned him to face her with gentle hands, only to find them slick with the blood that covered every part of his visible skin and stained his sodden T-shirt.

"Please, wake up. You can't leave me. Not like this." Through tear-blurred eyes, Maggie knelt by his side and battled the tidal wave of grief that crashed into her.

They'd been too late.

She'd failed Leon.

And now she and Ashton would die, too. All because of her.

Maggie craned her neck to the stars and blinked through the tears that streamed down her face. The little balls of gas twinkled down at her, the crystal-clear sky giving way to their brilliance as they witnessed Maggie's entire world crumble into nothing but ash.

"Enough," came a voice behind her. Maggie spun and saw Tahiil arrive to spectate the ordeal, a smug, satisfied smile tugging at his lips.

Without thinking, she got up and charged the man, ready to gouge his eyes out with her bare hands.

Yasir's men intercepted her before she got very far, pulling her back like they were trying to draw back a wild animal.

Tahiil stood unmoved and unimpressed. "Not so fast, Ekaterina, or whatever your name is. We're not going to kill you that fast. You haven't dug out your graves yet." Tahiil clapped his hands. "Get to work."

He gave orders to the men, some of whom followed behind him as he returned inside the compound, leaving Maggie, Ashton, and the two dead bodies with the six remaining armed soldiers.

They released Ashton and ushered him forward with their guns, yelling at him and pointing to the shovels.

Ashton swore and spat at their feet before collecting a shovel and coming to her side.

"Mags," he said, words thick with emotion. "Maggie."

He shook her shoulder, but she didn't budge, too lost in the cataclysm before her.

"I'm sorry, Ash," she murmured.

Ashton knelt and wrapped an arm around her. "None of this is your fault. None of it, you hear me?"

But it was. She knew the risks involved in coming here. Maggie should never have allowed Ashton to take them. "You wouldn't be here if I hadn't suggested it," she said, unable to look him in the eye.

"Yes, I would," Ashton said, a single tear trailing down his dust-covered cheek. "We tried, Mags. We did all we could, but it just wasn't enough this time. Now, come on, you need to get up."

One of the men barked at them and zipped his lips as a sign for them to be quiet.

Maggie put a hand over Leon's chest, ignoring them. They didn't matter. Nothing mattered anymore.

"Leon, I—"

She straightened at the feel of it, the shred of hope pulling her out of the whirlwind of grief and despair. The faint thuds of a heartbeat thrummed under her fingers.

Leon wasn't dead.

He was far from fighting fit, but she hadn't lost him. He was alive.

Maggie released another cry, this time one of sheer relief. No one seemed to notice the change as her mind kicked back into gear and took stock of their situation. Her hand tightened around the fabric of Leon's shirt as resolve washed over her and solidified into clear intent.

Leon was alive, and she was going to ensure he stayed that way.

Pulling Ashton down into a seemingly sorrow-filled embrace, Maggie brought her lips to his ear. "He's not dead," she whispered.

Maggie felt Ashton's tense muscles relax a little as he let out a relieved shudder.

"We've got to find a way out of this," he replied.

"We will. We've come too far for it to end here. I won't allow it."

"Me neither."

Maggie kissed his cheek. "On my move."

They untangled themselves from each other and got to their feet again.

One of the soldiers grew impatient with their lack of digging and stepped forward. He brought a hand across

Maggie's face with a hard smack that almost floored her, but she didn't retaliate. Not yet.

Maggie turned back to him, holding the side of her face as blood trickled down her lip. She displayed the shock and fear the man expected to see.

He would soon live to regret his blow, though not for long.

In the meantime, Maggie collected a shovel, and she and Ashton got to work on digging one of three graves that would remain empty. They needed to play it smart and bide their time. Taking out six armed men wouldn't be easy, and there would be plenty more inside the heart of the compound.

Sweat fell in beads down her forehead by the time they'd finished digging the second hole. Figuring it didn't much matter now, she tugged off her wig and tossed it into the growing pile of earth she and Ashton had excavated from the packed ground.

The soldier who'd hit her clicked his fingers and pointed to the lifeless body of Ugaas. His gesture was clear enough, despite the language barrier.

Dropping their shovels, Maggie and Ashton dragged poor Ugaas from where he'd been dumped and carried him down into a hole. Maggie closed his lifeless eyes and hoped that his family would be safe from Yasir's wrath now that they knew he was an infiltrator. People like the terrorist cell leader didn't stop at killing those who'd wrong them. They went after everyone you loved and wiped them out with ruthless disregard.

Once Ugaas was lowered into his final resting place, the soldier in charge pointed to Leon next.

"He's going to be too heavy," Maggie said, formulating an opportunity to strike.

Ashton nodded without comment and took his position at Leon's head. Maggie moved to his feet, and together, they made their fake attempt at heaving Leon up off the ground.

She hoped their struggle didn't hurt him or worsen his injuries. With so much blood and in the shadow-laden area the overhead security light created, it was hard to tell the extent of the damage Yasir and his people had inflicted.

The soldiers laughed at their struggle at first, but the head's impatience flared again, and he soon sent two of the other five soldiers to aid them with Leon's large frame.

Maggie tipped her head to the man at her right. Ashton nodded in understanding and reached for the shovel, his knuckles turning bone white as he gripped the handle, ready when she was.

Though the men still wore their rifles strapped around their shoulders, they needed to abandon their grip on the weapons to help out. As expected, they split up, one coming to either side of Leon, which was exactly what Maggie had anticipated.

They only had one shot, and Maggie made the most of it.

As soon as both soldiers bent down to tuck their hands underneath Leon, Maggie and Ashton wielded their shovels in unison and brought them up against their targets.

Maggie put the entire weight of her body behind the blow and sent the metal edge of the spade into the man's neck.

A sickening squish was accompanied by the spurt of arterial blood as it rained from the gash in the man's throat, the end of the shovel scraping the bone of his spine as it cut through muscle and sinew.

Ashton's adversary didn't fare well either, both soldiers bleeding profusely and summarily incapacitated. Seeing the fate of their comrades, the other soldiers reached for their guns.

Maggie knew this was coming and spun behind her dying victim. She wrapped her arms under his armpits and bore his weight to keep him from falling. Now the perfect shield from the bullets that flew from the other terrorists, Maggie reached for the AK-47 and took aim.

Ashton had hold of his soldier's gun, too, and together they released a tirade of bullets at the enemy, stepping out of range from Leon to ensure no stray bullets sunk into him.

The body of her human shield slammed into her with each bullet it took on her behalf, the force of it a very real reminder of the peril they were in. One round from one of the rifles was enough to end you, quick and clean.

Maggie fired at the soldier in charge, paying him back for the slap by sinking three rounds into his chest. With all the men down, both ex-agents turned to Leon and hoisted him up from the ground. There was no time to celebrate—already cries from within the compound rang out in response to the storm of gunfire.

"Which way?" Ashton asked, taking in the towering, impenetrable walls that ran the length of the compound in each direction.

Leon was in no fit state to risk the wilderness behind them, and they were too far out in what appeared to be a barren stretch of terrain for them to easily disappear.

"We'll need to go straight through."

Ashton set his jaw in determination, and they rushed forward, fast as possible given the load they had to bear. Leon was a lot of things, but small wasn't one of them, and Maggie's muscles strained under his weight with each step.

Footsteps sounded from behind the door they'd been brought out of, and they shared a look.

"I've got him," Ashton said, taking on the full burden of Leon. "You take care of them."

Maggie nodded, her heart close to bursting as Leon raised his head a little and planted his feet on the ground, roused by all the commotion. It was a good sign. Now they just had to make it out alive.

Men burst out from inside the compound, slamming the door against the wall as they charged toward them.

Thanks to the narrowness of the door, Yasir's soldiers were forced to exit one at a time, allowing Maggie to clip them with relative ease. The first one fell flat on his face, causing the next man to stumble while the rest struggled to jump over them both. They were all dead in seconds.

Maggie didn't think twice about stepping over the dead bodies of terrorists to enter the compound. She crept through the door, gun at the ready for anyone who dared get in their way. It was shoot to kill, and Maggie was an excellent shot.

More charging footsteps resounded from both ends of the hallway. Ashton dropped Leon on the ground, resulting in a pained groan from the injured man. Noise was good. It meant he was still alive.

The approaching men arrived at Ashton's side first, and Maggie helped him send round after round into the heads, necks, and chests of each one.

"I'm out!" Ashton called, pulling the trigger of his pilfered weapon. Maggie's rifle hadn't fared much better, and she checked the magazine. One bullet left.

"Leave it to me." Pressing her back to the wall on her right, Maggie inched to the corner of the hallway where the next set of terrorists approached from.

Maggie waited until the last moment, clutching her rifle like a baseball bat.

Without thinking better of what she was about to do,

she pivoted, turned the corner, and rushed the first man she met with a vicious swing.

The hilt of the gun collided with her enemy's jaw with a crunch that sent his teeth flying.

Before he knew what had hit him, Maggie twirled him around, shoving him into the next attacker while simultaneously snatching his rifle.

A symphony of bullets from the remaining men rang through the hallway, and Maggie dived behind the wall, falling on her back and aiming with her new and fully loaded gun. Expecting her to still be standing, the men weren't looking at the floor when they rounded the hall.

Blood spattered the walls in garish red, falling over her in warm raindrops as each man fell lifeless around her.

Ashton whistled in appreciation. "Well, that's one way to clear a room, Mags. Now, let's bounce."

Maggie got to her feet, almost slipping on the blood, and hurried to help her friend with Leon. Leon groaned again, coming to as they hoisted him back up and around Ashton's shoulders. "Maggie?"

"Yes, it's me," she replied, caressing his face as his eyes blinked open. "Ashton, too. We're getting you out of here." Maggie turned to Ashton and pointed down the left branch of the hallway. "Take him down that way and out into the courtyard. There are plenty of cars."

Ashton balked. "And what the hell do you think

you'll be doing while I get the big man into a getaway car?"

"I'm going to finish what Leon started. Yasir and Tahiil need to be stopped." Maggie handed Ashton her rifle now that they had more than enough to choose from. "Go! I'll be right behind you."

"Are you insane?" Ashton shouted as a lone soldier stumbled into Maggie's massacre. He gasped before reaching for his gun, but Ashton released shots into his leg, arm, and chest before he got the chance to strike. "We need to get the hell out of here before the rest of Yasir's brainwashed troops come and blow holes through us all."

"We can't allow them to live. Not after the damage they've done."

A bullet zipped between their faces. Ashton hissed as plaster flew off the wall upon impact and scratched the side of his face. Blood dripped down his cheek in crimson tears.

Another bullet grazed the top of Maggie's arm as she spun to take on the attackers. The force of the hit sent her reeling back as the wound burned and sent a searing pain down her firing arm.

"I don't think we have much of a choice in that matter," Ashton said, struggling to hold up Leon as he sent a string of rounds into the shooter. "What's important is that we all get out of here alive. Yasir and his weasel of a wee brother can be dealt with later, and by someone else. It's not your job to take them out. Not anymore."

"But—"

More footsteps thundered toward them, interrupting Maggie's protests.

"You know I'm right. Leon needs you more than his mission does. Sometimes you can't beat the bad guys."

Maggie huffed. It wasn't in her nature to run away, but Ashton was right. They were outnumbered and still in the thick of it with no guaranteed exit strategy. "Fine," she snapped, taking half of Leon's weight over her uninjured shoulder.

Leaving the rushing footsteps in their wake, the pair struggled down the opposite end of the compound with Leon and barged into the courtyard. With most of the residents heading to the location of the prior gunshots, the outdoor space was clear of enemies. For now.

Half dragging, half carrying Leon, they made it to the nearest jeep and opened the unlocked door. No need to lock up when the vehicle was inside the heart of a terrorist camp.

"There's no key," Ashton swore, checking the ignition, sun visor, and anywhere else someone might have left keys.

"It's fine, I've got it," Maggie said, nudging him out of the way. "Get Leon in the back." She then ripped the cover off the side of the ignition and hotwired it.

"I'll take a look at him," Ashton announced. Of the

two, he was the better medic. Maggie was more into inflicting injuries than healing them.

"Keep an eye out for any visitors, too." The last thing they needed was to miss an oncoming attack while trapped in the confines of a car.

The engine purred to life, and Maggie tilted her head back in temporary relief.

A blast echoed behind them, and the entire back window collapsed into a thousand pieces.

"We've got company," Ashton said, ducking behind the seat.

"No shit," Maggie said, suppressing the strange sensation to laugh. She put the jeep into reverse and slammed her foot on the gas.

Catching a glimpse of the terrorists running their way through the courtyard, Maggie turned the wheel and surged back until the rear end of the jeep slammed into them and trampled over their bodies.

Ashton whooped, getting a front-row ticket to the hit-and-run. "Strike!"

"Let's hope the gate falls just as easily," Maggie said. She switched gears and carried them forward, full pelt, towards the front gates of the fortress.

In the rearview mirror, Maggie spotted Yasir stomping out into the fray and throwing his arms around while yelling orders, his sniveling little brother following at his ankles. She gripped the wheel, still annoyed at leaving the men behind to carry out more atrocities.

"Hold onto him," Maggie ordered Ashton as they neared collision point pushing fifty miles an hour. Maggie fumbled with her seat belt, and it clicked into place just as the jeep crashed into the gate.

The force pushed back the metal until it bent and snapped, causing the gates to fly open and the jeep to careen out of the compound and into the open landscape.

"Hey, big man, lie down," Ashton said, trying to coax Leon onto his back. Leon wasn't having any of it.

He rasped something unintelligible between hoarse coughs that left blood on the back of his hands.

"What was that?" Maggie asked, trying to concentrate on the road while worrying over the roaring engines that started inside the compound, ready to give chase.

"The detonator," he repeated, clearer this time, rummaging inside the compartment between the two front seats and bringing out a small remote in his big, tremoring hands. "I wired the whole compound before I tried to take out Yasir."

Maggie let out an involuntary laugh, a mixture of relief and shock. Talk about beating a terrorist at his own game.

Ashton kissed Leon's forehead and cheered. "Leon, my man, you are a fucking genius." He took the remote from Leon's hands and eyed it with clear, boyish glee that set a flame in his otherwise blue eyes.

Ashton, forever the pyromaniac, pressed the button with a satisfying click. "Boom!"

Boom, indeed.

After a two-second delay, an earth-shattering explosion thundered through the sky as the entire compound erupted in a mushroom cloud of brick, mortar, and most importantly, pieces of Yasir Osman and his fellow terrorists.

Chapter 12

Maggie wasted no time in returning to the airport. There wasn't much air traffic in Mogadishu, and the pilots were more than eager to leave as soon as possible. Within ten minutes of arriving back on board, they were off without hesitation.

With the help of Ashton and a surprisingly unshaken Craig, Maggie hefted Leon onto the couch behind the seats and got to work. They stripped off his sodden, blood-soaked clothes and examined him for vital injuries requiring immediate attention.

Wiping away the layers of blood and dirt from Leon's dark skin, Ashton stopped at each wound that required extra care, cleaning out cuts with vodka from the bar and stitching them up with the supplies from the plane's first-aid kit. Maggie assisted while he worked, efficient but gentle with his friend, checking with Maggie first before examining Leon's more intimate regions. It wouldn't be the first time in history torture had turned sexual or sadistic, even if just to break the captive completely so they would tell everything they knew. Thankfully, it had not happened in this case.

Together, they spent the next hour tending Leon's injuries. Leon tried to brush them off, but Maggie hushed him and ignored the murmured protests as he slipped in and out of consciousness. Maggie could only hope this was from sheer exhaustion and nothing worse.

"If this was left any longer, he could have bled out," Ashton said, tying the end of his stitch work and snipping off the rest of the thread. The deep knife wound to Leon's thigh had knicked an artery and was the source of most of the blood. It seemed one of his torturers got a little carried away with his work.

They'd left him to bleed out in the dirt.

Maggie battled with the rage inside her and waited until it settled enough to reply. "He's alive; they're dead. They got what was coming to them."

There was no way of knowing the full extent of the damage caused by Yasir's splinter cell throughout its short but violent life. No way to heal the hurt of the families of those whose lives they had stolen. Of the hundreds, if not thousands, of innocent Somali people who perished by their hands. Or the British soldiers they'd murdered for trying to help. At least now, they couldn't hurt another living soul. Their personal reign of terror was over.

Maggie's dark thoughts were interrupted by Leon stirring awake. Once his eyes fluttered open, he shot up on the couch to a sitting position and darted his wild gaze around the jet while he gulped down panicked breaths.

"Hey, hey," Maggie said, cupping his face. The bristles of his beard were familiar and rough in her palms, longer than she'd ever seen it. "It's us. You're safe."

Sweat beaded across Leon's forehead and glistened on his exposed skin. "I thought it had been a dream."

For a moment, Maggie couldn't speak. She'd come so close to losing him, to one of her most terrifying nightmares becoming a reality. Seeing him there, injured yet alive, hearing his deep, rumbling voice brought her to the brink of losing it. Her arms ached to wrap around his neck and never let go. To never allow him out of her sight again. To protect him and keep him safe with her always.

Leon winced and groaned as he sat up straight, shivering under the blanket they'd put over him. He pulled it up to his chin.

"A dream? You never told me you dream about me," Ashton teased, lightening the mood as Maggie got herself together. "What was I wearing?"

Leon peered down at his bandaged, stitched, and bruised body. "What's the damage, Ash?"

"Well, they beat the shit out of you, that's for certain. The good news is most of your cuts and abrasions are superficial, and nothing appears to be broken." Ashton took a flashlight and flashed it into Leon's eyes, his right one bloodshot and surrounded in swelling. "No concussion either, from the looks of it, but I can't be sure of any internal damage. Best to get you checked out by a doc when we get back on solid ground."

"Thanks, Ash," Leon said, words that would never have escaped his lips only a few months ago when they were still estranged. Some rift a few years back when Ashton left the Unit meant my two best friends were no longer on speaking terms.

"Anytime, big chap." Ashton shook his bottle of pain pills he'd been taking for his broken ribs. "Take some of these. You won't feel your face, but from the look of you, I'm guessing that's a positive."

Maggie wasn't sure if the drugs were strictly legal, but Leon was in a lot of pain, no matter how hard he tried to hide it. She knelt next to him and handed him a cold bottle of water, taking the cap off first. "And drink this. All of it."

Leon winced as the liquid slid down his throat, residual pain from whatever torture methods Yasir had used on him.

"I never told him a thing," he said after draining the bottle.

Maggie took it from him and replaced it with a pack

of ice Craig handed her. "I always tell you that you're stubborn."

Leon hissed when he placed the ice over the nasty gash in his thigh but kept it there to manage the swelling. "Sometimes it pays off." He met her eyes, those warm, molten, dark irises boring into her soul like only he could do, seeing past the tough exterior she fought so hard to maintain.

"Sometimes." Maggie smiled, her heart warming under his attention. Ashton cleared his throat, breaking the moment with a cooling pad to soothe Leon's forehead.

Leon didn't like to be fussed over, so the fact he allowed Ashton to place it without complaint said more than his visible wounds did.

"How was I compromised?" he asked. "And how did you both learn about it?"

"All of that can wait until later," Maggie said. He didn't need to be troubled with the code red shitshow they were dealing with just yet. His head would be aching enough as it was.

"Please. I need to know. It's my job."

Maggie didn't argue much. She would be the exact same in his position, so she filled him in on what he'd missed with Ivan Dalca, the hack and release of agent names, and her reunion with the Director General.

"Have they released any names other than mine?" Leon asked, gripping the edges of his blanket with clenched fists.

"Jim Hunter," Maggie replied, thinking of the lost agent's kind face. "He was murdered before the Unit could pull him from his mission in China."

Leon's jaw clenched at the news. "Let me borrow your phone to call Helmsley. We need to stop them." He tossed his blanket off and attempted to get to his feet.

Maggie intercepted his ascent and pushed him gently back down onto the couch. It wasn't hard, given his shaky legs and fever. "We do, but right now you need to sleep so you can heal. Try to get some rest. We've got a long flight until we're back home. The rest of it can wait until then."

Leon's shoulders slumped. He knew as well as Maggie did that he couldn't do anything to help right now. Not in his state, and not in the early morning hours while stuck on a plane. Instead, he sprawled across the couch, his bare feet dangling off the end. He reached out with his calloused hand and entwined his fingers with Maggie's.

"Thank you, Maggie," he said, quieter now that Ashton had taken his seat up front and was partaking in some flirtatious conversation with Craig, the flight attendant. "I'd be dead if you hadn't come for me."

Maggie gave his hand a gentle squeeze. "I'll always come for you," she vowed. "No matter what."

"I feel the same way."

"I know," she said, sitting at the edge of the couch and rubbing her thumb over the back of his huge hand. "You believed me when no one else at the Unit did, and I'll never forget that."

He directly ignored his orders to hunt her down when Bishop and his cohorts had framed her for murdering the mayor of London. Instead, he'd come to her aid when she needed him most. He needed no explanation from her about what really happened; he required no irrefutable evidence to prove her innocence. He knew her well enough to know she'd never do such a thing, and that was enough for him. Enough to risk not only his job but his life, too.

"When are we going to talk about us?" Leon asked, still as ruggedly handsome as ever, even covered in fresh battle scars.

Maggie loosened her hold, but Leon held her still, his intense gaze imploring her not to shut him out. The way she always did, even after their last brief affair in Venice. After she'd learned she was carrying his child but lost it before she got the chance to tell him.

She should have told him, even after the fact. It wasn't just her loss, and though she knew it may hurt him to learn the truth, it was *their* truth. It was the reason why it hurt to get too close to him, and why it hurt not to be near him. It was the thing that held her back—not wanting to be hurt like that again, even though it wasn't his fault. Wasn't her fault.

Maggie gave his hand one final squeeze, trying but

failing to convey emotions she didn't have words for yet. "Once this is over and done with. I promise."

Leon rested his head on the pillow and sighed, but he didn't push her. "Okay. Wake me up before we land."

"I will," Maggie replied, making a vow to herself to tell him everything. Once they were safe.

Chapter 13

New Delhi, India

Secret Agent Prisha Patel knew something was wrong the minute she arrived to set up the transfer.

She'd memorized the account numbers given to her by the Unit. Had smuggled a gun inside her briefcase, just in case. And made sure she wasn't followed to the meeting point.

Up until then, her targets had been more or less jovial with her, helped by the fact they were all making a lot of money together. Or so they thought.

Yet when she arrived like always to make the payments, there was a distinct difference in her targets' attitudes. Their body language spoke volumes, and Prisha wasted no time getting out of there as soon as she could.

Now they were following her.

Prisha kept her pace casual so as not to alert the men she was aware of their presence. They weren't doing much to conceal their stalking; no slinking behind buildings or keeping a safe distance to stay out of sight. If anything, they were getting closer, their gaits more intent the farther Prisha walked through the city streets.

With the Indian government cracking down on counterfeit money by no longer continuing with high denomination notes, it left the forgers with the conundrum of what to do with their fake currency. It didn't take them long to come up with the enterprising idea to exchange the Indian rupees to pounds sterling and launder the cash through the UK banks before transferring it back over, effectively robbing Britain right under its nose.

Hence Prisha's presence in India's capital.

Things had been going well the last three weeks. Under the guise of a black-market accountant with particular expertise in making money disappear into practically untraceable offshore accounts, it didn't take long for her to wrangle her way into the fold of the largest counterfeit ring in India. What they didn't know was that she was transferring the stolen money back to the UK.

Another week at the most and she would have had enough for the Indian government to move in and take down the ring from their end, while the British narrowed in on those at the other side back home on the ring's payroll.

Prisha's phone rang, a temporary one solely for the purpose of her mission. Taking it out of her pocket, she frowned at the name on the caller ID: Dad.

It was a cover name to conceal the true identity of the person at the other end in case the forgers had searched her device, too. Which they had.

In her real life, Prisha had never met her father. He'd abandoned her mother and left them for another woman in India while her mum was pregnant with Prisha back in Britain.

It had been just the two of them Prisha's whole life, and she was keen to return to her, having been worried sick at the lack of news from the nursing home. Any unnecessary contact was far too dangerous to initiate back home, and though the Alzheimer's meant her mum wouldn't miss her, having forgotten Prisha's face many months before, not being able to visit or call was the toughest part of her work.

If Dad was calling, her suspicions of something being wrong was not a case of paranoia.

"Yes," Prisha answered.

"You've been compromised," said Director General Grace Helmsley. "Get out. Now."

Prisha stole a look over her shoulder at the approaching men. "Affirmative."

Without another word, Prisha hung up and tossed

the device down the nearest drain in case the forgers were using it to track her. Rounding the next street, she opened her briefcase and collected her gun, the metal cool and reassuring in her grip. Abandoning the briefcase too, Prisha hurried along the street and took a right, now as familiar with the local area as she was with her own neighborhood back in Soho.

It was early afternoon, and the market was packed. An infusion of spices wafted through the air, reminding her of her mum's home cooking. Cumin, turmeric, garam masala. It mixed together with the sizzling of spiced meats cooking on open flames and the crisp freshness of new material from rows of clothes and rolls of bright fabric in every color as entrepreneurs peddled their wares.

Prisha weaved between the shoppers and stalls, ducking under a clothing rack long enough to snatch a turquoise silk scarf to throw over her head and shoulders to conceal her identity.

She'd been so careful. So precise in her movements and what she'd said. Where had she gone wrong? How had she managed to mess things up? She'd never compromised herself before. Not once.

Prisha pushed those self-reprimanding thoughts to the side. It didn't matter how she was found out; what mattered was that they knew she was not who she claimed. A fact they seemed less than amused with given the number of men tailing her.

She'd counted five in total on her way to the market, though there could be more. Resisting the panic that spurred her to run, she kept a steady pace as she trailed through the crowd, not allowing herself to check if her pursuers still followed.

A souvenir shop selling tinctures and mementos to passing tourists caught Prisha's attention, and she navigated her way toward it. Stepping inside, she slipped down an aisle and snuck behind the counter to the back of the store. A door lay ajar to allow in some air, and Prisha exited through it into an alleyway.

Voices asking questions about a woman carried out from the shop, and Prisha took off at a run, the scarf slipping from her head and falling to the ground in a waterfall of silk.

Footsteps thundered behind her as the men spilled from the shop and charged after her. Using the precious few seconds she had to her advantage, Prisha hurtled over a pile of garbage and broke out into the street parallel to the market.

It wasn't anywhere near as crowded, and Prisha darted into the entrance to a block of flats as a resident was leaving, shoving them out of the way. She ran down the passage and swore at the discovery of no back door.

Turning on her heels, she made to leave and head back out to the street, but the men crashed through the flat doors, blocking the way.

Prisha turned and took the stairs to the floor above

three at a time, firing her gun behind her as she did. A cry came from one of her pursuers, telling her she'd landed a hit, but there were still four men after her.

All the doors were closed, and Prisha found the nearest to be locked. Ignoring the rest, she carried on up the next set of stairs and didn't stop until she reached the very top. A single door awaited her, and she shoved all her weight into it, dragging the heavy metal door open with screeches of rusted protest.

A breeze caught her loosened hair as she stepped out onto the flat rooftop. The skyline of Delhi stretched before her, illuminated in all its glory by the radiance of the sun above and coated in a layer of haze from the infamous smog. Prisha sent a silent prayer to the gods to guide her steps.

A stitch in her side nagged at her to stop and breathe, but if she wanted to continue breathing at all, she needed to keep moving. Sliding the door shut again, Prisha dragged a breeze block from a pile nearby and positioned it in front of the door. It wouldn't hold the men back for long, but a few seconds could mean life or death in her current predicament.

Adjacent to where she stood was another rooftop, about six feet lower. It wasn't connected to her building, but Prisha could make the jump. She'd managed farther before.

The same whines from the metal door screeched again, and Prisha was off. Taking a run at it, she sprinted to the end of the roof and leaped into the air. She'd managed a good spring in her jump, and a shred of hope danced inside her.

As she descended through the air, a crack sounded behind her, and a searing pain erupted in the small of her back.

Prisha had been an agent long enough to know what a gunshot felt like.

The hit interrupted her momentum, and her body gave an involuntary jerk mid-flight. Prisha reached forward as the breath was knocked out of her from the impact.

She landed with a hard thump against the side of the building with only her arms landing on the roof.

Prisha tensed her muscles and hung on, trying to pull her dangling body up.

"No," she gasped. Her arms began to slide, her body going into shock from the bullet in her back as it tried to retain the energy she needed to roll onto the roof.

Arms turned to fingers, and Prisha's palms scraped against the rough brick.

One of the men landed beside her on the adjacent roof with easy feet. He grinned as he straightened and stared down at her.

Prisha's fingers shook violently, but still, she held on for dear life.

The familiar tang of blood coated her clenched teeth, and she screamed as the man stomped on her fingertips with his boot and twisted his toes until he broke the skin around her nails.

When he let go, Prisha could hold on no longer, and she lost her desperate grip on the roof's edge.

Prisha thought of only one thing the whole way down to the hard concrete below.

Who will look after Mum?

Chapter 14

London, Great Britain

The sneer Director General Grace Helmsley wore as they arrived wasn't the welcome back Maggie had expected. Not that she'd been hoping for balloons, a nice cuppa, and some Victoria sponge.

"What is he doing here?" Helmsley asked, narrowing her eyes at Ashton, who waltzed into the Unit like he owned the place.

"The prodigal son has returned to make sure he and none of his friends are exposed thanks to your negligence," he replied, not missing a beat. "Really, Grace, have the Unit's standards plummeted so much since my departure? If you can't keep something as simple as a computer safe, what chance do your deluded agents have?"

"Hey," Leon said, "I'm one of those deluded agents, in case you've forgotten."

"No offense, mate, but there's really no excuse for what's happened." Ashton turned back to Helmsley. "Have you never heard of a firewall? Seriously, I can nip down to the shops and get you one for like twenty quid."

If looks could kill, Helmsley would have assassinated Ashton on the spot. "You haven't changed a bit, Ashton Price. I am not in the mood for your antics, today of all days, so I suggest you get out of my sight before I—"

Maggie stood between them and swiped the air. "No, we're not doing this. Ashton, stop goading Grace, and Grace, if it weren't for Ash, Leon would be dead right now. His name is on that list, too, and believe it or not, he wants to help."

Helmsley shook her head in disgust. "He can help by staying away from—"

"If he's out, so am I," Maggie warned, deadly serious as she hovered by the door of Leon's office. When none of them argued, she poured herself a cup of tea from the freshly brewed pot and sat herself down at the conference table. "Now, if you two kids think you can play nice for the limited time we need to work together, I'd like an update on the situation and then to discuss what we're all going to do to stop Ivan and his people."

Ashton slumped down next to her. "I will if she will."

"She?" snapped Helmsley, still standing.

Leon hobbled to the table, in clear discomfort, and sat across from Maggie and Ashton, pulling out the chair beside him for his superior. "Grace."

"Fine," she said with a huff, taking the offered seat. "Let's get this over with."

An awkward silence fell over the room as each of them filled their cups, Maggie pouring Leon's for him. He'd fought off their protests to head straight to a doctor, insisting that he attend the meeting with his boss. He was the new Unit chief and should be there to have his voice heard. Maggie had enough battles to contend with and therefore allowed Leon to come, making him promise to be seen to straight after.

Ashton passed the little milk jug over to Helmsley when he was finished pouring a dollop into his cup. "Nice suit, Grace."

"It's Dolce," said Helmsley, taking the milk and plopping a sugar cube into her tea.

"I know." Ashton pulled out a business card from inside his jacket. "Give my tailor a ring. He can get you next season's line before it goes to market."

Grace pursed her lips, and Maggie refrained from laughing when she took the card and slipped it into her pocket without a word. If there was one thing Grace enjoyed more than ordering people around, it was impeccably cut power suits.

"We've had another name announced since you've been gone," Helmsley announced to the table, connecting her tablet to the projector once more. "Another agent is dead."

Maggie sobered.

"Who?" Leon put down his cup and rubbed a hand over his head. The swelling in his face had lessened a little thanks to Ash's efforts, but it had given way to large patches of bruised skin down one side of his face and along his neck. He didn't say how he'd gotten them, and Maggie didn't ask. The visual was bad enough.

"Prisha."

Prisha Patel was one of the newer agents recruited to the Unit, barely two years out of training. Maggie hadn't gotten to know her all that well, but she had been an eager young woman and highly intelligent. Bishop had had high hopes for her future. Now she didn't have one.

"Did they send another video?" Ashton asked. He was the only one in the room who didn't know Prisha, having left before she graduated from training.

"Yes. It's much the same as the others."

Maggie didn't need to see it, but Helmsley played it for Leon and Ashton who had yet to view any of the videos. It was the same as the other two she'd watched, the demands unchanging.

"Who's the girl?" Ashton asked.

Helmsley paused the clip just before it ended, the girl's face taking up most of the screen. "We don't know, though I suspect she's one of Dalca's trafficked girls. She doesn't appear to be there willingly."

"And the analysts?" Leon asked. "How far are they from tracking down the filming location?"

"They've been working day and night, but the videos are encrypted and sent through a web of IP addresses that ping from one continent to the next. They'll track them down, but we need time."

Maggie leaned back in her chair. "Which is precisely what we don't have." All this sitting around and talking was doing little to solve the problem.

Ashton slurped the last of his tea and took his second biscuit. "So, what's the plan?" he asked, chewing with his mouth open.

"We follow the breadcrumbs. There's no way an operation as large as Dalca's can carry on with their business and not leave some kind of trail."

Maggie had tracked down people on less before, including the assassin handler Viktor Fedorov and German businessman Herman Vogel, both of whom played a role in framing Maggie just weeks ago.

"There's no guarantee we'll find them in time," Leon added.

"Right now, it's all we have." Maggie kept her hands under the desk to refrain from reaching over to him. Something was up with him, and it wasn't just the death of his colleagues and the close call with Yasir Osman.

"They both died under my watch," he said. His jaw

clenched as he continued to avoid eye contact with any of them. "I should have been here."

"You were busy trying to take down Yasir," Ashton said, though Maggie stayed quiet.

She agreed with Leon. In his new role as chief, he had no business running off on a mission. His job was to stay at headquarters and be the home base for all active agents. Maggie stole a quick glance at Helmsley to gauge her reaction, but whatever she thought about the situation, she was keeping it to herself.

A knock came on the door, breaking the building tension in the room.

"Go away," Helmsley barked. "I asked not to be disturbed."

"Sorry, Director General," said a muffled voice, "only this is something you'll want to see."

Helmsley swore under her breath. "Come in, then, and be quick about it."

The door opened and Tom Wilson, one of the Unit's techs, scampered in. "Thank you, Director General, ma'am."

Helmsley spun in her seat to face him with those hard, scrutinizing eyes of hers. "Spit it out, Wilson. We haven't got all day."

"Yes, of course. Well, you see, I was analyzing the last video and found something." Wilson connected his laptop to the projector as he prattled on and brought up his desktop. "It's quite genius, actually, and I would never have found it if I hadn't—"

"Today, please, Wilson," interjected Helmsley, arms crossed.

"Oh, right." After some fumbling on his keyboard, Wilson brought up a folder on his desktop. "The latest video sent to us had another file piggybacking it. A hidden one. Nice piece of code. Anyway, it's better if I show rather than tell you."

Wilson clicked on the hidden file, and a new video appeared on the screen.

Like all the others, it showed the same young, petite girl as before, only this time no one from behind the camera yelled orders at her. She pulled the camera close and kept her voice to a whisper.

"My name is Tamira Kapoor. My friends used to call me Tami before I was taken. If you are watching this, I am sorry for what they have forced me to do. I did not want to say the names of those agents, and I fear they are dead now."

There wasn't much to see with the camera being so close, but it appeared to be filmed from the same spot as the other videos, with nothing but bare walls behind her. The camera shook under her hold, her eyes wide with fear. Yet still, a determined fire lay behind them. She bit at her lip and checked over her shoulder before continuing.

"I haven't been here long, and I don't know where *here* is. It's all a blur, and I think I was drugged on the way. I know little, but I have to hope that someone out there sees this video and sends help. Girls come and go in a revolving door, and I don't know how long I have left. I am one of the few girls the men don't touch. Another like me thinks they've been warned not to in order to keep us 'pure' for potential buyers."

Her voice wavered at those last words, but she continued on.

"Most of my captors don't speak a language I understand, but I know they're from Romania. One of the other girls spoke a little English before they took her away. She said she overheard the men complaining about having to go to Amsterdam again. The next day, she and a group of girls were taken away with those men, and I haven't seen any of them since. That was a week ago."

Maggie leaned forward on the desk. Amsterdam. If Ivan's trade was predominantly in sex trafficking, it made sense for him to ship some of the girls there.

"If you are out there watching this, please send help," Tamira pleaded, tears streaming down her cheeks. "I will try to learn more, but for now, I must go. Someone's coming."

And with that, the video ended, and the screen turned black.

Helmsley was the first to speak.

"Well done, Wilson. I want you to find all you can

about this girl. Where she's from, and how did she come to be taken by Dalca's operation."

"And us?" Leon asked, getting up from his seat and gritting his teeth through the pain it caused, unable to hide it, though Maggie was sure he was trying to.

"You're staying out of this," she said, joining him on her feet.

That stubborn look crossed his face. "You know I won't do that."

"You're hurt. You have to sit this one out. Help out around here if you must, but let me and Ash handle this one."

Leon raised his voice, losing his patience. "I am the chief of this Unit, and it is my duty to help every agent at risk. I refuse to sit back and watch while you go out risking your life yet again for all of us."

"I quite agree with Maggie on this one," Helmsley said, calm in her seat as she looked her newly appointed chief up and down. "In case you haven't noticed, someone appears to have given you a right kicking."

Leon shook the bottle of pills Ashton had given him. "They did, but thanks to these, I don't feel a thing. You put me in charge for a reason, Director General. Please allow me to do my job."

Helmsley studied him for a moment before coming to a decision. "Very well. I hired you for a reason, and if you believe this is the best approach, then so be it."

"You can't be serious," Maggie protested, looking to

her best friend for help. Maybe he could make Leon see sense.

"Oh, I love Amsterdam!" Ashton practically squealed and pointed to the bottle of painkillers. "If you think those babies are good, Leon, wait until we get there."

Helmsley's patience from before seemed to have cracked as Ashton reminded her of his presence. "This isn't some seedy lads' holiday where you can go and get high on hash brownies and frolic around getting up to no good."

"I don't frolic," Ashton retorted, seeming mortally offended by the very idea.

"You frolic a little," said Leon, smiling for the first time since they'd saved him from Yasir's grasp.

Ashton shot him a dagger of a look. "Traitor."

"If you're coming," Maggie said, getting back to the problem at hand, "I need you to follow my lead. You're a liability in your state, and there are too many lives at risk for you to try to be the hero. You're injured, and if you insist on helping, you can, but on my terms."

Leon opened his mouth to argue but instead gave her a single nod. "Fine."

"I'll call Craig and have him get the pilots ready," Ashton said, ducking out of the office to make the arrangements.

"Okay, then, we leave for Amsterdam as soon as possible," Maggie said, already going over potential ways to track down the traffickers once they landed. “Grace, please keep us updated on any progress you make.”

“Likewise,” the Director General said. “And let us hope you find Dalca’s people before any more names are released from that list.”

Chapter 15

AMSTERDAM, NETHERLANDS
13 JULY

They booked themselves into a hotel near De Wallen, more commonly known as the Red Light District. Like always, Amsterdam was overstuffed with tourists of all kinds, from sightseers strolling through the canal-lined streets and enjoying a drink in the old-school bars, to those seeking a more "hands-on" experience of what the city had to offer.

Unlike many of the patrons visiting the array of pleasure establishments that surrounded their hotel, Maggie didn't associate Amsterdam with a good time. Her job had brought her here on too many missions for her to see beyond the dark and seedy underbelly that did little to hide itself. Where most cities hid their sex trade down dark alleys, within the inconspicuous walls of illegal brothels and the back rooms of strip clubs, Amsterdam proudly advertised theirs in glowing neon signs and glass shopfronts with girls on display as items to be purchased.

Maggie saw little to be proud of in an industry the government profited from through taxation under a guise of protecting sex workers, despite the growing number of vulnerable people lured into the trade and held there by circumstance or force. Though prostitution was legal, sex trafficking was still an ongoing and grossly overlooked problem in the city.

In short, it was the perfect place for people like Ivan Dalca to thrive.

Maggie paced the hotel room and worried at her thumbnail.

"He'll be back soon," Leon said from the couch.

Maggie had made him sprawl across it and get some rest until they were ready to act. Leon would need all his strength if he insisted on being on the front line with her, and a team was only as strong as its weakest link.

"He's been gone a while," Maggie replied, itching from inactivity. They'd already lost time making travel arrangements, arriving and settling in, then catching up on some much-needed rest for the night. Now this. A new name could leak any moment.

Leon sat up and tried to hide the wince it caused. "You know Ash."

A doctor on the Unit's payroll had checked Leon over for signs of serious injury before they left London yesterday. Thankfully, he hadn't sustained any damage that would cause lasting effects. Yasir and his men had done a number on him, though. Behind his macho front and stubbornness to be included in Maggie's hunt for the Romanians, Leon was still in real pain.

His leg was causing him issues, especially as the meds wore off. He walked with a limp, though a night's rest had done a world of good, along with the antibiotics the doctor had prescribed. Maggie was at least glad Leon hadn't lost his appetite and had made sure he ate the large breakfast she'd ordered from room service, as well as lunch of vegetable soup and a club sandwich.

Leon didn't complain at her nursing and fussing over him, so she didn't complain at his insistence on being there. Much.

"If he's not back in ten minutes, I'm going to look for him," Maggie decided. Ashton had been gone most of the afternoon.

She could have gone with Ashton but didn't like the idea of leaving Leon alone. Pain, Leon could handle. A significant part of being a good and effective fighter was the ability to take a beating and remain standing. It was a part of agent training Maggie certainly did not miss.

It wasn't Leon's physical condition that worried

Maggie, though. Something was off with him, and it had nothing to do with his near-death experience. Both of them had endured plenty of those. This was something else, and whatever it was, Leon was trying his best to hide it.

Like any agent worth their salt, Leon was skilled at concealing his emotions. Maggie doubted many others would notice his imbalance, but she knew Leon too well for him to hide it from her.

Maggie was about to broach the subject when Ashton decided to return.

"God, I love Amsterdam," said the Scot, barging in and kicking the door closed with a back heel.

Maggie's relief at seeing her friend safe and sound mixed like a bad cocktail with her annoyance at him for taking so long. "What did you find out?" she asked, instead of reprimanding him for not answering his bloody phone.

Ashton dropped an open box of brownies on the coffee table, then plonked himself on her bed with a childish giggle. "I visited a few places a contact of mine suggested and asked around about new girls."

"And made a stop at a bakery on the way back?" Maggie had a strong suspicion the brownies weren't the only thing baked.

Ashton's grin widened. "A few. I do love brownies." He took another bite to prove his point and proffered the remaining half. "Want some?"

Maggie pursed her lips. "No. Someone needs to keep a clear head on this trip."

Leon laughed from his spot on the couch and Maggie shot him a glare. The last thing Ashton needed was encouragement.

"It'll chill you out a bit, Mags," Ashton said, tossing a pillow at her. "You've been awfully uptight since you got back from your vacation."

"With good reason." Maggie caught the pillow and aimed it back at him, concealing a smile at Ashton's dramatics when she hit him in the head. "Now, give it a rest and tell me what you found out."

Ashton sobered and sat up from playing dead. "One of the proprietors I paid a visit to told me a friend of his was expecting some new girls. Dutch guy called Samuel Thomas. He owns a strip club a few streets away and pimps the girls out on the side."

"Isn't all that stuff regulated over here?" Leon asked. "He'd need permits, employee records."

Maggie sat on the edge of the couch. "Not as regulated as you might think, and any documents he needs for the girls can be easily forged."

"Idiotic law," Ashton muttered. "Like any of the people working the trade are there through anything other than circumstance and desperation. And that's those who willingly partake. From what I hear, there's not many of them left."

They'd all witnessed the effects of human trafficking

firsthand through the years. It was a scar in their memories time couldn't heal. Leon shook his head. "So many lost girls and women out there."

"Men and boys, too," Ashton added.

"Yes." Maggie shuddered at the memory of a past mission that still haunted her. "Boys, too."

Needing to do something other than sit around, Maggie got up and rummaged through her suitcase for supplies. Unsure of what or who she'd need, she'd made sure to overpack enough for any situation before leaving London for the second time in as many days.

"A lot of the window fronts are closing, so it's becoming more underground again," Ashton continued. "This Samuel guy has a sort of private members' club in the basement of his strip joint."

Maggie sat in front of the large dresser by the window and laid out her things. "Guess I'll be paying him a visit, then."

"Who are you going as?"

Maggie threw one of her passports over to Leon.

"Celine Delacroix," he read before examining the rest of the ID. "This isn't the work of our guy at HQ."

"It's one of the new ones Ash got me." Maggie had a whole host of aliases under her sleeve, but the mess with Bishop had caused her to adopt some new identities the Unit didn't have on file. Of the three Ashton had his personal forger Gillian design, Celine Delacroix was the only one Maggie had yet to try out.

"What did your side manage to find out about the girl?" Ashton asked Leon.

Maggie got to work while the boys spoke, starting with her eyes. Celine had hazel eyes. A small detail given the fact Maggie doubted she'd ever see this Samuel Thomas again after tonight, but standards must always be maintained, no matter who she was dealing with or how inconsequential the target. While Samuel may be one of many sleazeballs Maggie had the displeasure of encountering, Celine would undoubtedly leave an impression on the man once Maggie was finished with him. Celine's wouldn't be a face Mr. Thomas would forget anytime soon.

"From what we can gather," Leon said, "Tamira Kapoor is an Iranian national. Nineteen. Her father was Javad Kapoor, a noted journalist and political commentator known for what many in the country deemed as radical views, thanks to his criticisms of the establishment and their control over media and broadcasting."

"Was?" Ashton noted.

Maggie blinked the contacts in place and checked them in the mirror. Her blond hair was pulled back in a ponytail, her face free from makeup—both of which would need to be fixed.

"Six months ago, he was found dead in his home along with his wife and the younger of his two daughters," Leon replied. "Officially, they were murdered by unknown assailants during a burglary of their home in

Tehran. Unofficially, they were assassinated by those he opposed."

"A government hit," Ashton said, none of them strangers to the concept. "What about Tamira?"

Brushing out her hair, Maggie pulled it tight and secured it at the back of her head. Celine was blond like Maggie, which thankfully saved her from having to wear a full wig for a change. Summer was in full swing and though it wasn't nearly as uncomfortable as the heat in Somalia, using her own hair was one less discomfort to put up with on the job. Attaching a blunt fringe piece at the front and a long extension to her ponytail at the back, she was beginning to appear more like the infamous madam in her passport photo.

Leon continued to update Ashton on the intel the Unit had gathered on Tamira. "She was missing, presumed dead until now. She was attending university in Istanbul when the hit on her family was carried out. According to the school, she went missing soon after. My guess is whoever killed her parents and little sister sold her off to traffickers."

"Why not just kill her?"

"Money would be my guess. Especially if the hit was contracted. As long as Tamira was out of the picture, her father's enemies would be satisfied, while those carrying out the dirty work stood to make some extra cash by selling her instead."

Maggie finished off the bright red lip she'd painted

with a beauty spot above it to complete the severe face Celine wore. It matched her profession as a premier dominatrix and supplier of girls-for-hire through her own high-end and, most importantly, discreet agency, which made her the ideal persona to adopt when dealing with Samuel Thomas. If Gillian the forger had done her job as she had with the other two aliases Maggie had used, he would have heard of Celine Delacroix—and her reputation—before.

"That would explain how Tamira came to be trapped in Dalca's operation," Maggie added.

Ashton rubbed the nape of his neck. "Poor lassie."

"That's everything we have on her so far," Leon finished.

Ashton sat for a moment, taking it all in. "What was she studying at university?"

"Computer science," Maggie said, getting up and selecting her clothes for the evening. "She's some kind of prodigy."

Ashton's eyes lit with a conspiratorial glow. "Tech whiz. Well, here's hoping she gets back in touch soon with more information."

Maggie didn't have time to wonder about that look on her friend's face. She'd witnessed it enough to know when Ashton was thinking ten steps ahead of the game. Instead, she ignored him and headed for the bathroom to change into Celine's outfit. "In the meantime, we'll follow your lead, Ash. Let's see what Mr. Thomas has to say."

"And if he doesn't talk?" Leon asked.

Maggie imitated the cracking of a whip. "I'll make him squeal."

Chapter 16

Clad in a black leather pencil skirt, killer heels, and a sheer white blouse with spikes around the collar, Maggie marched to the front of the strip club entrance and ignored the line of eager patrons waiting to gain access.

"Wait in line," barked a burly bouncer in broken English.

Maggie arched an eyebrow. Celine was the one who gave orders, not the other way around. "Do I look like the get-in-line type?" she asked in heavily accented English, allowing Celine's French nationality to shine through in both her voice and the tilt of her nose as she regarded the bouncer.

Holding the man's stare, Maggie waited without saying a word. After a few seconds, the bouncer averted his eyes and swung the door open for her without another word.

Either Samuel wasn't paying his hired muscle enough to care, or he was paying too much for an incompetent member of staff. Either way, Maggie clacked past the bouncer with a deliberate sway that made the long, sleek ponytail down her back swing like a pendulum.

Samuel Thomas's place was like many strip clubs the world round. It had the universal scent of stale, over-priced beer and cheap perfume that clung to your skin, just as much as the clouds of opaque cigar smoke that billowed around the raised stage the dancers performed on.

Celine was no stranger to clubs like these. For her standards, Samuel's establishment could be considered quite tame, catering to a vanilla crowd looking for a cheap thrill. Celine's area of expertise could be regarded as more *niche* and *alternative*.

Like arms dealer Ekaterina Kovrova and Felicity Greene the jewel thief, Ashton's forger had fabricated a detailed life for Celine Delacroix. Counterfeiting official documentation like passports and driver's licenses was one thing, but it was the mark of a truly gifted forger when they could create a reputation for their aliases. The Unit was skilled at it, of course, having the right contacts and ample resources to make it happen, but so far Gillian the unassuming housewife from the countryside had more than proven the worth of her substantially priced wares.

By nature, the criminal underworld preferred to keep itself private and off the radar, and on the whole, it was populated by a relatively small circle of nefarious key players. Word of mouth and general gossip was rife among its members, and it was important to at least be a name others had heard of if you dared enter their world, if not perhaps someone who they'd had direct dealings with.

Maggie trusted Gillian's talents, having relied on them to clear her name with the Unit just weeks before, so she wasn't worried about Celine going unrecognized. It was pulling off what she had planned that concerned her.

It was verging midnight, and the club was near capacity, a sea of heads shrouded in the dim light as they all faced the strippers dancing and twirling around the poles with expert dexterity. While most of the observers were focused on the girls' bodily assets, Maggie couldn't help but note the vacant expressions behind many of the women's eyes. Either through defeated resignation, the haze of drugs, or a concoction of both, many of the girls had removed themselves elsewhere, in mind if not in body.

Maggie made sure to retain Celine's unaffected façade and harsh yet mischievous expression at the curve of her lips and behind her own watchful, present eyes.

Being around working girls was all in a day's work for Celine, just like any pimp.

"Champagne," Celine ordered, slinking through the huddle of men waiting to be served at the bar. "Dom Perignon, if you have it." Charisma oozed from a woman like Celine, who was more than aware of her sexuality and how to use it to her advantage. She smiled at the group of men she'd skipped by, and none of them muttered even the slightest complaint, their gazes lingering over her with hunger.

"How many glasses?" asked the barmaid.

"Two," Maggie said. Celine had no intentions of drinking alone.

"We have no tables available," the barmaid warned, aware someone with Celine's order would expect one to be provided.

"That's quite all right," Celine replied.

A man in his thirties sitting next to her on a bar stool slapped his thigh. "You can sit on my lap."

A few of the surrounding men laughed, their boyish bullshit almost causing Maggie to break character and curse them out. Fortunately, Celine was no stranger to dealing with men. She turned to the man in question and leaned in close, so her lips brushed his ear, and allowed him a moment to breathe in her sweet perfume and feel the heat from her body.

Just before the man had time to enjoy the sensation, Celine grabbed a handful of his crotch and squeezed.

The man yelped and tried to break free from her hold, but Maggie held him in a vise grip and whispered. "Of all the people I'd like to sit on, you are most assuredly not one of them."

His eyes bulged, face growing red as she squeezed harder. Then, as quickly as she had grabbed him, she let the idiot go.

Celine ignored him as he fell to his knees and cupped himself, nodding to the barmaid. "Put my drink on his tab." She stepped over him and slinked into the now-vacant bar stool and sipped the glass of bubbles the barmaid slid in front of her.

The rest of the men ignored her after that and returned to ordering drinks and drooling over the girls who wouldn't crush their junk, unless they wanted them to, of course. Maggie sipped her champagne and examined the room, searching for her target.

It didn't take long to spot him.

Samuel Thomas was a large man in all aspects. His booming laugh rang through the music in a huge, barrel-chested cackle that drew attention from his girls on the stage. He sat surrounded by a group of women, all of whom Maggie suspected worked for Thomas, which was their only reason for being there. His thick hands and wrists were encrusted with garish gold jewelry that glittered when the overhead lights touched them and matched the gold tooth that winked at Maggie as he smiled over at her.

Celine raised her glass and took a deep drink, locking eyes with Samuel only to turn her head away as if shy or intimidated by his attention. It wasn't exactly in Celine's character to react in such a way to a stranger's interest, but Maggie knew from experience that it would garner her the results she required.

It was an old trick, but highly effective. If a mark believed it their idea to approach you, they never suspected anything untoward until it was too late. Especially from a woman.

Samuel Thomas got up from his booth near the stage and headed straight for her with singular intent. The buttons on his expensive floral shirt stressed over his ample gut, his neck so engulfed by a second chin that it would make breaking his neck difficult.

Difficult, though not impossible.

A further two bouncers stationed by Samuel's abandoned booth watched as their boss crossed the room toward her. They assessed Maggie for a few seconds before disregarding her as a non-threat and settled back to their long shift of babysitting the strip club owner and deterring punters from starting any trouble.

They had no idea.

"Hallo," Samuel said, sliding up behind her and leaning a meaty arm against the bar.

Celine ran a hand through her hair and allowed the ponytail to fall over her shoulder and past her chest. "Bonjour."

"French?" Samuel said, seeming surprised. He took her hand without permission and kissed the back of it with his thin lips. The bristles of his unkempt beard prickled her skin like tiny needles.

It took everything in Maggie not to punch the man in the throat for touching her, but she kept her cool and played along. Samuel was nothing but a pawn in the deadly game of chess she'd found herself in, and she needed to learn what she could from him. There'd be plenty of time to punch him in the throat after the imminent threat was handled.

"Yes," Celine replied in English. "Drink?"

"Please, allow me." Samuel took the chilled bottle from the bucket and topped up Maggie before pouring his own glass of champagne. "I enjoy a woman with taste," he said, regarding the bottle.

Celine tilted her head to the side and leaned closer to him. "What is life for, if not to indulge in the pleasures it has to offer?"

"I'll toast to that," Samuel agreed, and clinked his glass against hers. "I'm Samuel."

"*Oui*, Samuel Thomas."

"You know who I am?" Surprised again, Samuel's wide grin indicated he was more than a little glad Celine knew of him.

"Of course. Your reputation precedes you. My name is Celine Delacroix."

Samuel's bushy eyebrows rose to the top of his balding, gel-covered hair. "My, my, what a pleasure to have you visit my establishment, Ms. Delacroix. A real pleasure, indeed."

"You're too kind," Maggie replied.

"I hope you don't think me too forward, but—"

Maggie placed a hand over Samuel's arm. "I like a man who gets to the point."

"In that case, might I inquire your reason for being here? Business or pleasure?"

Celine nibbled her bottom lip and held her glass between them. "I was hoping for a bit of both."

Hunger rose behind Samuel's watery blue eyes, taking Celine's not-so-subtle flirting as an invite. "Why don't we go to my office?" he offered, licking his lips. "It's more private, and we can talk business. And pleasure."

Maggie tossed back the remainder of her champagne. "Lead the way."

Samuel ordered another bottle of Dom and led her through the club and downstairs to the floor below. One of Samuel's guards left his station to trail behind them, close but not too close to impose. Maggie kept an eye on him, noting his position, and the silhouette of the gun outlined against the fabric of his suit jacket.

"You have girls down here too?" Celine asked, peering through an arched entrance guarded by another bouncer whose broad shoulders took up most of the space. That made at least two downstairs, one upstairs by the stage, and the man at the front door. Four wasn't so bad. Maggie could take four, even without her gun.

"For VIP members," Samuel replied, unlocking his office. "It caters to those of us who like to keep our activities discreet."

Celine gave a knowing nod. "Discretion is my middle name."

"So I've heard, though I've heard rumors about some of your clients and their proclivities." Samuel held open the office door and gestured for her to go before him.

Maggie entered the predatory lion's den, but Celine Delacroix was no lamb. "I can assure you none of it has come from me. My clients pay for my silence more than anything, which I provide. Loose lips could get a girl into a lot of trouble."

"Trouble isn't always a bad thing," Samuel said behind her, closing the door.

Maggie walked past the desk that had seats at both ends for when Samuel held meetings. She sat on a red leather couch at the back of the room. "Oh, I know."

Samuel followed behind her, sitting closer than necessary. He opened the second bottle of champagne and refilled their glasses. "So, what can I help you with?"

"I'm in need of girls," Celine said, allowing her foot to brush over Samuel's, each movement deliberate and entrapping the man's interest. "The Hungarians I use were arrested a few months back, and it's been difficult finding someone I trust who can supply what I need."

"Which is?" Samuel asked, sobering a bit. The man wasn't a complete fool, and while his intentions toward Celine were clear, he was still a businessman. Money was a much more tempting mistress to a man like Samuel who had his choice of girls at his disposal.

Celine enjoyed money a great deal. Much more than sex. Having been a working girl since the age of fifteen, sex was more of a transaction to a woman like Celine. A means to an end.

"Girls who will do what they're told. Girls who won't be missed."

It hadn't been easy working her way up from streetwalker to madam. Not many girls would survive what she'd gone through to get there, and such trying hardships had turned Celine cold and harsh, like any good pimp. Her girls were the product, and she the supplier.

"What makes you think I of all people could help?" Samuel asked, putting down his half-full glass. The hint of mistrust danced across his features, eyes narrowed ever so slightly. "I'm sure you know others who could fulfill your needs."

It was true. Celine had a vast network of contacts at her disposal. After all, creating an empire such as she had required the use of others, even if she never trusted any of those she worked with. From the directors of her snuff films and dungeon masters who provided rooms for her girls to take clients with more peculiar needs, to her peers in the kink scene and those who navigated the Dark Web where girls were bid on and sold like items off eBay. Yes, she had contacts, but Celine was in the market for a new business relationship.

"I have it on good authority that you have connections with a Romanian syndicate. Ivan Dalca. I've had some minor dealings with him in the past but have been unable to reach him."

Samuel nodded as understanding washed over him. He picked up his glass again and took a deep drink. "The British have him in prison."

"A pity," Celine replied with a sigh. "But his people are still active?"

A setup like Dalca's wouldn't stop just because its leader was imprisoned. Ivan Dalca wouldn't be the first criminal to leave prison richer than he had arrived, thanks to the hard work of his underlings looking to prove themselves in their leader's absence.

"Yes," Samuel admitted. "In fact, I've been meeting with them over the past week on some business of my own."

"Then I'd like you to make introductions." Celine inched closer, holding Samuel's stare like a snake enrapturing its prey before lashing out. "I'll provide you with a fair facilitator's fee, of course."

Samuel cleared his throat, his cheeks turning red as he pulled at his shirt collar. "And what kind of payment would you suggest?"

Celine trailed a finger down Samuel's chest and

stopped above his belt. "I'm sure we can think of something."

Samuel swallowed and leaned toward her with a conspiratorial glow. "I must admit, I've not had much experience with your side of the industry."

"We could start slow," Celine purred, luring the man closer. "Handcuffs. Toys. Chains."

Oh, there'd be chains all right.

"That, uhm," Samuel stuttered, reaching for her with his meaty paws. "Well, that could be nice."

"Oh, it'll be far from nice." Celine hiked up her skirt and straddled Samuel. She pinned his arms down with her legs, which resulted in a groan of exhilarated shock from her target. "A man like you is used to having to be in charge all the time. Let me lead the way and show you things you've only dared fantasize about."

Maggie slipped an arm behind her back and reached for the syringe tucked into the back of the waistline of her skirt. Samuel squirmed with pleasure under her and Maggie tried not to gag. It would be over soon.

"You know, I've always wanted to—"

Whatever lurid activity Samuel had always wanted to do, Maggie never found out. Before he could admit to idealizing some weird kink or another, Maggie thrashed out and jammed the syringe into Samuel's neck.

The effect was instant.

Samuel's eyes widened, and he shoved Maggie off him, his superior strength sending her to the floor in his panic. He struggled to get up from the couch, wriggling on the seat as the drugs began to circulate through his bloodstream.

"Help!" Maggie yelled, loud enough to be heard from outside the office. "Somebody please, help!"

The security guard outside barged through the door and strode past Maggie who hovered over Samuel in fake panic. He shoved her to the side to reach his boss, now convulsing on the floor and clutching at his chest. He ripped the buttons from his shirt with thick fingers, like he was trying to claw out the pain.

The second guard arrived at the foot of the door, eyeing the scene before him.

"He's having a heart attack!" Maggie yelled at him. "Call an ambulance!"

The guard fumbled with his phone and called as ordered.

"How long?" the first guard asked, trying to calm Samuel down and place him in the recovery position.

His colleague hung up the phone after relaying Samuel's state to the phone operator in rapid Dutch. "Ten minutes."

Ten minutes was all Maggie needed.

Four minutes later, a pair of footsteps herded downstairs.

Two emergency medical technicians were led into the office moments later by the second guard who wrung his hands as he followed behind. The paramedics bent down next to Samuel, ushering the first guard out of the way, and got to work.

"What's happening?" Maggie asked, still in her role as the panicked Celine, playing up the dramatics for her audience.

"We need to get him to a hospital," replied the EMT in charge, his Dutch accent thick.

The EMTs left Samuel to drag in a stretcher they'd brought downstairs with them. With the help of the bouncers, they hoisted Samuel on top and strapped him in.

Maggie trailed behind the four men as they carried the ample Samuel up the flight of stairs to the main floor of the club and rushed him through the crowd. The ambulance was waiting out front with the engine still running, and Maggie climbed in the back with Samuel and made a show of crying over his convulsing body.

One of the EMTs jumped into the driver's seat up front and prepared to leave. Samuel's main guard called something to the others as he got in the back of the ambulance with them, barking orders.

With no time to waste, the driver pulled into traffic, sirens wailing like a mourning banshee.

The guard asked the EMT dealing with Samuel a question in Dutch, but he ignored the towering man and turned to Maggie.

"What are we going to do with him?" he asked.

Maggie shrugged, and both she and the EMT regarded the guard like an unwelcome guest.

"Sorry, pal," said the EMT, "but you're not invited to the after-party."

Before the guard had time to react or comprehend what was happening, Ashton smacked the man's nose with a crushing fist and aimed a brutal kick to the solar plexus while Maggie swung open the back door of the ambulance.

The guard reeled, and Maggie shoved him with all her might. The guard toppled back and fell from the ambulance onto the hard street they were rushing through, landing with a heavy *thump* at the side of the road.

Leon glanced into the rearview mirror from the driver's seat to catch a glimpse of the guard and whistled. "That's going to hurt in the morning."

Chapter 17

Maggie doused her captive with a bucket of ice-cold water.

"Wake up."

Her voice echoed against the naked walls of the abandoned warehouse they'd hauled up in for the interrogation. It wasn't as secure a location as Maggie would have liked, but she doubted Samuel would have many of his people looking for him. He didn't have the level of resources or loyalty from his people that someone like Ivan Dalca benefited from. Samuel's men were work-for-hire at best.

Still, she had Leon keep watch through one of the slatted windows at the entrance in case their presence alerted the police or any of the homeless who called the surrounding area home. He'd done well playing his part as EMT, though he'd needed to sit and catch his breath after they'd dragged an unconscious Samuel into the building.

"I said, wake up!"

Maggie emphasized her words with a hard slap to the face this time, which seemed to do the trick. Samuel Thomas awoke, a thick droplet of saliva dripping from his gaping mouth as he sucked in a deep, panicked breath.

Eyes blinked open, and for a moment, Samuel appeared confused. Considering the drugs Maggie shot into his system, he should be. Imitating a heart attack wasn't the safest method of extracting a target, but it certainly did the trick, and no one would be shocked at the man's sudden health turn, given his physique and party-boy lifestyle he'd continued well into his forties. A bad bump of cocaine or an overzealous encounter with a lover could have been enough to cause a heart attack in a man like Samuel.

"Where am I? What's going on?" he slurred. Samuel moved his arm and the rattle of chains chinked together. His stare sharpened when he spotted the chains attached to the metal cuffs securing his wrists, fully awake now that the reality of his current situation settled in.

Thanks to one of the many sex shops in Amsterdam, it wasn't difficult to gather a few supplies to keep up Celine's persona. Securing Samuel against the support pillar hadn't been easy given all the dead weight, but the three of them managed to pin him in place without too many bumps to Samuel's head.

Maggie paced in front of him, back in character now that he was awake. Celine's hand wrapped tight around the leather handle of the whip she held, from which sprouted multiple tails.

"I'll ask the questions, Monsieur Thomas."

Her heels clicked against the stone floor like a ticking clock, counting down the minutes until Samuel broke and told her what she needed to know. How long that would take depended on him.

"What is the meaning of this?" Samuel practically spat the words, spittle spurting from his mouth with the water that drenched him from head to toe. While it wasn't winter, night had fallen and the temperature with it, which would only add to Samuel's discomfort.

"Tell me everything you know about Ivan Dalca's operation."

"I told you already, the Brits have him detained."

Maggie inspected the whip, running the individual tails through her gloved fingers. "I'm aware. It's his people I'm interested in. You said you met with them this week. Are they still in town?"

Samuel sneered and tried another futile attempt to break free from the chains. "Why should I tell you after this?"

Without another word, Celine cracked the whip across Samuel's face with a sickening snap. Samuel yelled out in pain as red lines instantly swelled across the side of his face and cheek.

Any remorse Maggie contained within her wasn't wasted on a man like Samuel Thomas. People like him used their power to exploit others and take advantage of the vulnerable and desperate. A couple of knocks around the head was the least he deserved for the many lives he'd undoubtedly ruined.

"If you don't want to talk, I'll gag you. I'm not a fan of pigs who don't squeal."

Celine clicked her fingers and Ashton came into view from the dark corner, out of his ambulance uniform now, and handed Maggie the ball gag, a black leather number with a pink ball in the center.

Candles burned around them, the fire reflecting off Celine's harsh face and creating distorted shadows as the flames flickered in the light wind circling the derelict building. It slipped through the cracks in the walls like phantoms warning Samuel of what was yet to come, should he decide to remain tight-lipped.

"What was the purpose of your meeting with them this week? Did you order a new batch of girls?"

Samuel pursed his lips in protest and Maggie thrashed out with the whip again for a second lashing, harder this time across the man's thighs.

"Yes, yes, I did," Samuel stuttered, wincing through clenched teeth. "They didn't give me an exact date, but they said I'd get the girls soon."

"How soon?"

"A week or two? They weren't specific. Complications arise all the time when smuggling the girls in. You should know that." A line of confusion crossed his forehead, but Maggie continued before Samuel could ponder on that little note.

She stepped closer to him, jabbing the whip into his chest. "Are Dalca's people still in the city?"

"I don't—"

Maggie tutted in a very French gesture her language tutor used to give her back in her agent training days. "Don't lie to me, Samuel. You've been doing so well up until now. Where are they?"

Distrust oozed from the man like a bad smell. "Why do you want to know?"

"I need to reach them." Maggie turned her back on him and walked over to a makeshift table where an array of toys and implements were displayed for Samuel to see. She hovered her hand over them, as if debating which one to try first.

"So, you kidnapped me? Tied me up?"

"I needed to make sure you wouldn't bullshit me. No pimp worth their salt would ever share their supplier. You would have kept Dalca to yourself."

Samuel's silence was answer enough to that. Sure, he would have enjoyed Celine's seduction attempt, promising her anything to get what he wanted, but handing over his supplier? Not a chance.

"Now you have more of an incentive to share." Maggie decided on a rather large set of needles that looked more useful for knitting scarves than inflicting pleasure. She never understood the whole pleasure-pain thing herself, but to each their own. Her choice certainly did the trick once Samuel spotted them, the metal glinting in the fire's presence. "So, spill it. Is the syndicate still in Amsterdam?"

Samuel's voice shook, and it wasn't from the chill of his damp clothes. "I'm not a fool, Ms. Delacroix. Whatever your reasons for wanting to reach them, your intentions are far from good. If I tell you their whereabouts and it comes back on me, they'll kill me."

Maggie strode over to him and pressed the needles against the region south of his belt. "And what do you think I'll do if you don't tell me?"

"Okay, okay. They left a few days ago." Samuel squirmed, sweat beading across his head and top lip.

Maggie rolled her eyes. Men and their penises. "And went where?"

"Back to Ferentari. In Bucharest." Samuel rhymed off an address that Maggie stored in the back of her mind.

"You're sure?" The Romanian capital seemed too obvious a hideout given their recent exploits. It would make more sense to avoid their home turf given they were taking on an entire government. Then again, it said something about the syndicate's cockiness and gall to remain. Plus, the home side always had the advantage in any game.

"Yes," Samuel said, speaking freely now to avoid an

unfortunate mishap with the needle. "I had to arrange collection of my last batch of girls and get them through the border myself."

"What? They didn't offer a delivery service?" The way Samuel and his ilk spoke of other human beings like they were items, like he had simply ordered some pizzas, made Maggie's skin crawl. She had to work hard to keep her face impartial. It was the language Celine used, too. A way for traffickers and pimps to detach themselves from those they exploited.

"Not then. Ivan had just been arrested, and they were lying low."

They certainly weren't lying low these days. Far from it.

Maggie stepped back and took her needles with her. "See, that wasn't so hard now, was it?"

Free from the threat of skewering, her captive regained some of his balls and spat out at her. Luckily for him, he missed.

"You are a real bitch, Celine Delacroix."

"And don't you forget it, Mr. Thomas," Maggie replied over her shoulder, making a show of removing her gloves. "If you so much as bleat a word to Dalca's operation about our little chat, I will come back and take great pleasure feeding you your own cock, after I castrate you."

That sobered him again, and his shoulders drooped as his short-lived bravado died away. "I won't say a word."

"There's a good boy."

Maggie waved Ashton to follow her like he was one of her goons and they made for the exit.

"Wait!" Samuel called.

Maggie stopped and turned on her heel. "Hmm?"

His face was pale. "Aren't you going to let me go?"

She smiled at him, sweet as treacle. "I'll make sure your security knows where to find you."

In a few more hours, of course. In the meantime, Maggie had a plane to catch.

Chapter 18

Essex, England
14 July

Secret Agent Janice Harris hung up the phone as the call went to voicemail. Again.

She redialed. "Come on, Paul, pick up. Pick up."

No answer.

"Shit." Janice tapped the side of her phone with her fingers. "Could you hurry, please? It's an emergency."

"I'm going as fast as I can, love," the taxi driver quipped, taking a left turn as Janice had done countless times on her commute, eager to get home after a trying mission or enduring long hours in meetings at HQ.

The Director General had been good about keeping Janice close to home after she told her about Paul needing to go out of town quite a bit for his new job. Janice had been so relieved and enjoyed the opportunity to get home most nights so she could tuck the kids into bed before going back out. After years of being away from them for days, sometimes weeks at a time, it was a blessing to be able to spend some much-needed quality time with her children.

Now it felt like a curse.

Her phone buzzed, and she answered immediately with tremoring hands. "Paul?"

"You've been compromised," Grace Helmsley said, to the point as always.

Janice checked over her shoulder for the hundredth time to ensure no cars followed her. "I know. I managed to get out."

The job had been straightforward enough. Surveillance took time and patience, but it was paying off, and Janice had garnered enough intelligence to systematically take out key players from the gang in London's East End. Run by the notorious Frank Fletcher, the gang laundered their cash through a private security firm. When the receptionist job came up, the Unit had jumped at the chance to plant one of their own inside Fletcher's camp, a move that proved to be lucrative in getting some heavy hitters off the streets. Until now.

"Come in," Helmsley said. "We'll ensure no one can reach you."

Janice itched to hang up on her boss. Paul might try to call back, and she must warn him. She pinched the bridge of her nose and tried to remain calm. She should never have taken on a case so close to home.

When news broke in the office about Jim Hunter and the list of agent names being exposed, Janice had asked Paul to fly back from his business trip in Abu Dhabi without delay. He knew she worked with the government, and though she wasn't able to tell him the specifics about her job, she'd made sure to emphasize that it came with an element of danger. Too much information, really, but when Paul had proposed all those years ago, Janice wanted to make sure he knew what he was getting into.

But Paul never asked for this. Neither did the kids.

"Okay," Janice said, resigning herself to uprooting her family and going into hiding until things blew over. Their safety was paramount. "I have to get Paul and the kids first, then we'll all come in."

Helmsley's voice sharpened. "Agent, report to headquarters immediately. I'm sending a team to collect your family."

"I'm almost there," Janice said, the driver now only three streets from her house. She checked her watch. The kids would be home from gymnastics by now, likely sitting with Paul on the couch watching cartoons before dinner.

"Janice, listen to me," Helmsley said, deadly calm. "It's too dangerous. Stay away from your house. That's an order."

Janice shook her head. She had to see for herself. Had to be the one to get them to safety. She didn't trust anyone else. Especially now, after Brice Bishop's massive betrayal. For all Janice knew, the leak of the list was an inside job.

The taxi took the last turn, and Janice instructed the driver to park a few houses away as a precaution. Nothing appeared untoward from the outside.

"I've got to go." Janice tossed some folded bills to the driver, not caring what she gave him, and got out the car. "We'll be at HQ as soon as we can."

"Agent Harris. Janice!"

Janice hung up, the first time she'd ever defied Grace Helmsley, a woman she respected and had looked up to her entire career.

Skipping the front door entirely, Janice slipped down the back of her next-door neighbor's house and crept into the garden, using the fence to shield her from being spotted by any lookouts to the back of the property. The kids weren't playing outside, but that wasn't odd. Trying to get them out for fresh air was always a battle, both too preoccupied with their tablets to bother looking up from their screens most of the time.

The chirping of birds enjoying the extended hours of daylight sang through the air, high-spirited laughter coming from the park across the way from children happy to be free from the shackles of school. The light breeze carried with it the scent of burning coal as people made the most of the change in weather, knowing it was on borrowed time, and fired up barbeques, which were lucky to be used more than a couple of times a year.

Normal. From the outside, at least.

When she was certain no one was watching, Janice easily scaled the fence into her own garden and landed on the soft grass. Keeping low, she pulled out the gun from her handbag and abandoned the rest by the back door. She could come back for it once she made sure the coast was clear.

The twin doors leading into the kitchen were glass and Janice risked a peek inside. No sign of trouble. She pried open the door, glad she'd oiled the hinges not too long ago. The back door slid open in silence and Janice slipped out of her shoes, tiptoeing inside and closing the door behind her.

The house was quiet.

With two kids under the age of ten, it wasn't a common phenomenon in the Harris household. The washing machine churned in the corner, meaning someone had been there to put it on. Less than thirty minutes ago, given the timer setting.

Had they left? In her panic, she hadn't noticed Paul's car, too busy scanning for suspicious-looking vehicles or unknown faces pacing the street. A stupid slight on her part.

Janice had found herself in countless predicaments and dangerous scenarios, able to keep a steady head. It was what she was trained for. All of that flew out the window when said danger involved the ones she loved most.

The pounding of her heart rattled her chest, like it could break through her rib cage at any moment, the beats thundering in her ears and disrupting her attention. If anything happened to them, it would be all her fault. Why hadn't she left as Maggie had? Gotten out when she first discovered she was pregnant with Emily? Why hadn't she just gotten a desk job somewhere?

Janice pressed her back against the wall and moved into the hallway. No voices, no racket from the television. The kids' jackets were hung on the pegs by the front door, but that didn't mean much. It wasn't raining today, so there was no need for heavy coats. She'd laid out shorts and T-shirts for them before rushing out the door that morning for her shift at the security firm.

"Paul?" Janice called, unable to stand it any longer. "Honey, are you there?"

No answer. Her legs threatened to buckle as real, unfiltered fear coursed through her.

"Emily? Justin?"

Nothing. Had they gone out? Maybe for a drive or to

get some ice cream? If Paul was driving, he couldn't answer the phone.

"Paul?"

Gun at the ready, Janice moved down the hall in stocking feet and nudged open the door to the living room with the barrel of her gun.

It inched open, and her heart sank to the pit of her stomach as her entire world stared back at her from the center of the room. Paul and the kids were bound to chairs dragged in from the dining room, their eyes wide as soon as they spotted her.

Janice ran toward them, instinct taking over as her worst nightmare played out before her. She got to her knees and fumbled with the zip ties locking her boy and girl to the chairs, their little wrists red from how tight they'd been secured. Paul was screaming something to her, but the thick tape over his mouth blocked the words.

Before she could decipher them, Janice felt the presence of someone behind her, her usual keen senses picking up amid her collision of shock and fear that crashed through her mind like waves in a raging storm.

Something switched in her brain then. The fear on her family's faces. The blood trickling down Paul's temple from where he'd put up a fight. Someone had hurt her family. Entered their home and violated them in the one place they should feel safe. A familiar sensation overthrew all other emotion. One the Unit had cultivated in her and turned into a weapon.

Rage.

Janice spun on her right knee and swiped her left leg across the carpet, catching the intruder off guard, sending him to the floor with her. Without even thinking, she fired her gun and sent a bullet into the side of the man's head before she even registered his face.

"That's quite enough of that, Kerry. Or should I say, Janice."

Janice looked up from the dead body beside her, his blood spattered across the cream-colored carpet. The children wailed innocent tears behind her, and she longed to wrap her arms around them and promise them everything was going to be okay. She didn't dare move.

Frank Fletcher had his own gun trained on her; a man and woman stood at his sides. Janice recognized them from the security firm, along with the man she'd just taken out. They were killers—Frank's crew he dispatched when things turned sour between him and his business partners, or when his verbal threats weren't enough, and someone needed roughing up or removal from the picture entirely.

"Drop the gun," Frank ordered, his hoarse voice carrying over the whimpers of the kids and Paul's futile attempts to free himself from his chair.

With three guns aimed at her, Janice did as she was told. If they fired, one of them might miss and hit the kids.

"Don't harm them," she begged Frank. "Please. This

is between you and me. They have nothing to do with this."

She got to her feet, holding her arms up to show she had no intention of fighting. He had her, and she would follow his orders to the letter if it meant saving her family. Or until an opportunity arose to take the three of them out.

"You should have thought of that before you crawled into my life and fucked things up for me," Frank spat in his cockney accent. He wasn't known for his mercy or forgiveness. You didn't mess with a man like Frank Fletcher and get away without being made an example of.

"I admit, I've helped get some of your people arrested, but you're safe," Janice insisted, slowly creating as much distance from Paul and the kids as she could in an attempt to lower their risk of becoming collateral damage to any punishment Frank chose to inflict on her. "You know how careful you are. How everything is set up, so it won't lead back to you. I have nothing on you," she lied. "I was to do what I could about those on your payroll and then get out. They're giving up on trying to pin anything on you."

Frank growled. "Lies."

"You're eating up too many resources without enough results. It's not a good look for my employers." Janice analyzed the room, searching for anything she could use to her advantage. A makeshift weapon. Something she could use as a barricade to block bullets while she charged at the gangster and his cohorts. But there was nothing. Nothing close enough she could reach without taking a bullet first.

Frank glared at her, though he remained calm for a man who just found out he was being spied on by the government from the inside. He'd been monitored for months now so they could finally remove him from the picture and ruin the criminal empire he'd established in his corner of the city.

Janice knew more about him than she was letting on. She'd seen the pictures of the bodies found in the Thames. The pieces of those who'd dared betray him, found in the forest by a dog walker. People who went after Frank didn't live to tell the tale once they were found out.

"Please," Janice said, tears falling down her cheeks now. "Take me away to do what you will. Just let my family go. Don't make them watch this."

The kids would never recover from what they were about to see. They'd witnessed enough already. Paul looked at her with glossed eyes, defeat shining through as he understood her meaning.

Janice wasn't walking away from this. Frank wouldn't allow it. Couldn't. She would be yet another example, a cautionary tale to anyone who thought twice about going after him. Not even the government could take him down.

Little did he know Janice had sent enough intel to put him away for life, but she omitted that detail. As pleasing as it would be to wipe that smug look off his hard, brutal face, his wrath would be worse.

Besides, he'd find out soon enough. A little pang of regret stirred in her at the thought of not being there to see it. She turned to her dear children and loving husband. She wouldn't be there to see a lot of things.

"I won't make them watch," Frank said.

"Thank you," Janice said, relief flooding through her. As long as her family was safe, she could handle the rest. As long as they weren't hurt for her actions. As long as they lived.

Frank raised his gun, along with his two colleagues, and each of them aimed to fire.

"No!" Janice screamed, moving too slow to do anything.

The shots tore through the air and embedded themselves into her family with sickening proficiency.

Janice fell to the floor by the chairs, covered in blood. Her entire world, gone in an instant.

Frank Fletcher crossed the room and stood above her. Janice peered up at him with resignation.

"I told you I wouldn't make them watch."

The last thing Janice heard was the blast from a gun, and everything went black.

Chapter 19

Bucharest, Romania

Janice Harris was dead.

Leon swore and leaned against the hood of their rental car, ducking his head into his arms. "They wiped out the whole family," he said, rage shaking his graveled voice, knuckles whitening as he clenched the phone he'd just gotten the news on. "Husband and two kids."

"This needs to end." Maggie knew Janice. Had even been on a couple of missions with her over the years. She was a good agent and was always open to help Maggie in her early days, Janice being almost ten years her senior and vastly more experienced at the time.

Another agent down. How many more would the Unit lose before it was all over?

Ashton patted Leon's back. "Come on, big guy. It's time to get moving."

Leon inhaled a deep breath and straightened up, gathering himself and regaining his composure. He'd always been closer to his colleagues than Maggie had. "Brothers and sisters in arms," he'd say, an ideal picked up from his days in the army. "Got to stick together and look after each other." Now that he was the man supposed to oversee their care, the continued deaths, and threat of more to come, was taking its toll.

Maggie knew Leon well enough to know he was blaming himself for all this. Part of her longed to reach out and comfort him. To wrap her arms around his broad shoulders and promise him everything would be okay.

But that would be a lie.

Things were far from okay, and the time for grieving and blaming himself could wait. Right now, they had a job to do, and the sooner they completed their task, the sooner the needless violence and deaths would stop.

They'd parked on the street when Helmsley rang with the news, already on their way to the address Samuel Thomas had given under duress. Though just over three miles from Bucharest's city center, Ferentari appeared like another world.

The scenes from outside switched from a well-kept and busy metropolis to a run-down ghetto not even low-end supermarket chains dared to set up shop in. The stunning architecture of the Romanian Athenaeum and the colossal parliament buildings, the quaint little cafés under the yellow glass of the Macca-Villacrosse Passage, and high street stores in the Old Center were replaced with the telltale signs of poverty, from discarded piles of garbage littered through the streets to the scattered high-rise apartment buildings marred with age and neglect.

"This place gives me post-apocalyptic vibes," Ashton commented, rolling up his window from the driver's seat once they got back into the car.

Maggie sat in the back with Leon and placed her hand over his. Hers appeared so small against his strong and capable fist. She longed for those hands. For his touch. Yet she refrained from inching closer to him and tried to focus on their reasons for being in the slums. Their relationship and her worries for Leon's mental well-being had to wait. Especially when all of their lives were in imminent danger.

Maggie ran her fingers over her gun as they drew closer to their destination. She hadn't had the pleasure of visiting Ferentari before, but it was a familiar sight. There were places like this everywhere in the world, outer city areas where money, opportunity, and education levels were low, and the drug use and violence that came with it were at an all-time high.

Though most of the wealthy and more fortunate residents of Bucharest would like to forget that Ferentari existed, covering it up like an unsightly blemish on an overall beautiful city, it was a vital and necessary part of the city's makeup. Without the poor, there could be no rich. Without people to exploit for cheap labor and to sell things to, the wealthy couldn't live their lavish lifestyles, so they merely pretended ghettos like Ferentari didn't exist, in the same way they walked past the homeless outside their favorite restaurants and designer stores. They were invisible to people who didn't have to worry about where their next meal was coming from. Out of sight, out of mind, tucked far enough away from their daily metropolitan lives so as not to be a problem.

Ashton stopped the car a few streets away and made sure to park behind a row of garages. The rental was a basic Volvo, old and unassuming to match the rest of the cars there. The paintwork wasn't chipped or rusting, but Maggie kicked in a few dents soon after they left the lot. If they required a quick exit, the last thing they needed was to run to their getaway car only to find someone had stolen it.

Ashton had tried to pay cash for the car, but Maggie let Leon cover it with his fake Inked International company card. If they were out risking everything for the Unit, the least the government could do was pick up the bill for any damages sustained to the vehicle. Ashton ran the keys across the doors when Maggie pointed this out, his little act of rebellion reminding them that while he may be helping by working with the Unit, there was still no love lost between him and his former employer.

And so, the waiting started. Four hours of it to be exact.

Maggie fidgeted in her seat, repositioning herself as she leaned forward to get a better look at the top floors of the building through a set of binoculars. None of the lights were on in any of the apartments, but it didn't mean no one was there. Still, it gave Maggie pause.

No one came in or out in the time they kept surveillance. Ideally, they would spend a few days keeping watch and recording any movements. Looking for patterns and discussing the best approach to get inside and what to do once they breached the entrance. Time wasn't a luxury they had at their disposal, however, and four hours already felt like four days, the ticking clock in Maggie's head counting down the minutes until another name was exposed.

"We can't wait any longer," she said eventually, and got out the car. Wind whipped through the street and collected garbage along the way, crushed cans and old plastic bottles rattling across the broken tarmac of road like a sorrowful marching band. Mothers yelled from apartment windows of neighboring blocks to herd in the kids as night began to fall.

Maggie zipped up her leather jacket and hugged herself from the chill, feeling the change in temperature even more due to their recent stops in Mogadishu and

Amsterdam. Taking in her surroundings, she could see why Ivan Dalca would use this part of the city as his base. Ghettos were the ideal location to hide in plain sight. The general public from the city center and other nice surrounding areas ignored it, not to mention the government. The police would avoid venturing into it if they could help it, especially at night.

As for the residents, they'd have learned to keep their heads down and their mouths shut concerning anything about Dalca's operation. Making examples of a few people early on in their setup would have put a stop to any interference from the locals, and many of them would be on the payroll. If Ivan were bringing money into Ferentari, families wouldn't be quick to offer him up to the police. To some around here, Ivan would be crowned a hero.

Leon opened the trunk and began dishing out the contents. Maggie accepted the sawed-off shotgun from him and pocketed extra ammunition. While she preferred the Glock at her waist, the Remington gave a far more dramatic visual for anyone at the unfortunate end of the barrel. Plus, it fit with their cover. The plane ride had allowed them ample time to come up with a plan of attack.

"Nope." Maggie snatched the grenade Ashton tried to slip into his jacket pocket and returned it to the trunk.

Ashton huffed and opted for a pistol and nasty-looking blade instead. "You never let me have any fun."

Maggie ignored him and focused on Leon. "Are you sure you're ready for this?" The apprehension of Samuel Thomas had taken a lot out of him, no matter how much he denied it. Even with the questionable pain pills Ashton was giving him, he still walked with a limp from the gash to his thigh. "You can stay in the car and be our lookout."

Leon groaned in frustration and slammed the trunk closed. "Don't patronize me, Maggie. I'm injured, not incompetent." He walked ahead of them as they rounded the garages and headed toward one of the tower blocks across the way.

Ashton arched an eyebrow at Maggie, but she didn't bite back at Leon. He was a grown man, and if he said he was good to go, then she wasn't about to question him again over it.

Their presence hadn't gone unnoticed. Heads popped out from behind lace curtains only to quickly close again once Maggie noticed and craned her neck. Community was all places like Ferentari had, and unfamiliar faces weren't a welcome sight. Maggie could only hope their presence would remain unreported until they could do what they came to do and make a swift exit.

Their footsteps were light, the street deserted now that the sun had given way to a dark moon. The lamps around the undeveloped fields surrounding the apartment buildings and the streetlights blinked and buzzed pitifully, most of their neighbors having blown or died out long since.

Taking advantage of the darkness, the trio made good pace and reached the tower block farthest away from the others, its back facing a field of wasteland covered in weeds and tufts of dying grass, the soil beneath barren. It made sound strategy to haul up there. The tower's distance from the others, as well as its high vantage point, allowed the syndicate the isolation needed to carry out business while simultaneously providing the perfect watchpoint for any unwanted arrivals.

Well, most unwanted arrivals. Maggie may have given up her official title as agent, but she might as well have chosen a career as a party clown if she wasn't able to approach undetected.

Cloaked in shadow, they pressed against the once-white walls of the building and rounded to the back entrance. If Dalca's team were on the watch, the back would be less guarded than the front, especially given the ruined terrain behind them. Any assault would most likely come from the front, and anyone enterprising enough to approach from behind would be spotted long before they made it to the foot of the building, easily picked off by a sniper from one of the upper levels.

"Ready?" Maggie asked.

Both men nodded, and Maggie pulled the balaclava over her head.

Dalca's goons would recognize their faces from the

stolen files, and if things went south, they didn't want their mug shots to be the next ones to leak in retaliation. Better to have Dalca's crew think they were robbers trying to steal either the girls or the money than reveal themselves. Enough agents had been exposed already.

Maggie raised her fingers and counted them down from three. The familiar gesture brought her mind to another time in another place five years before. A mission with three of her colleagues, Leon included. Brazil in the middle of the summer. Sweat beaded across her forehead and dripped down her back as she kicked the door of the bank and barged inside, locking it behind her so no one could get in or out.

Their target had an appointment with his bank manager that day. A corrupt politician who accepted handouts whenever and wherever they came. After many compromising situations arose that had resulted in a few dead bodies, the Brit made a swift exit to South America. He'd managed to evade the government's attempts to capture him. Until the Unit stepped in.

Collateral damage. That's what people were to think. An unfortunate soul caught in the crossfire of a robbery. A tragic case of the wrong place at the wrong time.

The niggling itch of that day scratched in Maggie's mind. Bishop had given the orders to take him out. Maggie had been the one to pull the trigger. Bishop's favorite, as the other agents liked to tease. Had the politician really been corrupt? Or was he one of the many people Bishop had his agents eliminate to line his own pockets? Had Maggie killed an innocent man?

Another innocent man?

"Mags?" Ashton asked, Maggie's fingers stuck on three.

She blinked away her thoughts and focused on the here and now, shoving her past deeds to the recesses of her mind where they belonged. Locked away where they couldn't come back to plague her mind with every mission she carried out. Since learning of Bishop's betrayal and her role in his side operation, Maggie had lain awake at night trying to decipher which of her missions were legitimate and which weren't. Trying to tally how many innocent people she'd killed. Trying not to think of the countless lives ruined as a result of her actions.

Confident the building wasn't tricked out with the latest high-tech security system—if the building had smoke detectors, Maggie would be shocked—she approached the back door and turned the handle.

"Locked," she whispered.

"I bet you wish I'd brought that grenade now, don't you?"

Maggie fished out the pins inside her jacket and got to work on the lock. In less than a minute, and with significantly less noise than a grenade, the lock clicked open, and they were in.

The ominous darkness beyond lingered like thick

smoke, Maggie's eyes taking time to adjust. Leon switched on a flashlight from behind her and raised it over his head to illuminate their path, checking vital entry points and doorways before they ventured farther in.

Stone walls and flooring made their careful footsteps echo like a giant's thundering stomps, her very breathing feeling far too loud against the eerie silence that engulfed them.

Maggie tightened her grip on her shotgun. One blast would be enough to announce their presence to the entire building, but she'd fire if she had to. Together, they reached the foot of a staircase leading up to the second floor. It also continued below to a basement level with a steel door at the bottom.

Leon aimed the flashlight up the flight of stairs to find them empty. No noise came from above. No shouting or music. No footsteps or closing doors. Nothing.

"I don't think anyone's home," he whispered.

Maggie had to agree. It wasn't late enough for the building to be so quiet or encased in darkness. The air wasn't stale, and there were no layers of dust coating surfaces, but the place had an empty feel to it. "If Samuel Thomas has lied to us, I am going to strangle him. Slowly."

"He might like that," said Ashton, with a playful elbow.

Was this some wild-goose chase? Had Samuel tricked

them? Hell, were Dalca's people even in the country, never mind Ferentari? The sleazy pimp had more balls than she thought if he had fooled them. Not that he'd have them for much longer once Maggie returned to pay him a visit.

Leon moved his focus downstairs. "It's worth a look."

Taking the lead, Maggie descended and was yet again met with a locked door.

Ashton tapped the metal door with the toe of his boot. "Your little knitting needles aren't going to get through this bad boy."

"You're not going back for that grenade. Stand back," she warned.

"Spoilsport," Ashton whined, but he moved back up the stairs to stand with Leon who kept an eye out for any signs they weren't alone.

Maggie aimed her shotgun at the lock and let loose. The air exploded as a great boom ricocheted off the walls and reverberated through the building like the enraged cries of an unforgiving beast. It did the trick, though, as the bullet blasted off most of the lock, allowing Maggie to smack the rest of it clean off with the butt of her gun.

It was even darker within, the basement free from any natural light coming in through windows or glass doors. The indicators of life emanated through the room. The smell of bodies. The remnants of food beginning to rot.

People had spent a lot of time down here, and recently too.

Leon arrived and brought his light with him to reveal rows of bunk beds, lined up as close to each other as they could and filling the room like an overcrowded army barracks, only much messier. They'd left in a rush and from the discarded clothes across the floor and some personal items on dressers, they hadn't taken much with them.

"They kept the girls down here," Maggie said, running her hand along the thin fabric of the unmade beds.

Ashton called over from deeper inside, using the light on his cell to guide him. "And filmed the videos over there."

Maggie and Leon followed his voice into a new room, smaller than the living quarters of the low-ceilinged basement, if you could call it that, and entered what appeared to be their tech room. A camera setup lay in one corner, the scene familiar from the videos featuring Tamira and the syndicate's demands.

Computers, still wired up and with screen savers on glowed in the darkness, coating all of their faces with a haunting blue glow. While the living quarters held only the bare minimum to sustain life, the syndicate had spared no expense on the makeshift control room equipment. Maggie wasn't a whiz like the techs and analysts back at Unit HQ, but she knew enough about computers to know Dalca's crew were working with some serious hardware.

Ashton shook his head in disbelief. "They hacked the Unit mainframe from this shithole."

Maggie wasn't so sure. Yes, they had some high-tech stuff to play with, but the Unit's firewalls were some of the toughest in the world to get through. Something wasn't right about it all.

"Looks like Tamira left something," Leon said, camera in hand. A sticky note was stuck onto it with Tamira's name written in clear haste.

Maggie switched the camera on to search through the recordings saved to the memory. "Another message?"

"Could be," said Leon over her shoulder.

Maggie leaned into him without realizing it, the gesture so natural for them, their intangible and inevitable pull as strong as ever.

"Wait, do you hear that?" Ashton asked, looking up from a computer he was trying to hack into.

Maggie reached for her gun. "What?"

Ashton frowned and got up from the desk. He walked back through to the bunks with Maggie and Leon close behind him. "I thought I heard—"

Right then, the basement door crashed open and in poured a gang of who Maggie assumed were part of Dalca's syndicate. She swore and cursed Samuel Thomas.

They'd been ambushed.

Chapter 20

Maggie lost count of the number of footsteps, each new arrival too entrenched in the surrounding darkness to tally in her head.

"Next time, I'm bringing that grenade," Ashton vowed somewhere to her left.

"Turn your light off," Maggie warned Leon.

"We won't see them." Leon shifted on his feet, his flashlight catching glimpses of men spilling in from the entrance and coming toward them.

"If you keep it on, they'll know where to fire." Maggie gripped her shotgun in one hand and tensed her muscles, ready for the inevitable showdown.

Leon placed the flashlight onto the nearest bed and positioned it toward the door, giving them a line of vision to see those who came out as well as their only exit to escape. As one, all three of them moved back from the light and into the shadows.

Such close quarters didn't offer much room.

Maggie reached out and shoved Leon behind her, then Ashton. Without a word, she aimed her shotgun in front of her, making the most of the confined space, and fired.

The sawed-off barrel made the gun less precise, but it also meant the range was wider. From the resulting yells and cries that came after the ear-ringing shot, Maggie managed to hit more than a few of their enemies.

The sounds of pain from the syndicate acted like a war call for the three trained assassins, and they darted toward their victims like sharks smelling blood in the water.

Shotgun out of ammo, and with no time to stop and reload, Maggie launched the gun into the fray of opponents and switched to a pair of knives, yanking them out from the holster at her thigh. Her Glock was a last resort, gunfire far too risky amid the darkness when she couldn't be sure where her friends were situated.

Maggie charged into battle thrusting out with her knives to land wherever and on whomever they fell. Blade met skin, and she pushed forward, shoving the knife into flesh until it buried up to the hilt. A whimper gasped from surprised lips as hot blood spilled over Maggie's hands. The person fell forward, and Maggie yanked out her weapon and stepped to the side before the dead man toppled her over.

A fist caught her at the back of the head, the impact vibrating through her entire body and making her mind swim. Hands grabbed for her, thick and strong as an ox, and found purchase with the back of her jacket.

Allowing her adversary to pull her toward him, Maggie used the momentum and swept her blades behind her, sinking the blade into what she guessed to be a thigh and abdomen.

A yell came from her left, and Maggie's heart skipped a beat. Leon.

Not wasting time to celebrate her fatal hit, Maggie abandoned her opponent to die alone and shoved her way toward Leon.

Grunts and the smack of flesh meeting fists and feet played like a horrible soundtrack to the carnage.

Maggie caught sight of Leon as his body passed by the beam of light from the flashlight, along with two attackers who were ganging up to take him down.

"Oh, no you don't," Maggie said through gritted teeth. Leon had been hurt enough, and those men were going to feel her wrath for daring to touch him.

With one of the men's backs facing her and still within range of the light, Maggie closed the distance between them by throwing one of her knives. The blade flew through the air and embedded itself into the man's spine.

By the time he fell to his knees, Maggie had retrieved her knife from inside him and turned to face the second of Leon's assaulters.

Leon was locked in a tussle with him, both men scrambling for advantage. Dalca's men were brawlers, street fighters with more brawn than brains. Even in his condition, Leon gained the upper hand and wrapped his arm behind the fighter's neck. He cupped the man's chin and twisted his head in an unnatural angle, the snapping sound confirming the break.

"You good?" Maggie asked, panting heavily.

Leon brushed his fingers against hers.

Before he could answer, another three of Dalca's men were upon them. One caught Maggie by surprise and got in a good smack to her jaw, filling her mouth with the familiar coppery tang of blood.

Two of the three lunged for Leon and left the other to handle the woman. That was their first mistake.

The second was thinking a single punch to the face would be enough to stop her. Maggie faked a fall and instead raised her knee and crushed it against the man's groin, doubling him over. Next, she balled her fist and reciprocated the blow to the face with an uppercut.

The blow impacted her opponent more than his did Maggie, and she wasted no time slamming her palm into his nose. She felt the bone break and was on to the next guy as he crumpled to the floor next to the others.

"Ash?" Maggie yelled, having lost him in the confusion.

"Yes, dear?" cooed a Scottish accent.

Maggie tried to clothesline an oncoming syndicate member, but he foresaw her tactic and ducked, spinning on his heels and kicking her square in the stomach. Maggie stumbled back, and her heels met the back of one of the bunk beds.

"Just making sure you're alive," she called back.

The man lunged for her, and she threw herself back onto the mattress. She kicked out at him, but missed, the lack of light making her sloppy. The man swung for her, and she caught his arm in a hold, followed by his free arm as he hit out again.

With both arms in her grasp, Maggie pulled him toward her with all her strength. A clang rang through the air as his head rattled against the metal bars of the top bunk frame.

Maggie released her hold. Scurried off the bed. Got back to her feet.

Her foe landed hard on his back, and she stamped her boot into his face to make sure he wouldn't get back up.

The grunts were fewer now, and Maggie had to step over squirming bodies splayed out on the floor to reach the last man standing who squared off with Ashton, Leon having dispatched the two gang members he'd been dealing with.

"Wait," Ashton warned, as Maggie grabbed the Romanian by the hair. "He could tell us what he knows."

Maggie took out her Glock, safe in the knowledge the others were out of commission, either dead or incapacitated. "Do you speak English?" Maggie inquired of the man as Leon collected his flashlight and shone it over their captive.

Either he was pretending not to speak the Queen's English, or he had no clue what she was saying. He wriggled in her hold and reeled off a string of rushed sentences, begging from the cadence and look on his bloody face.

Maggie tried French, Russian, Japanese, and some sketchy Portuguese to no avail. After Leon and Ashton exhausted their roster of languages, it was clear the man spoke his home tongue and nothing else.

"Worth a shot," Maggie said, still out of breath from the fight. She raised her Glock and thumped the last gang member on the back of the head with the grip, efficiently knocking him out. "Everyone okay?"

"Yup," said Ashton, hands on his hips as he admired their handiwork. "These lot weren't trained."

Maggie rubbed her jaw, irritated at the blood filling her mouth. That one guy had clipped her good.

Leon sat himself down on one of the beds, his forehead shiny with sweat. "Any more of them, though, and the outcome could have been very different."

Remembering the camera, Maggie returned to the

tech room and switched it back on while Leon and Ashton kept watch over the carpet of bodies in case any of them decided to get back up for round two.

The latest video on file was time stamped. It was recorded yesterday, late at night when Maggie and her boys were waiting to get back in the air after their little talk with Samuel Thomas.

If they'd been faster in obtaining the address, they could have gotten here in time to stop the syndicate from leaving. To prevent them from leaking any more names. Maggie ran a hand through her hair, then pressed Play on the clip.

"My name is Tamira Kapoor, and I am being held against my will by sex traffickers. If you are watching this, then I beg you to hand this footage over to the authorities in the hopes they can find me and the rest of the girls before we are sold off."

Maggie closed her eyes. The girls. For all she knew, Tamira and the others who'd been held prisoner down in the basement were sold off already. Lost for what could be forever in the cruel underworld of sex work.

"I don't have much time, but here is what I know: I'm being used to read out demands to release a man called Ivan Dalca who I understand runs this operation of trafficking people. He is currently being held prisoner in London, England, and his people are trying to blackmail the government through terrible means to release him."

Tamira's eyes filled with tears as she spoke, her words rushed.

"I've helped to cause the deaths of the people Dalca is exposing. From what I understand, they are covert operatives, and their true identities are being outed to the targets of their undercover assignments. I didn't want to do it, but they made me read out those names. Made me show their pictures to the camera."

"None of this is your fault," Maggie said to Tamira's unhearing ears as she watched on. Tamira was a victim in all this, just like the lost agents and their families.

"One of the Romanian girls said she overheard them talking, and that they're taking us to Belgium. They've secured buyers for us. I don't know what it is, but something seems to have them angry and shaken. We're leaving earlier than they said."

Tamira sucked in a breath and fumbled with the camera. The recording ended, and the screen paused showing the poor girl's terrified face.

"Good girl," Maggie said. Even in the midst of such a horrific ordeal, Tamira was helping them track down Ivan's people. The girl had guts, and Maggie could only hope she'd reach her on time before she was sold. Even then, Maggie could track her. Save her from the nightmare she was living.

If she made it through this alive, that is.

The men left behind in Ferentari were street thugs, not important enough to be taken with the others as they crossed Europe. It was the leaking of her name she was most worried about, and the abundance of enemies who would stop at nothing to put her head on a spike for her actions against them.

"Tamira said they're headed to Belgium."

"Belgium it is," Leon said, groaning as he got up from his seat on the bed. "I'll call the Director General and see what she knows about traffickers there. My bet is they transport the girls by boat or ferry across the Channel. Easier to get through customs compared to flying."

"Let's get going, then," Maggie said, keen to get out of there.

The casualties were still down, most of their complaints and squirming dying down now. Maggie ignored them, guilt-free knowing what these men did to those girls, and countless others who had the misfortune of passing through those doors.

"Hey, where did you get that?" Maggie asked, stopping halfway up the stairs.

Ashton pretended to be embarrassed, like a little boy caught in the middle of sneaking a bar of chocolate before dinner. "I told you it would come in handy."

Maggie shook her head and continued upstairs with Leon, leaving him to it.

Ashton pulled the pin from the grenade and tossed it behind him before closing the door and jogging upstairs. They may not have arrived with a blast, but they certainly left with one.

Chapter 21

Amsterdam, Netherlands
15 July

Maggie kicked down the bedroom door and stormed inside. After one too many flights and nowhere near enough sleep, she was in a foul mood for having to return to Amsterdam.

Samuel Thomas woke with a start and sat up in his bed. Maggie drew back the curtains to let the morning sun pool in. As Maggie was kitted out as Celine again, Samuel roused from his slumber and yelped at the sight of her.

"Bjorn! Johan! Help!" Samuel scurried from the tangle of sheets and pressed himself against the headboard, curling up as if to create as much distance from the dominatrix madam as he could.

"They're a little tied up at the moment, Monsieur Thomas," Maggie informed him, standing at the foot of his bed.

"Get out of my house," Samuel demanded, jabbing a finger at the door.

Maggie waggled a gloved finger in the air and tutted. "I warned you to keep your mouth shut. It was foolish of you not to adhere to my strict orders. Now you must be punished. Boys?"

With a clap of her hands, Leon and Ashton entered the room and snatched Samuel from his bed.

"I never told anyone anything." Samuel fought in earnest to escape their clutches, but he was scared, disoriented, and most likely still suffering aftereffects from the potent drugs Maggie injected into his system on their last visit.

"No?" Maggie said, pausing at the sincerity behind Samuel's terrified eyes. Maggie prided herself as an excellent reader of people, trained in body language and nonverbal cues. "You never let Ivan Dalca's people know I was asking about them? Had acquired their address?"

"I got the message loud and clear, Celine. I promise I didn't say a word."

"Hmm," Maggie said, swinging the same whip she'd used on him before. "What to do with you, then. I want to believe you, but then how can I trust you when we were ambushed at the address you gave to us?"

Samuel paled. "I know nothing about that."

He may be a corrupt, morally deficient excuse for a human being, but Samuel was no liar. At least not a good one. His face was too animated, too much of a window into his mind. Maggie was willing to bet he hadn't spilled his guts to Dalca's gang. But if Samuel didn't let them know they were on their way, how did Dalca's thugs know to be there?

Unless they'd been positioned there. Left behind in case the Unit tracked them down and arrived to take them out just like Maggie had planned. A backup crew watching and waiting to trap and take out anyone suspicious who turned up at the apartment building to snoop around.

Whatever their reasons, Samuel not being the one to alert Dalca's crew to their arrival meant the members in Belgium didn't know about their little visit. Or at least, didn't think it was Celine who was the one to call on them in their home base.

Thanks to Ashton's lack of ability to do as he was told, the grenade had solved the issue of any surviving members reporting back to the heads in Belgium. Even if the residents of Ferentari alerted the rest of the syndicate about the massacre left behind, they had no way of knowing for sure who was responsible. Meaning Celine

Delacroix, and Samuel Thomas for that matter, were still of use.

"Perhaps you're telling the truth." Maggie shrugged. "I don't know, but we're here now, and I do hate the idea of a wasted trip." Maggie turned her attention to Leon and Ashton. "Handle him and be quick about it."

"Wait, wait," Samuel pleaded. "I can help you. Please, I'll do anything."

Celine cocked her head to the side. "Anything?"

Samuel shrunk under her stare and ducked his head to avoid eye contact. "Well, nothing sexual. Not after last time."

Maggie suppressed an amused laugh. "You need not worry your little head about me requesting anything of that nature from you. Believe me."

Samuel dropped to his knees and clasped his hands together. "Tell me what you want, and I'll do it."

"First, put some trousers on. My eyes are hurting." Much to Maggie's disgust, Samuel slept naked.

Leon tossed him some trousers and Samuel did as he was told.

"Are you still after some girls?" he asked after he was decent. "You can have some of mine. Take them. Free of charge."

Maggie pretended to consider. "Generous, but I still want what I came to you for. I want a fresh supply from Dalca's syndicate. You are going to set up the meeting."

The same resistance stirred in Samuel as last time, his jaw tightening. "I am?"

His hesitation was understandable, even in his current predicament. If Celine were planning something untoward against Dalca, then Samuel would be implicated and in turn, face the same wrath if Ivan and his crew sought vengeance for Celine's actions.

"Unless you want me to leave you with my boys, of course," Maggie said, reminding him of the more imminent threat to his well-being.

Samuel rubbed his face where a bruise had blossomed from the lashing she'd given him. "All right, all right. I'll do it. Just say where and when."

"I have it on good authority the syndicate are in Belgium." With any luck, Tamira and the other girls would still be there, too.

"Fine," Samuel said, resigned to his forced fate. "Let me get my phone, and I'll set up the meet."

Leon hoisted him back up from the floor with ease, as if Samuel were a small child. "After that, pack a bag," Leon told him.

Samuel froze, and his face fell. "Why?"

Maggie shot him one of Celine's devious smirks. "You're coming with us."

Chapter 22

Zeebrugge, Belgium
16 July

Samuel scheduled the meeting for the next day, giving them time to fly in, find a hotel, eat something, and then fall into bed for some much-needed rest. Maggie slept a full eight hours and woke up the next day refreshed and ready to take down a syndicate of sex traffickers.

Dalca's crew agreed to the meeting without any push-back or questions, indicating the extent to which Samuel had dealt with them in the past. Thankfully, his shady dealings worked in their favor, and they were set to come face-to-face with the people who had put in motion the series of events that had killed so many of Maggie's former colleagues.

They'd arrived at Ostend-Bruges International Airport under the guise of Celine and her entourage, continuing the charade when checking into the hotel for both Samuel's benefit and to keep up appearances for anyone paying them unwanted attention. You never knew who could be watching. Though they may work together when required, criminals didn't trust each other as a rule, and Dalca's men could have lookouts to spy on Celine Delacroix. Especially since they'd never done business before.

Samuel's involvement would help, but they'd be smart to be suspicious, and as much as Maggie would like to think she was up against a collective of foolhardy petty criminals, Ivan's syndicate was highly organized, powerful, and well connected. They were the real deal and would do anything to protect their organization at all costs.

"They've paid off the coast guard," Leon said, sitting next to her on the beach that stretched across the coast adjacent to the port. It had taken a while to find the traffickers in the chaos of the busy port, but they were right where they'd told Samuel the day before.

"And whoever's in charge of customs here," Maggie agreed.

Zeebrugge was located on the coast of the North Sea and had the most important port for Belgium's fishing industry. As well as fish, they also acted as the central port for many of Europe's automotive manufacturers, held terminals for passenger ferries, and apparently now facilitated the transportation of trafficked girls.

At first, Maggie assumed the syndicate was selling the girls to buyers around western Europe and using Belgium as a temporary central base, being so close to many neighboring countries. The fact they were in Zeebrugge port changed that and proved Leon's theory correct. They were moving the girls by the sea. Given the proximity to Britain, it was a safe bet that's where they were headed.

"You think they'll go through Hull?" Maggie asked. The P&O ferries carried British tourists from Hull to Zeebrugge every day in their overnight route. Not that the syndicate would use the ferry to move the girls.

Leon passed her the binoculars. "My bet's Southampton. Closer to London."

They'd slipped out of the hotel through the back entrance as Celine and one of her goons, making sure no one tailed them. Once they were sure they hadn't been followed, Maggie changed into her normal attire to keep tabs on the syndicate and scope them out before the meet. Ashton was back at the hotel babysitting Samuel until showtime later that night. He was a shifty character, Samuel, and Maggie didn't doubt he'd at least consider trying to escape, but no one was shiftier than Ashton.

Maggie peered into the binoculars and watched a line

of sailors, ship workers, and other miscellaneous men waiting for their turn. Even at this hour, Dalca's crew were selling the girls, using the large intermodal containers in the loading bay as makeshift rooms, the men coming and going as casually as if they were visiting the barber for a haircut.

A deep fire raged within Maggie as she watched, sitting so close and unable to stop it there and then. To barge in and save those poor girls who'd already been through too much. To make the men forcing them into it know what it felt like to be powerless and terrified for their lives.

"I can't watch this anymore," Maggie admitted, palming her eyes like she could remove the images from her memory.

Leon's arm wrapped around her tense shoulders. "We'll get them out. They'll be safe soon."

Maggie leaned into him, careful not to put too much of her weight against his battered and bruised body. The sun was out and warmed her skin as the gentle coastal breeze brushed through her hair.

"How are you holding up?" she asked him, watching the waves sway back and forth. With Samuel around, they'd been unable to speak freely. Even without the pimp about, Leon had been closed off since they'd left Somalia. A wall was there that Maggie wasn't used to, constructed somewhere between then and the last time she'd seen him, at Bishop's funeral. With her, Leon was always open and frank with his feelings. Maggie was never the best at reciprocating such honesty, a facet of her personality that made her the perfect candidate for the Unit, but she was getting better at opening up.

Leon shrugged off her question. "I've taken a few beatings in my time. I'll be fine."

"That's not what I meant," Maggie replied, more than familiar with avoidance tactics. They were her specialty.

His chest deflated as he released a deep, troubled breath. "I don't know, Maggie. It's just a lot."

"We'll get through it. Like we always do." Maggie placed a hand over his muscled chest, feeling the strong beat of his heart against her skin. A heart that she hoped would be hers once this was all over. Once they had time to discuss their future. If Leon still wanted a future.

Leon shook his head. "This time feels different."

Maggie sat up and met his deep, dark eyes. Eyes that had seen her at her best, and her worst. "We've taken down people like Ivan Dalca before."

For most of their lives they had taken down men like him. Defeated the odds. Defied what most thought possible to protect the innocent. This wasn't new ground for them, and though Dalca had managed to break into the inner workings of the Unit, he was just like the rest of the scum she and Leon had put away over and over again for years.

Leon avoided her gaze and stared out at the ocean

beyond, his mind somewhere else. His thoughts washed away in the tide and lost at sea. "It's not just them. It's everything."

"Hey." Maggie cupped his face, stroking the bristles of his newly trimmed beard along his chiseled jawline. "Talk to me."

Leon turned his head and broke free from her touch. He got to his feet, dusted sand off his jeans, and turned his back on her. "Come on. We best be getting back."

Maggie watched him walk away, more concerned for him than ever before. He was shut off from her. Unreachable.

Chapter 23

Night had fallen, and the setting sun had taken the heat with it. A cold chill swooped in from the North Sea and across the village of Zeebrugge in a change of weather Maggie hoped wasn't an omen for things to come.

They'd gone over their plan, using their burner phones to lay it all out via text messages in the presence of Samuel, who was none the wiser to their true reasons for wanting to meet with Dalca's syndicate. As far as he was concerned, Maggie's name was still Celine Delacroix, and he'd spent most of the day in a state of fear and thinly veiled contempt.

Samuel Thomas was a user and wielded power as a weapon against those who had none. It appeared he wasn't a fan of the switch in roles, displeased with getting a taste of his own medicine. The fact that Celine was a woman would make it a tougher pill to swallow, something Maggie took great delight in. Men like Samuel and Ivan Dalca viewed woman as less than human, and it was about time someone slapped them with a dose of reality.

"I don't like this," Samuel said, not for the first time.

"And I don't like you, yet here we both are," Maggie said, touching up Celine's makeup in the back of the car.

Sweat drenched Samuel's head, and they'd had to obtain a hat before arriving at the port to mop it up and hide the telltale sign of his building anxiety. The last thing they needed was for Dalca's men to get suspicious with Samuel's unfortunate perspiration. She'd already ordered him to stop wringing his hands, his nails nibbled down to the quick.

Considering he was in the dark for Celine's reasons for wanting to meet Dalca, not seeming to buy her story about needing to purchase new girls, he'd soon do a lot more than sweat. Maggie preferred a quick and clean approach to any job, but she had a feeling this one wouldn't go down that way. Her knuckles cracked in her balled fists. Dalca's crew deserved more than a little mess.

Leon and Ashton were up front in the car, taking on their roles as Celine's security. The man in charge of Dalca's operation in Ivan's stead was named Grigore Ursu. At the mention of his name at the gates of the port, they were allowed entry and given directions to the freight containers they'd scoped out earlier.

The loading bay was a small city, with towering

skyscrapers of piled containers, in different colors like a child's building blocks. The streets were tarmacked and kept wide enough to allow the cranes and machinery to transport the metal vessels in and out as they were needed, giving Maggie and her crew ample room to drive through the city until they reached their destination.

They made a quick stop and switched as planned, Maggie taking her place at the driver's seat with Samuel next to her as Ashton and Leon slipped out into the shadows and disappeared.

Maggie didn't like it, but the boys had the hardest job tonight. Celine was needed as the distraction while they worked, and she intended to do all she could to keep their presence a secret until the right moment.

Rounding a corner, they arrived at the location. Their little corner of the city was illuminated with outdoor lighting that hummed from the generator powering them.

Bile rose in Maggie's throat. The red-light district of the freight container city was busier than it had been earlier. It wasn't just punters from around the port giving the pop-up brothel their patronage. Word must have spread around town, and every creep in Zeebrugge appeared to have turned up to pay to take advantage of the young girls.

Maggie had left her gun at the hotel in preparation for the inevitable search by Dalca's men, and it was just as well. She may have gone trigger happy there and then at the sight of so many men eagerly waiting to gain entry to the rows of open containers, concealed with nothing but a dirty piece of fabric to curtain off what was going on inside.

Dalca's crew were easy to spot among the growing crowd. None of the Johns wore guns.

Unsurprised, yet still uneasy about them all being armed, Maggie turned off the engine and got out of the car. Two men were waiting for them and approached.

"Celine Delacroix?" one asked, both of them towering over her.

A scream came from one of the containers followed by the unmistakable smack of a slap. It took everything in Maggie at that moment to remain calm and stay in character.

Celine offered a tight-lipped smile. "The one and only."

"We need to search you," said the second man, his face hard like it was chiseled from stone.

"I charge men a lot of money for that privilege." Nevertheless, Maggie held out her arms and spread her legs to get it over and done with. Surprisingly, the guard never tried to grope her. A smart choice on his part.

Maggie used the time to take in the layout. From the size of the containers, not all of the girls were put to work. From what Tamira said, they had virgins they planned to sell untouched. Virgins were big money in the black market, and people were willing to pay huge amounts of cash to get their hands on them.

The others must be kept somewhere else.

"Come this way," said the gargoyle-looking guy after both Maggie and Samuel had been searched. "Grigore is waiting on you."

They were led through the camp, the noises coming from inside the containers almost sending Maggie over the edge. No matter what happened tonight, she would make good on her promise to Ivan to not only stop his crew from leaking any more names of agents but to tear down their entire operation and burn it to the ground.

Behind the occupied containers were a row of large trailers, the fleet of vehicles answering Maggie's question as to how Grigore Ursu transported Ivan's girls from Romania. If the crew took it in shifts, driving through the night, they would have reached Zeebrugge within two days, less if they only stopped to refill the vehicles and pick up supplies.

Maggie couldn't help but wonder how many girls had ridden in the back of those trailers. Watching helplessly from the windows as they were taken away to parts unknown, with no idea what awaited them when they stopped.

The first trailer was nicer than the others, a state-of-the-art affair with tinted windows and a glossy paint job in gunmetal grey. It came as no surprise to Maggie when the door opened and out stepped a man Samuel appeared to recognize. The current head of Dalca's syndicate enjoyed the top-of-the-line trailer for luxury travel while the girls were crammed into the backs of the others like commuters on the tube during London rush hour.

"Samuel," said Grigore, hopping from the trailer and coming over to welcome them. He offered his hand to Samuel and pulled him into a hug. "How are you, my friend?"

He spoke in English, a given when dealing with other Europeans. Other than Brits, most other European countries made concerted efforts to teach kids a second language early on in school, usually English, and most of the time well enough for them to be considered fluent.

Maggie was fluent in French, among others, but it was only after joining the Unit that she could string more than a few basic sentences together.

"Good," Samuel replied, not nearly blithe enough for Maggie's liking. "How is business?"

"Business is great. I expect my uncle will be very pleased when he returns."

Uncle Ivan. Grigore must be Ivan's sister's son, given the different surnames. He seemed so assured of Dalca's return that it made Maggie's stomach churn. Either he was incredibly arrogant, or he had more up his sleeve than what they'd currently attacked the Unit with.

"And you must be Celine Delacroix."

Maggie offered her hand for Grigore to kiss, holding it there when he hesitated and unflinching until he brought his lips to her gloved hand. It was a tiny power play, but even the smallest of victories won the battle in these types of negotiations. Even if Maggie were playing a part to stall for time, Celine would play every encounter with a business contact to her advantage. She was a dominatrix in all aspects of her life, especially when it came to her empire.

"Mr. Ursu. Thank you for meeting with me on such short notice."

"Of course. Anything for a friend of Samuel's."

Maggie made a show of shuddering and crossing her arms together. "Should we step inside? It's rather chilly out here."

"Please, by all means," replied Grigore, opening the door to his trailer and waving them in. "Ladies first."

For a man who made a living selling girls, he was terribly polite. Then again, from what Samuel had told him on the phone, Celine was interested in buying girls. Regardless of his feelings toward her, or his attitude toward women in general, Grigore was capable of putting on a charade if it meant he could profit from it.

Maggie stepped inside, hoping that this meeting would go much more smoothly than the one she had as Ekaterina in Somalia. Like Yasir Osman, Grigore wasn't short on security. As well as the guards who'd searched them, there were men stationed at each container, by the doors of the other trailers, and a further two inside Grigore's trailer. A lot, but if things went to plan, it wouldn't matter.

It wasn't lost on Maggie that none of Ivan's syndicate

members were women. He didn't respect them enough to have them work for him in any position other than on their backs. Perhaps if he'd hired some women into the fold, they wouldn't have been so easy to track and trick into a meeting.

Grigore opened a well-stocked minibar at the kitchen area. "Something to drink?"

"Do you have champagne?" Celine asked.

Grigore laughed. "I'm afraid not. We have vodka, though."

Celine sniffed and took a seat at the dining table, shoving Samuel in before her to make sure it forced Grigore to sit directly across from her. "No, thanks."

Grigore helped himself and poured Samuel one too without asking him. Maggie hoped it would at least calm the man down. He was already shaking his leg like a father afraid to enter the delivery room.

Maggie give him a swift kick under the table, and he stopped.

"So, Samuel tells me you were asking for me," Grigore said, taking a seat.

"For your uncle, yes," Maggie corrected. "Where is he?"

Grigore didn't miss a beat. "He couldn't make it, but he sends his sincerest apologies. I know he would have loved to meet you."

"A pity," Celine mused with a little pout. If only Grigore knew she'd had the distinct displeasure of meeting his uncle Ivan. His nephew wasn't as openly chauvinistic, but he shared the same calculating eyes that couldn't hide the hunger behind his stare, the predatorial glint that hinted he would go to great lengths to get what he wanted.

Too bad for him.

"I'm sure I can accommodate you in his stead. I understand you are interested in our supply."

"Perhaps," Maggie said, keeping it French. Part of Celine's allure and shrewd business tactics was her perceived disinterest in most things. Living the life she did, most situations were mundane and unexciting.

"Well, we have plenty for you to choose from. Other than those we have set aside for Samuel, the rest have yet to be placed with a buyer."

Maggie itched to throttle Samuel there and then. If he thought he was going to walk away with a new set of girls of his own, he was sorely mistaken. He'd be lucky to return to Amsterdam with his balls intact.

"And the less you need to take across the Channel, the better, yes?" Maggie said, instead of castrating Samuel where he sat.

Grigore shrugged, playing his own side of the game as negotiations started. "It's all the same to us. If you don't take them off our hands, one of our regular buyers will once we reach London."

So they were headed to London. Was it simply business as usual? Or did it run deeper? While Maggie didn't doubt they had a thriving business in England's capital—Grace Helmsley had said as much when telling Maggie about Ivan's operation—it did strike Maggie as a coincidence that they were headed to London during their blackmailing of the Unit. Like they expected to simply turn up at the prison and collect Ivan at the gates to take him back home to Romania.

What were they planning that made them so certain the British government would release their leader?

Even if Maggie broke her character and asked Grigore outright, she wouldn't have gotten an answer to her burning question. Shouting came from outside, and the door to Grigore's trailer flew open.

"Sir, we have a breach."

Grigore's eyes narrowed and pinned on Maggie.

Chapter 24

Maggie didn't need to speak Romanian to know what Grigore's orders were to his men as he left the trailer. *Keep them inside and don't let them leave.*

Even without fully understanding what was going on outside, Grigore knew to be suspicious. It was a little more than coincidence something bad happened while Celine Delacroix, a woman he had never met nor done business with before, decided to pay them a visit.

Maggie let him leave to lower the odds between her and the guards. Samuel was a big guy, but given how chalk-white and sickly his face had turned, she doubted he'd be of any help in a scuffle.

The door slammed closed, and yelling sounded from beyond. One of the men crossed the trailer and stood sentry by the door, blocking the only exit and leaving her cornered from both ends.

Maggie stood up, still playing Celine. "What is going on?" she asked, clutching her neck and playing up the scared woman routine men had a habit of falling for. "It is the police?"

"Sit," one of the men replied, emphasizing his command with the point of his gun.

"What is the meaning of this?" Celine demanded, tossing aside her act. No one ordered her about, never mind dared to point a weapon at her. How outrageous.

Knowing Grigore would want Celine alive even if they realized she was behind the commotion, Maggie risked approaching the man by the door.

He stayed where he stood, not in the slightest bit intimidated, and looked down his nose at her with a sneer. "I said sit."

Maggie dug in her heels and spat out a tirade of French at the man, waiting for the inevitable. It didn't take long.

Quickly tiring of the angry woman before him, the guard grabbed Maggie's shoulder to lead her back to her seat by force. Or so he thought.

The man's fingers buried into Maggie's shoulder much harder than necessary. Maggie shot him a wicked grin, and in that split second, he knew he'd made a fatal error.

She attacked, resorting to an old faithful by first

punching the mountain of a man in the throat, then pressing down on the area between his thumb and finger as hard as she could to free herself from his hold.

By the time she freed herself, the second guard was in attack mode. Maggie apprehended the gun from the man struggling to breathe beside her and ducked behind his bulk as a shield.

"Celine!" Samuel cried, struggling out of his seat and stumbling toward her. "Wait for me."

The second guard eyed Samuel, seeming to read the room wrong and thinking Samuel was charging at his colleague. He fired his gun, and Samuel stopped in the middle of the trailer, eyes wide. A bullet to the back was no joke, and before Samuel could mutter any last words, he fell forward and crumpled to the floor, dead before he touched the ground.

Maggie fired at the second guard from behind the first, sinking three bullets into his chest to take him down. The man fell to the floor with Samuel, and his gun skidded across the floor.

The remaining guard clocked it and dove. Maggie fired again, the man so big and close within the trailer he was a hard target to miss. Like the other men, he crashed dead on the ground.

A crashing boom rang from outside, and Maggie smiled despite herself. Ashton never made an entrance without a bang.

She collected the second guard's gun, the grip on

both weapons easing the tension in her muscles a little. Being unarmed left her uneasy.

The trailer door had a little window, and she checked through the slats in the blinds to get a read of the situation outside before barging into the fray. Like most things Ashton had a hand in, it was pandemonium.

The dock was lit up like a bonfire, and the explosions burst from all around like a chaotic fireworks display. People ran in all directions in the confusion—guards, half-dressed men, and girls who were already scared enough. Needs must, though, and the wilder things were, the less of a handle Grigore and the rest of Ivan's syndicate would have over the situation.

Maggie slipped out of the trailer and the smell of gasoline and burned plastic hit her senses from all angles. Containers were alight and blasting waves of heat across the port. They blew up like a row of dominoes in a symphony of explosions that sang through the air and illuminated the surroundings in a bright orange glow.

The armed guards were Maggie's first priority. The trailers behind Grigore's had been defended by a guard a piece, but some of them appeared to have left their stations in the midst of the attack. Only one remained, and Maggie took him out before he spotted her, sending a bullet through his temple.

Normally, Maggie would be concerned about killing people who weren't her direct target. Life was precious, a fact she was more familiar with than most having been so close to death and dealing it out too. If she had to kill someone, of course, she did, but if it could safely be avoided, a bullet to the kneecap was just as effective.

Maggie had no qualms killing these men. All of them played a role in trafficking the unfortunate souls who found themselves trapped in their clutches. A bullet to the head was the least they deserved.

She opened the door of the closest trailer. A huddle of girls was inside, each younger looking than the next. Maggie searched their faces for Tamira, but she wasn't among them.

"English?" Maggie asked.

One of the girls nodded and relayed Maggie's words to the rest.

"Stay inside." Maggie placed one of her two guns into a girl's hand, the calmest of the bunch with steady, serious eyes. "If any of those men come in, you pull that trigger without question."

Maggie left the girls and went in search of Grigore, Tamira, and her boys. Leon still wasn't right, physically or emotionally, and darts of fear for him pierced the corner of her mind.

Sirens wailed through the air and grew louder as the Belgian authorities and fire brigade rushed to the scene. Even less time than Maggie thought.

Girls in various states of undress and panic scurried through the lot of the makeshift brothel, screaming and sobbing amid the chaos playing out before them. Maggie ushered as many of them as she could toward the relative safe haven of the trailers.

Someone crashed into Maggie from the side and tackled her to the hard ground with a thud. The air swept from her lungs as a great weight pinned her down. Maggie wriggled under the man and caught the glimpse of silver as he rose the knife into the air to embed into her chest.

Her heart raced. She couldn't move fast enough as the blade cut through the air toward her. She twisted with everything she had and screamed as the metal sliced her skin.

Blood pooled across her abdomen within a matter of seconds, the slash long and deep, but not as deep as the man intended.

Maggie searched for her gun. It lay on the ground, just out of reach.

She stretched her arm, gritting her teeth as her fingers brushed the handle.

With the first blow missing the mark, her attacker aimed again. He shifted slightly and sat up to get a better view of Maggie's struggling form. Spotting her opening, Maggie launched her knee into his groin and sent the man doubling over. She rolled over, hissing at the burning pain in her stomach, and collected her weapon.

The man grabbed her hair and pulled her back, ripping locks out with his big fingers, but she allowed it, using the momentum to place her into position to release a bullet under his chin once she got close enough.

It took off half his face.

Maggie ran a hand over her wound, and her fingers came back slick and crimson. She swore and got to her feet, the mess of a man beside her already forgotten as she scanned the burning city of containers.

There.

Grigore, surrounded by a group of his men, running toward an SUV. He had someone by the hair, dragging them along with him.

Maggie strained her eyes, her mind growing hazy from the pain of her knife wound.

It was Tamira. She was sure of it.

She broke into a run and charged toward Grigore and his crew. Tamira was too close for Maggie to risk taking a shot at the syndicate's temporary leader.

A terrified-looking john with his shirt unbuttoned ran in front of her as he searched for an exit among the flames. Maggie shoved him out of the way, the effort sending stabbing jolts of searing pain across her open skin.

Grigore shoved Tamira into the back of the SUV and got in with her as the engine roared to life. Maggie sprinted as fast as she could, but she was too far away, and too slow thanks to her injury.

Tamira's face came into view from the back window, and she and Maggie locked eyes. The girl's hands pressed against the glass until a hand curled around her face and pulled her back and out of sight.

The driver put the pedal to the metal and hightailed it from the port, the tires screeching in their wake. Maggie got to one knee and aimed at the vehicle with one eye closed. She fired the rest of her clip at the car, sinking bullets into the wheels to stop them from leaving.

Maggie swore. The tires were bulletproof.

All she could do was watch as the SUV sped off into the night, taking Grigore and poor Tamira with it.

Chapter 25

Police lights flashed through the port as officers cuffed the collection of remaining guards who made it out alive and the johns who weren't fast or smart enough to escape in time. Maggie made sure no one went near the girls before she spoke with them, making it clear to anyone with a badge that they were not to be arrested. They were the victims in all of this and had been through enough.

Helmsley had made some calls to the Belgians to smooth things over, likely calling in a few favors in the process. Interpol were on their way, too. Apparently, they'd been investigating Ivan Dalca's operation but had lost sight of its whereabouts in recent months.

The authorities would be on the lookout for the SUV, Maggie having memorized the license plate number. Not that she had any hopes of them finding them, even with

CCTV at their disposal. The plates would be replaced out of sight from surveillance before the end of the night, if not the SUV itself for a less conspicuous vehicle.

Maggie sat in the back of an ambulance for the second time that week, only this time she was the patient, and not a very good one at that. She shooed away a man fussing over her in Flemish and pointed him toward one of the girls who had fallen in the chaos and broken her arm.

"I want you to do it," Maggie told him.

Leon eyed the paramedics. "They're better equipped."

Sweat beaded on Maggie's forehead, the loss of blood sending a chill through her that made her teeth chatter. "You're trained just as much as them. You know what to do."

Maggie didn't want anyone else touching her. The pain across her stomach, along with her failure to apprehend Grigore or save Tamira, stung like a bitch. She clung on to her last nerve to stop her from taking out said frustrations on everyone and everything in proximity. Except for Leon. Never Leon.

He brushed away her hand pressing over the wound and peeled back her blood-sodden shirt. "It'd be better if we had a doctor look at this. No telling how dirty his blade was."

"I'll get a tetanus shot," Maggie retorted. "Besides, we don't have time." Grigore would be extra pissed now that they'd ruined his uncle's trafficking operation, and she didn't like his attitude back in the trailer. He was too confident of Ivan's return. Even now, the Dalca syndicate still held all the cards.

"As long as you trust me," Leon said, meeting her eyes.

Maggie softened under his stare. Those dark, honest eyes captured her attention and calmed her down. "You know I do," she said, brushing a hand over his face. "More than anyone."

He had fared better than Maggie, a fact she was more than thankful for. She'd had a word with Ashton before heading out earlier to make sure Leon was on the sidelines of their plan as much as possible. Like always, Ashton had come through for her.

Right now, her best friend was mingling with the girls and making sure they were safe. Some of them appeared to speak one of his many languages, and he had them laughing, despite everything they'd witnessed and been victim to. Maggie smiled. Ash would never admit it, but he had a big heart.

Leon cleaned the wound with rubbing alcohol first. Maggie's knuckles turned bone-white as she gripped the sides of the stretcher.

"You okay?" Leon checked, his hands efficient yet gentle.

Maggie nodded, unable to speak around the sting of the alcohol, and let him work.

"It's deeper than I'd like, but it doesn't seem to have hit anything vital. Superficial."

"I wish it felt like that," Maggie said with a laugh, instantly regretting the swimming sensation it caused in her head.

She'd had worse, but her injury was ill-timed, and the threat of Dalca's syndicate was more pressing than ever. Now Grigore didn't have his girls to worry about; all he had was time to focus on getting his uncle back. If he made the connection between Celine Delacroix and the Unit, his retaliation could result in many more lives lost. If Grigore was anything like his uncle, he'd make sure his wrath would be felt by those who'd wronged him.

And Maggie had wronged him all right. She wasn't aware of how much each girl was worth to him financially, but whatever the monetary value, it was a lot for him to lose. Especially in the absence of his uncle, where Grigore was undoubtedly trying to prove himself as a worthy successor to the insidious empire.

"This is going to hurt," Leon warned as he prepared to make the first of what would be many stitches.

Maggie sucked in a breath as he stuck the needle into her skin and released it once it had gone through the other end. It was a sensation she'd experienced many times, but never got used to. Just like with Leon. No matter how many times he touched her, each time felt like the first. She watched him work, all of his attention focused on patching her up. His tongue poked out from the side of his full lips the same way it did when he was defusing a bomb or poring over the mountain of paperwork upon returning from a job.

"Feels like only the other day I was helping stitch you up," Maggie commented, her leg brushing against him as he worked. Even amid the pain and irritation, tingles in nervous excitement still danced within her at his proximity, his deep voice like music to her ears, sending thrills through her body.

Leon smirked and stole a glance at her. "That's because it was."

They'd spent more nights patching each other up than they had on dates in the time they'd known each other. You could learn a lot about a person by going out to dinner, but nowhere near as much as you did fighting for your lives together and risking it all. It was a shared past that could never be forgotten, not like some meal at a restaurant. It was imprinted in Maggie's mind, as was every scar Leon wore across his hard body, like a road map to his soul that she could follow with her hands. A battle-worn body that matched her own.

"How did the other guy fare?" he asked, keeping a steady and even pace with each stitch.

Maggie blinked away the sight of the man with no face. "Let's just say he's not on Ivan's payroll anymore."

Leon paused for a moment, and his face darkened. "Good."

"It had to be done," Maggie said, eager to change the subject. "How are you feeling?"

"You've been slashed and require"—Leon counted—"at least twelve stitches, and you're asking me how I am?"

"I'm worried about you," Maggie admitted.

Leon continued stitching. "I'm fine."

Maggie raised his chin and met his eyes, the white in his left one still bloodshot. "You're a terrible liar."

"I'm a great liar," Leon said, escaping her hold and returning to work. "If I weren't, *I* wouldn't be on *the Unit's* payroll anymore."

His tone was light, but he shifted on his knees before her and cleared his throat, visible signs of his obvious discomfort that he tried to conceal.

"True, but you've never been able to lie to me. I always know."

What Maggie didn't say was Leon had never had to lie or keep things from her. His stark honesty with her always left her taken aback. He never shied from professing his feelings or how he felt about her. Never kept anything from her, even when they were in the off periods of their on-and-off-again relationship.

Leon had always been open with her. Until now.

"Why did you take the job in Somalia?" Maggie asked, unable to hold herself back anymore. The question had been burning inside her ever since Grace briefed her on Leon's self-appointed mission back in London.

Leon's jaw tightened. "There was no one else with the right specs. Yonas Ibori's still on paternity leave, and we couldn't let an opportunity to get into the folds of Yasir's operation slide. He was too dangerous."

"You're supposed to be the new chief," Maggie continued, her voice rising as the fear of losing him came back like a haunting recollection. Of losing him before they got the chance to finally be together, to be happy. "It's a desk job. Bishop never went out in the field."

"Yeah, well, I don't think Bishop is a good example of what a chief should and shouldn't do," Leon snapped, snipping off the remaining thread after he tied the last stitch into a knot.

"You know what I mean. Grace told me the brief was to gather intel, that was it. You were supposed to come back home after that."

With the wound stitched, Leon rummaged through the supply drawers and found plasters to cover the wound. "An opportunity presented itself."

Maggie held up her wet, dirt-covered shirt for him to place the plaster over her newly sealed wound, his hands still gentle even as their tempers grew.

"To what?" she said. "Place yourself in immeasurable danger? You knew the risk you were taking by going into his compound. You're a lot of things, Leon, brave and stubborn among them, but never stupid. Why did you do it?"

Leon took off the disposable gloves and tossed them

into the ambulance's bin along with the bloody gauze and other items. "Someone had to do something. He had to be stopped, and I was in a position to do it."

Maggie tried in vain to see past the wall he'd constructed between them. "It was a suicide mission."

"So, I'm incapable now, is that it?" Leon's chest heaved as he stepped away from her. "Useless?"

Maggie's shoulders slumped, too tired to argue. "Leon, I didn't say that. You're more than capable, but not for a job with the odds against you like that. None of us could have carried that out and lived to tell the tale. You almost died."

"You could have done it."

Without another word, Leon jumped out the back of the ambulance and left her alone. A tear escaped from the corner of her eye, and she swiped it away. Maybe after everything they'd been through, they weren't going to make it. Not with Leon refusing to open up to her, and Maggie still keeping things from him.

Maybe, in the end, they were better off apart.

Chapter 26

London, Great Britain
17 July

Director General Grace Helmsley closed the door to her terrace house on Talbot Road, Notting Hill, and leaned her back against the solid wood. It had been a long, tedious day with no results. The worst kind of day. Unproductive and no closer to nailing the bastards threatening her agents.

She kicked off her high heels and released a sigh, placing her stockinged feet on the cold tiled floor of her hallway. Grace hated wearing heels, but they made her taller and more imposing, the ominous clack of her approach instilling fear in even the hardiest assassins she'd wrangled in her long government career.

The house lay in silence like it always did these days. Even three years after losing her husband, she still expected him to traipse downstairs from his home office and give her a warm, all-encompassing hug that, no matter how horrible a day she'd had, always managed to make her feel better.

When they first bought the house, it seemed grand, the perfect place to build a family. Now it felt too big. Empty and hollow.

Kids were never a part of Grace's plan when she was younger. By the time she'd gotten around to quite liking the idea of being a mother, she'd left it too late and wasn't able to get pregnant. Still, she had her Malcolm to come home to. Until she didn't.

Grace had fought many foes in her time, but cancer was one evil she couldn't take down. It got Malcolm in the end, after years of fighting, remission, and resurgence. It was a resilient disease with never-ending patience and a death stroke swifter than any killer she'd known.

Tossing her keys into the bowl by the door, Grace shrugged out of her jacket and hung it over the railing at the bottom of the stairs, bypassing the living room and heading into the kitchen.

It was two in the morning, far too late to cook anything close to resembling dinner, which she'd skipped earlier due to a meeting with the prime minister. With more agents meeting their untimely ends and the threat of exposure hanging over their heads, it was time to update the Tory leader on what was going on. She wasn't happy, but nothing was new there. Grace found it hard to decipher one emotion from the other with the PM's face stuck like that. It was as if she'd spent the afternoon sucking lemons and her face hadn't quite gotten over the fact. The meeting, as they tend to do, bled over longer than anticipated and ate into Grace's already hectic schedule.

Forgoing any thoughts of nutrition, Grace opted for a sharing-sized packet of cheese and onion crisps and a cup of tea. Sod the diet.

The security light illuminated her back garden, but it was only Stephen Dewan, her agent, and personal bodyguard, making his rounds. He gave her a curt nod and carried on his search.

Lisa was stationed at the front door for the night, with Daniel taking over in the morning. They were insistent on the extra security, even after she'd sent them to Spain to fetch Maggie Black, which left them with more bruises to their egos than their bodies. Still, they forgave her and carried out their duties as diligently as always, never once complaining about the longer shifts. She'd already seen to it that they'd each receive a raise for going over and above the call of duty.

Grace drained her cup, returned the half-eaten bag of crisps to the cupboard, then headed upstairs. She had an early start in the morning and wanted to try at least to get some sleep before then.

After a quick change out of her suit and into her nightgown, she turned off the lights and fell into bed. After Malcolm passed, she got rid of their king-sized within a week and replaced it with a smaller one, unable to sleep in the same bed he'd died in. The same bed they'd made love in, and spent stolen moments lounging around and reading the papers on Sunday mornings.

Sleep never came easy to her, especially now that the other side of her bed lay empty, without the comforting heat of the man she loved, his soft snores no longer soothing her into a contented slumber. She placed a hand on the vacant pillow and closed her eyes.

Grace hadn't been there in the end. In Malcolm's final moments. She'd been called into an emergency COBRA meeting, and by the time she'd returned home many hours later, he was gone. Since then, she'd never been able to forgive herself. While she may be one of the best ever to hold her position as Director General, she'd been a terrible wife. Canceled vacations, forgotten anniversaries. Through it all, Malcolm never complained or made a fuss, though it must have hurt him. He said he knew what he was getting into when he married her, and he was proud to have a wife who was so accomplished and who fought the good fight.

"Oh, Malcolm," she whispered into the night. It was

times like these she missed him most, when he'd comfort her and tell her no matter what it was, she'd figure it out.

"No, not Malcolm," said a voice in the darkness.

Grace sat up and strained her eyes in the direction the voice came from, her heart rattling against her rib cage so hard she thought it would burst. Her hand slipped under the pillow at Malcolm's side, and she watched, waiting for the slightest movement.

A figure stepped forward from inside her walk-in closet and Grace moved into action. Grip already wrapped around the handle of the SIG Sauer P226, she pulled it from under the pillow, aimed at the approaching figure, and fired.

The voice laughed, and a rain of unspent bullets fell across the wooden floor as he came into view, the streetlights from outside setting his face in an eerie yellow glow. "I removed the ammunition before you got home. And from the one inside your bedside table."

He was dressed in all black, only his face visible in the night. An ordinary-looking face. They always were. People expected villains to have grotesque features, or a scar across their face as if to highlight their intent. In reality, people were people, and even the plainest of men were capable of horrific deeds.

"Very good," Grace said, placing the gun on her blanket.

She didn't move, though her legs twitched for her to get up and make a run for it. While she was hardly an invalid, she was no spring chicken and knew well enough when she was outmatched. She was never one for exercises in futility, so she remained in bed with her back straight and controlled her voice to stay steady and unaffected by his intrusion into her home.

"Did you harm my agents?" she asked, thinking of Lisa and Stephen.

"*I* didn't," the man replied, his voice soft, yet it was clear he was enjoying himself. Like he could smell the fear Grace concealed.

There were more of them, then. Lisa and Stephen were likely dead.

She didn't need to ask who he was. His accent was answer enough, the lilt of his words matching that of his boss. Grace was good at sourcing accents. Had a knack for it, even when they were trained by the best to hide it.

"If you're waiting for me to scream or run in fear, you'll be sorely disappointed," she warned him.

"A pity," he said, pulling out her Smith & Wesson from his jacket.

Grace grimaced. He was going to kill her with her own bloody gun.

She knew this day would come. Had been waiting on it for years. Grace Helmsley long accepted the possible fate back when she was a young and eager agent in MI6. Had come to terms with it even more so when she took the position as Director General.

Leon had warned her to expect Grigore Ursu to

arrive on British soil within the next day or so, but what they hadn't accounted for was that others in Dalca's syndicate were already here in London and awaiting his arrival.

"Dalca will never be released. You know that, yes?"

The man shrugged. "Not my immediate concern."

Hitmen were all the same. Single-minded and focused on the task at hand. Others could worry about the greater plan. People like herself, and Ivan's nephew, who seemed to be running the ship while his uncle was under lock and key. This man wasn't here to solve the problem of Ivan Dalca's imprisonment. He was simply here to remove one problem from the bigger picture. Perhaps Grigore would use her death in the hopes of it tipping the scale and ensuring Ivan's release. Maybe he just wanted her dead for the sake of it, to take down the head of the Unit and hope the others would fold in her absence.

Not her agents. They were too well trained to allow her death to interfere with their jobs. She'd made sure of it. Had taken a hand in recruiting each and every candidate, whether they knew it or not. They'd take the syndicate down, even if she wasn't there to see it. Of that, she was certain.

"Shall we get on with it, then?" she asked, calmer than she thought she would be.

"Turn around," he ordered.

Grace raised her chin and shot him a glare her agents

knew all too well. “If you’re going to shoot me, son, then have the balls to face me while you pull the trigger.”

Her thoughts turned to the agents she’d lost, to her parents long since dead, and to her sweet, gentle Malcolm. She’d see them all soon.

Grace Helmsley stared her killer straight in the eyes as he raised the gun to her head.

Chapter 27

Zeebrugge, Belgium

Maggie woke to the sound of swearing.

It wasn't the most eloquent of statements, but the meaning behind it was clear. Something was wrong, and from the way Leon swore, it must be bad.

Forgetting her injury, Maggie kicked off the covers and jumped out of bed, instantly regretting it. Her stomach ached in complaint at the abrupt movement, the rest of her body still catching up with her from the sudden wake-up call.

She padded into the living area of the suite Ashton

had insisted on, the boys' rooms branching off at the opposite end. Leon was there, his face drawn.

He wore only his boxer shorts, giving Maggie ample opportunity to take in the various colors of his healing wounds against his dark skin. If Yasir weren't already dead, Maggie would have gone to the ends of the world to seek vengeance against him for hurting the man she loved.

Leon paced the hotel room with a hand over his head, and his neck craned back. "Send it over to me now and keep me posted. I want all updates sent to me the second you have them," he ordered to the person on the other end, and hung up.

"What?" Maggie asked Leon as Ashton came out from his room, dark hair sticking out at all ends and one eye still closed.

"Did someone burn the breakfast?" Ashton asked, breaking out into a yawn.

Maggie checked the clock. It was just after five in the morning, Belgium being an hour in front of Britain. Odd hours for a call from the Unit.

Leon sat on the arm of the couch and blinked in obvious bewilderment. "It's Grace."

"What about her?" Maggie asked, crossing the room to comfort him. She wrapped an arm over his broad shoulders and rubbed his bare back.

"She's been taken by the Romanians. They broke into her house, killed her security, and abducted her."

Maggie froze. Grace? How did they get to her? Surely her name wasn't on the list? Then again, if Dalca's people made the connection between the Unit and the Secret Intelligence Service, it was a sound bet to link Grace with managing both entities. Her name and face were all over the SIS website in the lame attempt to appear more transparent with the public.

The more this whole mess developed, the more Maggie couldn't shift the thought of the leak being an inside job. Someone in the Unit would be able to hand over Grace's address. They'd have access to all the right information Dalca and his syndicate needed to exploit the Unit.

"How do we know the Romanians did it?" Ashton asked, interrupting Maggie's thoughts.

Leon's phone pinged. "They told us."

They huddled around him as he brought up the video attached to the email he just received and hit Play. Unlike the other videos the Romanians had sent, Tamira wasn't the one shoved in front of the camera.

Maggie balled her fists. "Grigore."

London was an hour and fifteen minutes' flight away. He must have flown over soon after he'd made his escape, likely private as Maggie, Ash, and Leon had been doing for anonymity. Even then, the flight records must have been forged, if they were even filed at all.

Maggie shook her head. He would have been out of

the country before the Belgians even had time to set up an APW on him and his remaining crew.

"We have your leader, just as you have ours," Grigore said.

The camera shifted from Grigore to Grace Helmsley.

They'd done a number on her. Maggie knew Grace well enough to know she wouldn't have taken a beating without giving as good as she got, but she was older than most people assumed and small in height and size, despite her overpowering presence that could dominate any room.

Grace Helmsley wasn't the indomitable leader sitting there on the floor in her nightgown. She was frail and bleeding, blood sticking the front of her tangled hair together from a gash on her head, with a busted lip that was swollen and beginning to show signs of bruising.

"I'll kill him," Leon said, so low it was almost incomprehensible.

The camera continued to move along the room, the location masked as best they could by having the women sit against a plain, white wall and zooming in close to them to block any clues to where they might be.

Tamira sat to Grace's right, just as beaten and bloody. Tracks of blood ran from her nose, and her left eye was puffed out and blackened from a fist. Her entire demeanor had changed from the fighter Maggie recognized in the previous clips. Tamira had given up, the lost hope emanating from every part of her as she hugged her knees and looked into the camera when Grigore ordered her to.

"We know the girl has been sending secret messages, but even that won't help you now," he said, controlling the footage from what Maggie guessed to be a phone, judging by the dimensions of the screen. The camera they'd used before had been left behind in Ferentari by Tamira in a last-ditch attempt to seek help.

Maggie clung to the sides of the couch, willing Tamira to raise a defiant chin or for anger to flare in the one eye she could see through. All that peered back at Maggie through Leon's phone was a blank stare and a stricken face.

Grigore moved the focus back to him and continued his diatribe, his voice barely controlled. The screen shook from the anger vibrating through his entire body, the loss of his trafficked girls clearly having sent him close to the edge. Uncle Ivan would not be pleased when he heard about what happened at the port, and the blame would fall on his nephew's head.

"You have forty-eight hours to release Ivan Dalca, or we will publicly execute your Director General and stream the live feed out for the world to see. Then, we will leak the entire list of agents to the public at large and feed you to the wolves. Everything your organization has done will be released, along with the names of every employee so each of you will face the retribution you deserve."

They all tensed at his rant, the air changing in the room as Maggie processed the man's threat. From the venom in his voice, he was not calling their bluff. He was done playing games and meant every word of what he said.

"Send your response to the email we've sent this video through. For your own sake, I expect to hear from you soon."

Grigore ended the message, and Leon's screen went blank.

Chapter 28

They sat in silence as it set in. They had Grace.

It wasn't just Grace. They had the Unit by the balls, and they knew it. Grace *was* the Unit. The majority of the agents there had joined with Grace in charge. Taking the Director General was a symbol of Dalca's power over them. Grigore and the syndicate were calling the shots, and unless the Unit did what they demanded, they would destroy them from the top down.

"They're going to regret this," Leon promised.

Maggie got up and paced the room. "They're going to regret a lot of things once we're finished with them."

If Grigore was crazy enough to release the list, shit would well and truly hit the fan on an international scale. None of them would be safe. More agents would die. Everyone they had ever fought against would come after them, from criminals to entire governments. Every back-handed favor with apparent enemies and every job against allies would be exposed along with them, causing a diplomatic disaster on a scale unlike any seen before. All because one sex trafficking asshole got caught and imprisoned.

If any of it happened, if Grigore opened Pandora's box and unleashed their secrets to cause irreparable damage on the grandest of scales, then Maggie would make a point of making him and the rest of the syndicate pay, even if it was the last thing she ever did.

"I'm hardly besties with the old battle-axe, but even I admit this is too far. She's old enough to be my wee granny," Ashton said, fully awake now that reality had come to punch them all in the face.

Leon ducked his head and rubbed the back of his neck. "We have to stop them before it's too late."

Maggie gave up pacing and went to him, kneeling and squeezing his hand. "We will," she promised him. Promised herself. "Our new start hasn't had a chance to even begin yet, and I am not about to let anyone ruin it for us. You hear me?"

Leon brought her hands to his lips. "I wish it were that easy."

Ashton cleared his throat. "I'm going to speak with the pilots and find out how soon we can get in the air. Maybe arrange for my parents to leave Mexico and head to a safe house a mate of mine has in Belize."

"Good idea," Maggie agreed, on both counts. They needed to be in London as soon as possible, and there was no telling how all of this would end. It wasn't just the agents on the list who were at risk, but their families and loved ones, too. A safe house in the middle of nowhere was an ideal place for Mr. and Mrs. Price to lie low, and one less thing for Ashton to worry about while he and Maggie and Leon tried to stop the worst from happening.

He returned to his room to get changed and was out the door within five minutes, arranging the move of his parents on his phone the entire time. The door closed behind him, leaving Maggie and Leon alone.

The lock had barely clicked before the first tear fell down Leon's cheek, as if he'd been holding it in until Ashton left.

"Hey," Maggie said, leading him down from the couch arm to sit with her. "Talk to me. What's wrong?"

A redundant question, really, considering their entire world was crumbling before them. Still, Maggie had never seen Leon like this, never witnessed him so rattled and on the verge of breaking completely.

Leon pressed his fist against his mouth and convulsed as pent-up tears burst from him like broken floodgates, a pained, angst-ridden cry building in his chest.

"Leon," Maggie said, leaning over him and running her fingers over the short bristles at the back of his head. Tears pricked at her own eyes. She hated seeing him like this. "Tell me what's wrong, please."

Leon's shoulders shook up and down, and he covered his eyes like he was ashamed. Maggie pried his hands away to look into his eyes, to let him know she was there and always would be.

"It's just," he started, as more tears fell, the anguish on his face breaking Maggie's heart.

It took a few minutes for him to settle down enough to speak.

"Everything I thought I fought for was a lie. Bishop ruined everything, and now I can't even keep my agents safe in his place."

Maggie opened her mouth to stress to him it wasn't true, but stopped. How could she tell him otherwise when she felt the exact same way?

"We didn't know," she said instead, something she'd repeated over and over again to herself since learning the truth.

"We should have," Leon said, shaking his head in disbelief. "We're spies, for Christ's sake. How could we have been so blind?"

"We trusted him!" It was a simple truth, but a tough pill to swallow all the same.

Leon stared at his feet, elbows on his knees and eyes glossed with a real, gut-wrenching pain Maggie had been doing everything to push aside in herself. Seeing her turmoil reflected in Leon made it worse. Made it real, and unavoidable.

"He betrayed us. Betrayed us all. He sent every last

one of us on his side missions. Hid them in piles of paperwork and false evidence used to justify sending us to do his dirty work." Leon met her gaze for the first time. "There are so many of them, Mags. I've gone through them, over and over again. So many names written in black and white who shouldn't be there. So many innocent people dead by our hands. By my hands."

Tears fell as Maggie listened, her own pain rising from the depths where she'd shoved it away to be forgotten. To never be dealt with, like so many things in her life.

"How do I even begin to make things right?" Leon asked, pleading to her, like Maggie had the answers. "How do I wake up each day and do my job as if none of it happened? Like I didn't kill a good, honest man in Peru who left three children and a wife behind? Like the woman in Egypt who I killed to line the pockets of the very people we are supposed to be fighting against? How can I sleep at night knowing what I've done? How could you ever love me knowing what I've done?"

"What we've done," Maggie said, reminding him he wasn't alone. That this was as much her burden as it was his. "Up on the roof at Saint Paul's, Bishop admitted he'd sent me out the most on those missions of his."

"I know," Leon said, a haunted look across his handsome features. "It was all in his files."

Leon knew. Knew everything she'd done on Bishop's orders. Knew which of the missions she'd gone over and over in her head were legit and which were not. Leon knew her death toll of innocents, a number she couldn't bear to even guess. He knew it all, and yet still sat there with her instead of running.

"Is that why you stayed in Somalia instead of coming home when you should have?" Maggie asked. "Why you went at all instead of sending another agent? Guilt?"

"I had to do something. Had to make a difference to try to somehow make up for everything I've done under Bishop's leadership. To prove there was still something worth fighting for."

"By getting killed in the line of duty?"

"I sometimes think it's what I deserve."

"No, now you're being stupid," Maggie snapped. "If you weren't so beaten up already, I'd kick your arse, Leon Frost."

Leon gave a hollow laugh. "Thanks."

"Do you think I deserve to be punished for what I've done under Bishop's orders?" Maggie asked. If he felt that way about himself, what did he think of her when she had done far worse for Bishop than he had?

Leon leaned in closer to her, his brows furrowed. "Of course not. You didn't know."

"And neither did you," Maggie said, relief flooding through her at his response. "Why is it any different?"

"You'd do the same," Leon retorted. "The very things you praise me for are the same things you beat yourself up about. Killing, lying, spying, all of it. You have this warped image of me in your head that I'm some kind of hero, yet you can't see it in yourself. I'm half the agent you are, and even with Bishop's missions, you've done so much better for this world than bad. I wish you could see it."

"I understand why you went," Maggie admitted, avoiding the other stuff Leon said. She wasn't ready to see herself as a good person. Not after everything she'd done. Didn't know if she'd ever be able to see herself the way she saw Leon. "It was still bloody stupid of you," she continued, "but I understand. It was nobler than what I did. I ran away, telling myself I needed a vacation. I just couldn't face it, any of it. Knowing what he made us do. The lies he told us and the deeds we carried out without ever questioning him. We trusted him, and he abused that trust in the worst possible way."

"What now?" Leon asked, like a lost little boy, more vulnerable than she'd ever seen him.

"We do what we always do," Maggie said, knowing she needed to be strong for him. For herself, and everyone who depended on them. "We fight."

"I don't know if I have any fight left in me," Leon admitted.

Maggie leaned her forehead against his, so close their noses touched. "Well, you better find some fight. I can't take down Dalca's syndicate and save Helmsley and Tamira all by myself. I need you, Leon."

His dark eyes bore into her soul. "I need you too, Maggie. I always have."

"Fight for us," Maggie insisted, trepidation welling in her for what she was about to profess. "Once this is all over, we can be together. I'm done pushing away what I want. I'm done with the Unit, and all the bullshit that comes with it, including us not being able to be together. I love you, Leon, and I want us to finally give things a shot. A real shot this time, not just some fling in a foreign country before we go back to our lives at home. You are my home, and I want to be with you. If you'll still have me?"

"Now you're the one being stupid." Leon laughed amid his tears and wiped Maggie's from her cheek with a thumb, stopping at her lips. "You're all I've ever wanted, Maggie."

The undeniable pull between them drew them closer amid their heightened emotions, the thrill and fear in their honesty coming to a head and bringing them together.

Maggie opened her mouth and waited to taste his lips. Leon cupped her face, his calloused hands rough and familiar against her skin, and she leaned into his touch.

Unable to wait any longer, she bridged the short gap between them and kissed him hard and deep, putting everything she felt behind it. All of her emotion and love for him, and the hope she'd held onto for so long that they would one day be together.

Leon responded in kind, pulling her toward him and onto his lap. He was already hard, and Maggie writhed against him, resulting in a deep, sensual moan from him that sang like music to her ears.

They fell into a rhythm, old and new all at once. Leon kissed along her neck, knowing which spots made her squirm in pleasure, whispering his love for her as he did, his hands running down her back and along her aching thighs.

Maggie's stomach reminded her of her slash and the stitches holding her together, but she ignored it, her need for Leon outweighing the discomfort of her injury.

Leon helped her out of her T-shirt and tossed it to the floor, taking her breasts in his hands and kissing them, too. He continued south to initiate foreplay, but Maggie stopped him and forced him back against the couch.

"No, I need you inside me. Now."

She hopped off and freed herself of her pajama shorts, ridding Leon of his boxers next, and returned to him.

"I love you, Leon," she shuddered into his ear as he gasped in pleasure. She spent the rest of their time alone together showing him just how much.

Chapter 29

London, Great Britain

The pilots came through and managed to secure them a flight time as soon as possible, the short ride through the skies having them back in their home city by noon.

"They've really gone over and above," Maggie said of the long-suffering pilots and cabin attendant, Craig.

"And they're being paid nicely for it, too," Ashton assured, parking the car in the lot of Her Majesty's Prison Belmarsh.

Leon had arranged another meeting with Ivan Dalca, and this time all of them were done messing around. It was time to end this, once and for all.

Much to everyone's frustration, Helmsley's abduction didn't change matters much in the eyes of the government. At least officially. Dalca and his crew were deemed terrorists for their exploits, and the government categorically did not negotiate with terrorists. Behind closed doors, however, they were a mess. The ripple effect of the secrets the Romanians held over their heads was unprecedented, and all of them could agree those secrets must not be made public.

Unfortunately, it was the only thing they seemed to agree on. Meetings were called, debates were had, and still they couldn't agree on a plan, even if it meant protecting the lives of their agents. They'd called in experts, made reports, and done everything other than provide a solution.

They never argued as much with each other when it came to their own interests. When a salary increase for MPs was up for debate, they were all in agreement before noon and back to their second homes in time for lunch. Ensuring national security, avoiding international conflict, and saving key assets from being compromised? Well, that required thought. Time. And catered lunches and dinners.

Bloody bureaucrats.

Time was one thing they didn't have on their side, so Maggie made the decision to let the government officials fight amongst themselves while she and her boys made moves to put a stop to Ivan Dalca and his syndicate before they could ruin any more lives.

Leon rubbed his thumb over the back of her hand and stole a kiss to her cheek before putting his Unit chief face on.

Their recent reunion hadn't gone unnoticed by Ashton, who never missed a trick with Maggie. "Back to shagging, then?" he said with a grin. "About time."

Maggie hid a smile and freed herself of her seat belt to join Leon outside the car.

"Aren't you coming in?" she asked Ashton.

Her best friend shook his head. "No, thanks. I spend most of my time trying to avoid prison. I'm not about to walk into one of my own free will."

Maggie shrugged. It was a fair enough point. "Suit yourself."

Harold the governor waited for them by the entrance, the sky above overcast and blocking the sun. At least the rain had stayed away.

"Where's Grace?" he asked, eyeing them both.

"She's wrapped up in meetings, so she sent us instead." Leon held out his hand. "Leon Frost. This is my colleague, Maggie Black."

"We've met," Maggie said, avoiding the man's sweaty grip. 'Where is he?"

Harold took the hint and led them inside. "In his cell."

They'd given up torturing him, then.

"I assume he hasn't said anything of importance?" Leon inquired.

"Other than calling me everything under the sun, no."

"You'll love him," Maggie said as they passed through electronically locked doors and the general population wing. It was lunchtime inside, so most of the prisoners were in the cafeteria.

"We're moving him first thing tomorrow," the governor informed them.

"Why?" Belmarsh was a maximum-security prison. Even Maggie would have a hard time getting in or out unnoticed.

"We've had multiple threats, bombs and the like. Now we have news that the Romanians are here, and we suspect they may try to break him out. This mess is causing too much of a stir, and the PM wants Dalca moved out of the way without his people catching on."

Maggie rolled her eyes behind his back. "Glad she's decided to help. I wish she would bloody well give it a rest already."

"Where are you moving him?" Leon asked. They reached solitary confinement and were allowed through by an armed guard, their voices echoing off the bare walls.

Harold stopped by the door on the end of the cell block and turned to them. "Classified."

Leon arched an eyebrow. "Oh?"

"Yip." Governor Harold crossed his arms, looking very pleased with himself. "Everything's on a need-to-know basis. You understand."

"Of course. I wouldn't want to compromise your operation here," Leon said, somehow managing to keep a straight face. He nodded to the prison cell door. "Should we see if he's in, then?"

Harold motioned to the prison guard, and he unlocked the solid metal door that screeched open with a whine.

The stench hit Maggie first, and she recoiled. "You might have showered him."

"I would have thought you'd like it dirty," came the Romanian's voice from within.

Leon's fists clenched, and Maggie placed a warning hand against his back. This conversation needed to go well if they had any hopes of stopping Ivan's syndicate.

"Ivan," said Leon, stepping forward and taking up most of the door, "why don't we speak somewhere a little less confined."

The governor began to argue, but Leon stood up straight and stared him down. "A meeting room would be ideal, and please, get Mr. Dalca a warm cup of tea and something to eat. He's looking a little thin."

"Well, he should," Harold gruffed. "We haven't been feeding him."

"A meeting room, if you please," Leon repeated.

"Right, well, you can use our staff room."

"Lead the way," Leon ordered, emulating Helmsley in the way she assumed the role of being in charge wherever she went. "Come on, Ivan."

Maggie let Ivan hobble in front of her so she could keep an eye on him, even if it left her downwind of his unwashed body. She didn't trust him not to try anything, even in his current state. Almost as battered as Leon, he had an array of nasty bruises and abrasions peeking from the sleeves and collar of his orange jumpsuit, his face various shades of purple and muddy yellow.

The staff room wasn't far, but Ivan was out of breath by the time they reached it. They sat down, Ivan across from Maggie and Leon, though they'd foregone the need for handcuffs. It was a sad affair inside, the white paint yellowed and stained with splashes of tea around the kettle, the bin overflowing, and a stale smell to the carpet.

The tea was made, and a tray of the prison lunch was found for Ivan, which he wasted no time demolishing. They really had been starving him.

"That'll be all," Leon told the governor who made to sit, not paying the man any attention. Maggie knew what he was doing, making it clear to Ivan he didn't like the man who'd been in charge of mistreating him.

Harold left with his tail between his legs, slamming the door a little harder than necessary.

"Where is the Director General?" Ivan asked with a satisfied smirk once he finished eating.

"Busy," Leon responded, masking his rage well. "I've come to call a truce."

Ivan wiped the corner of his mouth like they were in some fine-dining establishment. "A truce?"

"This has all gotten out of hand, wouldn't you agree?" Leon asked.

"Yes."

"Then let's put a stop to it." Leon kept his voice controlled and amenable. Just a few people discussing business and trying to come to a mutual agreement. Only, the lives of countless agents, their families, and Unit allies and affiliates didn't hang in the balance of most business meetings. This was one deal they needed to secure, and fast.

Ivan sat back in his chair, and Maggie could just see him in a sleek suit instead of the standard-issue jumpsuit he wore. He was comfortable in these situations, no stranger to blackmail or negotiations over human lives. "I believe you already know what will stop London Bridge from falling down."

"I can't arrange for your release," Leon said, his tone reasonable. "You should have known that was never going to happen before you started any of this."

Maggie remained quiet, not trusting herself. Ivan was lucky she hadn't dragged him across the table already and choked him into submission. Leon had the cooler head, and she let him do his job as Unit chief.

"Stranger things have happened," Ivan mused,

brushing crumbs from his jumpsuit. "Don't try to tell me your government hasn't made arrangements like that before."

"Perhaps, but those instances could be kept under the radar. You, Ivan, have made that impossible, thanks to the news coverage your arrest garnered. We let you out, and there'll be a public outcry. People will want answers as to why the government let out a convicted sex trafficker. We can't very well tell them the truth."

Ivan laughed. "Why bother with the truth at all? Your country runs on lies."

Leon sat back, emulating Dalca's body language. "Look, I don't make the rules. I'm just here to facilitate a deal with you."

"There is nothing you can offer me other than my release that will put a stop to your predicament. My men are under strict orders to carry out my plans to the letter."

Maggie couldn't hold back any longer.

"Was it a part of your plan for Grigore to lose all of your new girls? They're with Interpol now, and Grigore seems to have done a runner," she said, throwing in the lie to test how much Ivan knew. If he knew she wasn't telling the truth, then someone was communicating with him. Either that, or he was still in the dark.

"Thanks to you, I have no way of fact-checking what you say without access to my lawyer, so I'm afraid I must conclude everything you say is bullshit until I am told otherwise from a source I trust."

Maggie suppressed a guffaw. There was no way Ivan was getting any kind of communication with the outside. No phone calls, and definitely no meetings with anyone from his camp. Even inside the prison walls, he still thought he had them over a barrel. It wasn't too far from the truth, but they didn't need to confirm it for him.

Leon nursed his tea. "People have died."

"On both sides," Maggie added, taking a sip of hers and eyeing Ivan's reaction over the brim of her mug. He blinked a little too much at that, though he hid the shock and recovered fast enough. Ivan was a pro.

He held his hands up like a haggler behind a market stall who had offered a fair price and was unwilling to lower it any further. "Let me walk free and return to my country, and all of it could end today."

"You know that's not going to happen," Leon reminded him.

Ivan shrugged. "Never mind. From the way you've come in here, it seems to me like I won't be in your custody much longer anyway. You're getting desperate."

"What I'm getting is tired of your shit," Maggie snapped. She slammed her fists on the table and sloshed the tea from their mugs everywhere.

Ivan's eyes narrowed. "There you are. The lioness. I was wondering when you'd show up to this conversation instead of playing assistant."

Maggie leaned forward. "We've been to your spot in

Ferentari. Left that basement of yours in a bit of a mess, though."

"Stupid girl," Ivan said, still unconcerned and leaning back on his chair. "That is but one arm to a much larger machine. Your efforts are futile, and one way or another, I will be free of these chains very soon. Perhaps then you and I could arrange a meeting in a more intimate setting."

"Now Ivan," Leon warned the muscles in his jaw twitching, "I've been reasonable with you so far. Don't force me to change that."

Ivan's mouth stretched into a wicked gash, a few of his teeth missing since Maggie last saw him. "Struck a nerve, have I? I see. How romantic. A shame you'll both be dead soon, Maggie Black and Leon Frost. Have my men released your names yet? Or are they saving you both until last? I bet a lot of your comrades have met an untimely end by now. But don't worry too much; you'll both be joining them soon."

Leon kicked his chair behind him and knocked the table away with one great swipe of his arm. "I wouldn't be so cocky, old man. We've taken down worse scumbags than you, and I'm going to take great pleasure in making sure you don't see the light of day ever again. It's over for you and your syndicate."

"Keep telling yourself that, Mr. Frost. If I were you, I'd be preparing to leave the country like I am. I don't believe you'll be a popular man after I finish what I started. Better to get a head start now. Though I doubt it will do you any good, but perhaps you and your bitch can enjoy a few days of stolen time."

Leon grabbed Ivan, dragging him off the floor with the ease of a bear ready to maul its victim.

"No," Maggie warned him. If the Romanians found out Ivan was dead, they would have no reason not to leak the names and execute Grace sooner than planned. The Unit needed as much time as they could get now that it was clear Ivan had no intention of coming to any form of agreement.

Leon dropped Ivan like a sack of potatoes, and he fell to the damp carpet with a thud. He glanced up at them with mirth and laughed, a real, joy-filled cackle that sent shivers down Maggie's spine. He truly believed he was getting out of this on top.

If she didn't think of something soon, he very well might.

They left him there on the floor, still laughing as the governor's guards came in and carted him back to his cold cell.

"He's blooming mad, that one," said Harold.

"What time are you moving him tomorrow?" Maggie asked. "We may need to question him further before he leaves."

"Sorry, but he's being shipped out at four bells. Avoids the traffic."

"That's too bad," she said, the cogs in her mind turning.

Leon eyed her, knowing that look on her face all too well. A plan was coming together. "Well, thanks for your cooperation," he said. "We'll leave you to it."

Chapter 30

Outside London, Great Britain
18 July

Thick smoke billowed from the open bonnet of the car.

"Great," Maggie said, leaning over to get a good look at the vehicle's internal organs. Everything appeared fine, but the trail of smog wafting into the crisp morning air told another story.

The rising sun glistened off the dew-covered leaves of the surrounding trees that encroached the narrow country road like angered gods ready to smite anyone who dared cross their path. Their branches twisted and snarled like damning fingers, watching and judging them for what they were about to do.

Leon joined her and checked his watch. "They left on the hour," he advised, having someone from the Unit act as lookout. "Should be here any moment."

"You hear that, Ash?" Maggie asked, her phone on speaker.

"Loud and clear, boss," came his voice, bright as a daisy considering the time of day. Maggie downed three coffees before leaving her apartment and still struggled to stifle a yawn as she and Leon waited by the car.

The Ford Fiesta they'd acquired through the Unit was a fifteen-year-old banger and looked closer to eighty. The once-green paint job was now a rusting riot of reds and oranges with only the hint of original color left. The wheels had lost their hubcaps over the years, and the sad excuse for a car barely looked capable of making it up a steep hill, never mind passing an MOT test.

True to its appearance, the car sat in a pitiful steaming pile in the middle of the road and blocked the road.

"Party's here," Ashton announced. "One big, two small."

"Got it," Maggie confirmed, and they moved into position. She got into the driver's seat, leaving the door wide open, and Leon took her place at the front of the car, waving the smoke from his face and making a show of his frustration at the dead car.

Right on cue, three vehicles rounded the corner of the winding road and slammed the brakes upon seeing them. The car at the front of the procession honked its horn at them. Leon popped his head out from behind the bonnet and shrugged. There wasn't much to be done with the state of the Ford Fiesta.

The driver rolled down his window and called out to them. "Move the car."

"I'd love to," Leon said. "Don't suppose you've got any jump cables on you?"

The driver groaned in frustration and spoke something into a walkie-talkie.

Behind them waited a black armored truck with another car taking the rear. Maggie wasn't sure how many were inside, but they were outnumbered at the very least.

The reverse lights of the back car came on, and the others in front followed suit to make a U-turn and reroute from the unexpected, unwelcome diversion. They didn't get very far before the last car in the line screeched to a halt and the others in front slammed the breaks to avoid hitting it.

Maggie watched from her rearview mirror as a van for Novatec Electrical Services blocked their way, parking in the middle of the road at an angle that clogged up any chance of a clean exit.

Having lost any reserve of patience, one of the men in the front car got out and shouted at the electrician to move out of the way, waving his arms and throwing around some choice words.

Maggie strained to see inside the work van from the distance between them. The door opened then, and someone got out to greet the enraged driver in charge of leading the escort to some supposed secure location.

The driver stopped when he laid eyes on the electrician. Instead of a tool-laden electrician the man behind the wheel wore a wide grinning mask synonymous with Guy Fawkes and the internet vigilante group known as Anonymous.

Ashton and his dramatics.

Clearly not green to the job, the approaching driver of Ivan's escort caught on quick to what was happening and ran back to the car, yelling the entire way. "Code red! Code red!"

Code red, indeed.

Maggie and Leon pounced into action. They would only have a short window before backup would arrive. Knowing the transport detail for Ivan Dalca would be ordered to shoot first and ask questions later, Maggie had brought along a deterrent to avoid any unwanted gunshot wounds. Her trio was injured enough, and she intended to get out of this mess without as much as an additional papercut.

Those inside the armored truck remained in position, their orders to ensure they made a swift exit from any altercation and kept their human package away from those who would want to take him. The guards in the cars were another story. They were the backup and first in line to engage with anyone dumb enough to try to intercept their prisoner transport.

Armed to the teeth with C8 carbine assault rifles, the detail spilled from their vehicles like synchronized dancers organizing themselves into a deadly formation.

Maggie brought out her deterrent and made sure each of her opposers caught sight of it. Its official name was the XM25 Counter Defilade Target Engagement System, an import from the US acquired by the Unit before the model went out of commission, and recently upgraded with SAGM rounds.

Soldiers in Afghanistan referred to the grenade launcher as the Punisher.

Maggie named hers Betsy.

A quick scan of the men and women taking aim at her confirmed they were army. Maybe SAS. Had the prime minister and her gaggle of advisors any clue about what they were doing, they would've handed over the responsibility of Ivan's transfer to the Unit. They of all people had reason to ensure he arrived safely and out of the Romanians' clutches.

Maggie waited until everyone from the car up front evacuated the vehicle to lay their assault on her and her team of two, then fired up Betsy. She'd never had reason to use the grenade launcher until now, and Maggie reveled with girlish glee at being able to pull the trigger.

Despite the model's apparent issues that had caused the US to decommission the line, Betsy worked like a dream. Maggie aimed true and launched a grenade at the empty car. It lit up like a bonfire on November 5th. Ashton would be jealous.

The car exploded and careened into the air, knocking everyone back with a wave of heat and giving Maggie, Leon, and Ashton enough time to duck and find cover before a rain of bullets poked holes in them.

The armored truck backed up and crashed into the car behind it, crushing it against Ashton's van as it tried to barge a path through. The road was too small, though. Maggie had chosen this spot on the prison's planned route for that very reason.

"Now!" Leon called, and out from within the trees and bushes slinked every agent the Unit had at their disposal close by, each of them armed with rifles of their own and, to Maggie's bemusement, the same Anonymous masks as Ashton wore. Silly man.

"Stand back," the man in charge of the detail called. "We will shoot."

"I think we've established I have the bigger gun in this pissing match. Now, be a good boy and order your team to drop their weapons and hand over the prisoner before I'm forced to put you and all of your troops into early retirement."

The only thing greater than any commander's bravery was their love and loyalty for their team. Maggie knew it, just like the man whose top lip glistened with sweat. The battle was lost before it had started. Anyone could see it, and with a deep sigh, the man waved down his troops and ordered them to toss their weapons aside.

Their egos would undoubtedly be bruised, and a severe bollocking lay in their future from their superiors, but at least they would all live to fight another day. Not that Maggie ever had any intention of harming them, but they didn't need to know that.

Things went smoothly after that, and once each of the soldiers were restrained with zip ties and left at the side of the road with the Ford Fiesta and the crispy remains of the blown-up car, Maggie, Leon, and Ashton said their goodbyes to the Unit agents and headed off into the distance in the armored truck with Ivan Dalca inside.

Chapter 31

East Sussex, Great Britain

The ride to Ashton's was uneventful. By the time Belmarsh Prison and everyone involved in Ivan's transfer realized things hadn't exactly gone to plan, Maggie and her team were long gone. The prison officials could track the van, but it was currently on its way to Scotland, and taking the scenic route at that. Enough of a distraction to keep them occupied while Maggie, Leon, and Ashton did the heavy lifting.

"A somewhat nicer spot than my last prison," Ivan commented as they yanked him from the back of the van and dragged him inside.

Nice was an understatement. Ashton's place was an expansive country estate two hours away from central London. Complete with twelve acres of woodland, twenty acres of farmland, three separate guest houses, a swimming pool, and stables for his mother's horses, the grade two–listed, ten-bedroom house was like something from a dream.

To Ivan, it was a nightmare.

While he seemed to fully expect his transfer to be intercepted, he got quite the shock when Maggie was the one to open the back of the truck.

"But a prison all the same," Maggie replied.

They were in Ashton's gym, Maggie deciding to avoid any room with easily stained carpets or light-colored walls that would be ruined with blood spatter. She didn't intend to beat Ivan further, but accidents happened.

Tied to a treadmill and leaning against the frame, Ivan sat slumped on a floor mat. Maggie pulled up a chair and sat before him with Leon and Ashton at her back.

"What now?" Dalca asked. "Are you going to kill me?"

His question seemed more out of curiosity than fear. Like Maggie, death must have felt like an eventuality rather than a possibility. You didn't live lives like theirs and not consider that your life expectancy was well below the national average, Romanian, British, or otherwise.

"No," Maggie admitted, though she wouldn't mind being the one to end him. "We're going to continue where we left off in Belmarsh and try again."

"You said it yourself, your government doesn't negotiate with terrorists, and as far as they're concerned, that's what I am."

Maggie wasn't about to argue semantics on what Dalca was. A terrorist. A gangster. A sexist pig. A trafficker. A monster. He was any and all of those things.

"The government won't negotiate with terrorists," Maggie said instead, "but I will."

"Ah." Ivan's eyes lit up like a kid in a candy store.

"Are you sure this is a good idea, Mags?" Ashton asked. Purely for effect, of course. Maggie had gone over her plans with him and Leon before they captured Dalca.

"Nope," she replied, crossing her arms, "but we're out of options at this point."

"This either works, or we're all as good as dead," Leon agreed, making a show of looking anything but happy about the situation.

Ivan's posture straightened, on familiar ground to his day job now. "In that case, Ms. Black, let's talk terms."

Maggie laughed. "I don't mean with you." Ashton handed her his phone, and she turned on the video recorder. "Make sure to smile for the camera."

She hit record and began the rehearsed speech she'd laid out with her boys.

"Grigore Ursu, my name is Maggie Black. If you've perused that list you stole, you may recognize my name and know what I'm capable of. I believe I don't need to introduce him."

She turned the camera from her to Grigore's uncle and stayed on him for a long moment before returning it to her face.

"You have our leader, and we have yours. We both have something the other wants, and I see no reason why we can't come to an arrangement that satisfies us all. The Unit has no interest in considering the British government's opinions when our very lives and those of our loved ones are at stake. So, I propose a simple trade-off. In exchange for Grace Helmsley, the girl Tamira, and all copies of the list of agents, we'll give you Ivan."

Maggie turned the camera back to Dalca.

"What do you say, Ivan?"

Ivan stared into the camera. "Do it, Grigore. That's an order."

The hint of a sly, satisfied smirk tugged at his lips, which made Maggie's blood boil. He'd known all along he would get what he wanted in the end, and here she was giving it to him.

"Oh, and please don't release any further information about our agents or hurt Grace and Tamira in the meantime," Maggie added. "If you do, I'll return your uncle to you in parts."

Threat made, she turned off the recording and handed it back to Ashton to forward on to the email address Grigore left in his last message.

The deal was on the table. All they had to do now was wait.

Chapter 32

And wait they did.

Maggie paced in front of the roaring fireplace in Ashton's study. It snapped and crackled as the time ticked by, each minute driving her closer to the edge. This was their last shot at fixing things, and if it failed, Maggie had no idea how they were going to get themselves out of this mess. She'd gone through so much, overcome obstacles when everyone else had counted her out, accomplished the impossible when others would have failed.

But this? This was different.

Information was power in today's world, and it was being used against them. Maggie couldn't punch, kick, or shoot her way out of their predicament. If Grigore didn't want to play ball, they were fucked.

"What's taking them so long?" she complained.

"Relax, Mags," Ashton said from his studded leather couch. "Here, have my whisky. I'll pour another one."

Maggie rubbed her head, the beginnings of a migraine threatening to take over. "I'm fine. I think I'm just going to lie down for a while. Wake me if they get in touch?"

"Of course," Ashton assured, draining his glass and pouring another drink anyway. "Well, Ivan, old chap. Looks like it's just you and me."

Dalca didn't respond, Maggie having gagged him hours ago. He may not have cracked under torture, but it would be interesting to see how well he did while spending any length of time with a whisky-filled Ashton having a one-way conversation with him.

Maggie went upstairs and knocked on the door to one of the many guest bedrooms. "Can I come in?"

"Of course," Leon replied, sitting up in the bed as she entered. He'd gone for a sleep, the events from earlier having tired him out. "How's your stomach?"

Maggie kicked off her shoes, lay down on the other side of the double bed, and ran a hand over her wound. "Sore, but I've had worse. You?"

He'd taken off his shirt, and she ran her hand over his chest, memories of their reunion stirring in her mind.

"Same," Leon admitted, taking her in his strong arms. "Any news?"

Maggie cuddled into him, his skin nice and warm

from being under the blankets. "None. I'm starting to worry."

Leon kissed her head, both of them melting into each other. "Ivan gave Grigore an order. He'll come through. They'll be letting us stew for a while to try to throw us off."

"Well, it's working," Maggie grumbled. She was sick of the power plays. Sick of all of it.

"It'll be over soon," Leon assured.

That wasn't what worried Maggie, though. It was the outcome.

There was no telling what would happen. So many things could go wrong. So many variables she had no control over that could impact how everything would go down with Dalca's syndicate. Their fate and any chance she and Leon had at a future teetered on the edge of a knife, and Maggie didn't know which side things would slice.

"I have to tell you something," she said, her mouth spilling the words before she had time to think otherwise.

"What?" Leon asked. His muscles tensed at her grave tone and a pit of dread weighed heavy in her stomach, like a sick reminder of what she'd been through. Of the secret she'd been harboring from him for months now. The secret that had caused her to shy away from him and avoid him at all costs. To refuse to let him in. To let anyone in.

Maggie hesitated.

"You're starting to worry me, Maggie. You've gone chalk-white." Leon sat up and released his embrace, concern mapped across his features.

She couldn't go back now. Not when things were so uncertain. This could be her last chance to tell him, and if things went horribly wrong and their plans failed, she didn't want to die without admitting it to him.

Maggie had tried so many times to tell him, but there never seemed to be a right moment. How did you broach such a subject when things between them were so strained and up in the air? When they tried their best to stay professional and ignore their feelings, knowing the Unit wouldn't allow them to be together. Knowing their lives were too chaotic and dangerous to settle down and be in a relationship.

Now that they'd confessed their feelings and things were different, Maggie couldn't go on without Leon knowing everything. She couldn't lie to him when all he'd ever done was be completely honest with her.

"After we got back from that mission in Venice last year, I—" Maggie paused and composed herself. She needed to get this out. "I found out I was pregnant."

Leon's eyes widened. "Pregnant?"

"But I lost it. After I came back from a job in New York, I visited the doctor. There were complications with the development—she said there was nothing I could have done, and I wasn't pregnant anymore."

Maggie couldn't see Leon's reaction from the tears spilling down her cheeks. She curled in on herself and hid her face, too ashamed to meet Leon's gaze.

He was quiet for a long time. So long Maggie didn't dare break the silence.

"You should have told me," he finally said, and then his arms returned around Maggie's shoulders and she completely broke in his arms.

"I know," she cried. "You had every right to know, and I was going to tell you."

"That message you left? The voicemail I asked you about when we were called in about the Charing Cross bombing?" Leon sniffed, but she couldn't look at him. Couldn't see him cry. It was too much. All of it.

"I found out I'd lost my, our, baby right after I'd called. After that, I didn't know how to tell you. It broke my heart, and I didn't want to do that to you, too."

Maggie beat herself up for months over keeping it from him. It was easier not to tell him. Easier to let him stay in the dark about it and hide from him, so he didn't need to carry the burden she did.

"I'm sorry you went through that alone," Leon said softly, never once letting her go. "I wish I could have been there for you."

"You're not mad?" she risked asking. Maggie thought he would hate her after she told him. That'd he'd storm off and never want to see her again.

"Mad?" Leon repeated, pulling her closer to him. "How could I be mad at you after what you've gone through? I'm devastated we lost it."

"Me, too," she said, calming down now that she'd gotten it out. It was never something she'd get over, but not bearing the burden alone took a weight off her shoulders she wasn't aware she'd carried until now. "I'd never given being a parent much thought until then," she told Leon. "I think I was starting to like the idea. I was going to leave the Unit and walk away from it all for our child."

Maggie still walked away from the Unit, but not the way she'd planned or wanted.

Leon wiped the tears from her eyes and gave her a gentle kiss. "For what it's worth, you would have made a great mum."

"I don't know about that," Maggie said, glad she didn't have any makeup on.

"I know so. And I know things are just getting started with us, but we have all the time in the world to have children. To start a family."

A family. Maggie hadn't had a family for so long she forgot what having one felt like. Even when she did, it was just her and her mother. Growing up in the system, she never allowed herself to even dream about one day having a family of her own.

Joining the Unit only made the idea more foreign to her. Agents had families, but it wasn't easy. Bishop was estranged from his daughters. Went through a nasty divorce. Even Grace Helmsley had her issues. Agents were married to the job first and their spouses second. Not to mention the element of danger that came with the career. Janice Harris and her entire family were just wiped out the other day.

"Grace said to me once, 'You enter this life, there's no getting out of it.' Do you believe that?" Maggie asked. Ever since the Director General said it, Maggie hadn't been able to forget it.

Leon mused over it for a moment. "I don't know."

"I thought I'd left for good, but here we are," Maggie said, bone tired of it all. "Just another day at the office."

"I guess for me, it's more about wanting to stay. There's still so much that needs to be done. So much to make up for after Bishop. That's me, though. What do you want?" Leon asked her.

It was Maggie's turn to pause.

"I don't know. While I was away on vacation, I felt lost. Who am I if I'm not Maggie Black the agent? What purpose do I have? What am I supposed to do with the rest of my life? Get a nine-to-five? Pretend that none of it ever happened?"

"You could always come back, but only if you want to, of course. You don't have to make any decisions straight away. Take more time to consider your options. Things should be clearer once we're through with this mess with Dalca."

The door knocked, and Ashton entered without waiting for them to answer.

"They want to make the trade," he said. "It's showtime."

Chapter 33

London, Great Britain

The meeting point was at an agreed location on mutual ground.

Maggie stood with Leon and Ashton in Hampstead Heath beneath the stars, one of the few places in London such a view was possible given the thick air and widespread unnatural light that kept the city alive long into the early hours of the morning. It was approaching midnight, and darkness embraced them like a well-loved cloak.

The Extension at the northwestern point of the park made for a sound strategic spot to make the trade. Of the 790-acre space, the Extension was created out of old farmland, offering open expanses of flat land so anyone in the vicinity could see approaching enemies long before they arrived. Other than the woodland area off to their right, which Maggie checked as soon as they arrived for any plants Dalca's crew may have snuck there, the area was as safe as they were going to get from unwanted surprises.

Grigore was late, but Maggie wasn't concerned overmuch. He would show. They had what he and the rest of the syndicate wanted. No way would he skip out on them when they were offering Ivan on a platter.

"So, what are you doing after this?" Leon asked, trapping Maggie against the car where they'd stored Dalca to avoid having to interact with the wretched man.

She reached on her tiptoes to wrap her arms around his neck and pull him closer. "Nothing, why?"

"I was thinking we could maybe go out for a drink or something."

"Or something," Maggie teased, the thrill of the impending meet coursing through her veins in an adrenaline rush like no other. There was something about deadly situations that made her feel alive, and now that she'd come out to Leon with the truth about her miscarriage, she could focus on their future and work toward accepting the past, no matter how horrific her ordeal had been. With Leon by her side, she felt like she could do anything.

Ashton turned back from his watch at the front of the

car and shook his head at them. "Come on, guys, be serious for one moment, please. You're supposed to be professionals."

He burst out laughing before even finishing the sentence.

"What do you say, Ash?" Leon said, freeing Maggie and slapping his friend on the back. "Drink after this? Supposing we don't die, of course."

"And play gooseberry to you two?" Ashton said, checking the magazine of his Glock 17. "No chance. If I don't die, I think I'll give Craig a wee call and see if he wants to join the mile-high club."

"Another flight?" Maggie would be happy if she never set foot on another plane again after all the traveling they had done. A week on the couch with Leon and some TV shows to binge sounded like heaven to her about now, and she longed to get out of her clothes and into her pajamas and housecoat.

"Someone's got to collect my mam and da from Belize. Might as well make the most of the trip." Ashton was never one to stay in one place for long. He was too hyper for that, always needing something, or someone, to keep him occupied. Having too much time on his hands often resulted in him getting into trouble. Maggie of all people should know, having to come and rescue his crazy Glaswegian arse on more than a few occasions.

"Those poor pilots." Leon laughed, and it made Maggie's heart soar to see him smile again. He was far from okay, the impact of Bishop's betrayal still a very raw and open wound for them both, but they'd make it through the storm. Just like they always had.

She ducked into the driver's side of the car and turned on the headlights. They created a path of light along the field. As well as providing a better visual of the approaching enemy, it also concealed Maggie's team of three, and everything around them, in a deeper shield of shadow.

Just in time, too, because more headlights peeked through the darkness beyond like monsters on the prowl. They approached in a pack of yellow eyes and narrowed in on them as one.

"So much for agreeing to one car," Leon muttered.

Maggie's lips thinned. Four Land Rovers pulled up and stopped sixty yards away.

"You don't think they'll have a sniper with them, do you?" Ashton asked, with just a hint of alarm in his voice. "I should have brought a grenade."

"There's been more than enough grenades in our lives recently," Maggie quipped. "We'll be fine. Just play it cool, and then we can get out of here."

She wasn't sure if she was saying it for Ashton's sake, or her own. It appeared Grigore had brought his entire team along with him.

Grigore and his men got out of the cars and stood before them with crossed arms, Ursu at the front, their shadows stretching across the field like distorted demons. "Where is my uncle?" he demanded.

"Get him out," Maggie said. Leon pulled Ivan out of the back of the car and brandished him before the syndicate.

"Your turn," Maggie called.

Grigore clicked his fingers, and his men brought out Grace and Tamira, both women as they were in the video. Maggie prickled with anger. They might have allowed Grace to change into something warmer and more dignified than her nightgown. One final humiliation before they handed her back.

Maggie had at least let Ivan wash and dress in fresh clothes before they left, to at least save them from inhaling his stench during the journey there.

"I don't suppose you want to tell me who in the Unit has been helping you?" Maggie asked Dalca while they waited to make the exchange. She was sure of it now. There was no other way Dalca and an operation like his could have infiltrated the Unit on their own. Though undoubtedly dangerous and formidable, they didn't have the sophistication to slip past the agency's wall, digital or otherwise.

Ivan glanced at her from the side of his eyes and bared his teeth in a conceited leer. "I would have thought an agent as smart as you seem to think you are would have already figured it out."

"Well, Ivan, I can't say I'm sad to see you go." Her

only regret was that it wasn't in a body bag. Maggie turned her attention back to Grigore. "And the list?"

Grigore slid a small object from his pocket and tucked it into Grace's cleavage.

"How can I be sure that's the only copy?" Maggie asked, instead of shooting Grigore right there on the spot like she should have done.

Ursu simply shrugged. "You have my word."

"That's reassuring," Maggie mumbled, then called back, "Fine. Let's make the trade."

She shoved Ivan in front of her and, not needing to be told twice, he sauntered off like he owned the place. "Farewell, Maggie Black. I'm sure we'll meet again."

"You better hope not," she responded, watching as Grigore's men let the women go. They ran across the grass field, passing Dalca without a second's glance.

Tamira arrived first, and Ashton ushered her behind the car, assuring her she was safe now and everything would be okay.

Grace reached them soon after and handed Maggie the flash drive containing the list of agent names and their case files. "What are you doing, Black?"

"Trust me, Grace. It was for the best. Are you okay? Did they hurt you?"

"We can't bloody well let them walk away," Helmsley said, ignoring Maggie's concerns and very much the Director General, even in a nightgown and bare feet.

It seemed Dalca had similar thoughts.

He arrived at his end of the field and spoke in rapid Romanian, his arms waving wildly in their direction.

Leon reached for his gun and turned the safety off. "That doesn't look good."

Maggie spun and watched as more men spilled from the cars, armed to the hilt with rifles, and charged across the field dressed in all black.

"Kill them all," Dalca yelled.

Chapter 34

Maggie watched and waited as Dalca's men raced toward them, guns at the ready, waiting until they were in range to let loose and send a tirade of bullets through their flesh.

Fifty feet away.

"Mags?" Ashton called.

"Wait," she ordered.

Forty feet.

"Give me a gun," Grace demanded, grim determination setting across her face.

Thirty feet.

"Now!" Maggie ducked and dropped to the ground, pulling Grace down with her.

Leon and Ashton followed suit with Tamira, knowing the drill, and shielded the girl with their bodies.

The second they touched the ground, cracks from

within the trees rattled through the park like claps of thunder.

One by one, the approaching assailants fell backward like they'd been punched by a ghost, crumpling to the grass. Lead slugs sank into their chests with expert precision, making short work of Dalca's shooters before any of them released a single bullet.

The last man standing among them watched as his team went down around him; he tried to run back to the Land Rovers for cover. A bullet zipped over Maggie's head and embedded into the man's back, sending him flying forward to land dead at the feet of Ivan Dalca.

Beyond, red-and-blue beacons flashed into the night, a chorus of sirens wailing in victory, as the cavalry headed their way, having been ready and waiting for the signal to join the assault.

From the woodland behind Maggie, men and women dressed in camouflage gear slid out of the darkness with their guns pointed at the remaining members of Dalca's crew.

The Romanians scrambled and made to escape, diving into their cars and revving the engines as they slammed into reverse. They didn't get six feet before the strike force of Unit agents blew out the tires and left them stranded in the middle of the field with nowhere to run.

Maggie got up from the grass and helped Grace to her feet.

"Not the most orthodox approach, but effective

enough," her old boss said, dusting the dirt from her bare knees with shaking hands, either from the cold or from pent-up adrenaline that no doubt surged through her frail, battered body.

"Everyone good?" Maggie asked, scanning over her small but effective team. Her stomach pulsed under her clothes and she unzipped her jacket. A few dots of red against the white cotton of her T-shirt let her know she'd popped at least a few stitches in her slash wound. All things considered, she'd take it as a win.

Leon helped Tamira to her feet and made sure she was unharmed. At least physically. The girl nodded, and Leon ushered her into the back of the car before walking over to his team of agents to congratulate them on a job well done.

"Here, Grace. Take my jacket," Ashton said, wrapping his coat around Helmsley's shoulders.

"Thank you," said the Director General, pulling it close and admiring the beautiful fabric with appreciative appraisal.

Maggie stared in bewilderment at the jovial exchange, but she didn't have time to marvel at the spectacle. There was still the Romanians to deal with, and Maggie wanted to personally make sure everything went to plan until the very end.

The police officers poured out of their cars with guns pointed and German shepherds barking as they circled the stranded traffickers.

It hadn't been easy to orchestrate, but with the help of Leon and more than a few heated phone calls with the prime minister's staff, they had managed to wrangle the Unit members once again to aid them, along with a fleet of Scotland Yard's finest who now surrounded Dalca and his men.

"What have you done, you bitch?" Ivan cried, getting out of the car and slamming the door shut as Maggie reached their side of the field.

Dalca's men followed suit and got out of the cars, followed by Grigore, whose face had adopted a greenish hue. Seeing your fellow syndicate members turned into swiss cheese will do that to a man. The dead Romanians were splayed between both sides of the fight like a macabre football team that would never kick a ball again.

"I would've thought a man as smart as you seem to think you are would have figured it out by now," Maggie replied, taking great pleasure in mirroring the man's words back at him.

Grigore may have invited a few more friends than they'd agreed to, but so had Maggie. She never trusted the syndicate for one moment to fight fair, so she made sure to play them at their own game. Sometimes to take down the bad guys, you had to think like them, and thankfully, it had paid off.

"Did you really think I was going to let you go?" she asked as Dalca's men were shoved against the cars face-first and handcuffed.

Some of the officers were being extra diligent in their duties and indulging in their right to issue force when their suspects resisted. The batons and pepper spray were a bit much, but Maggie wasn't about to tell the officers off over it. The Romanians had come for a fight, and they were getting one. Grigore tried to punch the officer cuffing him and won a vicious bite to the leg from one of the German shepherds prowling through the mob for signs of trouble.

Dalca screamed in frustration as his entire operation burned to ash before him. He lunged for Maggie but was held back by the officer restraining him.

"This isn't over," he promised, pushing and shoving at the officer so hard, another had to come and help restrain Dalca.

"Yes, it is, Ivan. You played with fire and now you've got to face the consequences." Maggie leaned toward him and reflected the smirk he liked to wear back at him. "I told you I would bring you down that first day in Belmarsh. You should have listened then and called it all off. Now you and your followers will never see the light of day again."

Maggie turned to leave, but Ivan spat out at her. "The list," he said. "You think that was the only copy made?"

Maggie glanced over her shoulder at him, like he was an afterthought. "It doesn't make much difference now.

With you and all your men going down, there'll be no one to leak the list even if you did make copies."

The rage inside Ivan's eyes told Maggie all she needed to know. There were no copies. Sure, it would take the Unit a considerable amount of time, money, and effort to ensure there weren't any loose ends remaining of Ivan's plans. The cleanup jobs over the names that had already leaked to the criminal underworld were just one example of the many messes Maggie was glad she wasn't in charge of overseeing. She'd leave that to Grace and Leon.

"Goodbye, Ivan," Maggie said, and walked away. She'd spent enough of her time on him and refused to give him any more of it.

Leon walked her way from across the field, battered, bruised, and all hers.

She couldn't wait to get home, take a shower, and lie in bed with him all day. They had so much time to make up for, and Maggie intended to make every second they had together count now that they'd accepted they needed each other.

It had been a long time coming, but if she'd learned anything in life, it was that some things were worth waiting for. With the Unit no longer an issue for them, and everything now out in the open, they had the rest of their lives to spend with each other. Maggie couldn't wait for what the future held in store for them.

Leon's face dropped as he approached her and stared over her shoulder. "Maggie, look out!"

Maggie spun on her heels and pulled out her Glock. Behind her, Dalca had fought free from the officers dealing with him and yanked a gun from one of their holsters.

He aimed it at Maggie and fired.

Maggie fired too, releasing three bullets in quick succession.

Dalca fell to his knees, blood oozing from the gunshot wound between his eyes and the two in his chest. His mouth gaped open, and he fell forward flat on his face as he released his final breath.

Maggie lowered her gun, her ears ringing.

Leon called out to her, but he sounded far away. Off in the distance.

Her stomach surged with pain, and she peered down to inspect the cause of the acidic agony that coursed through her body, wondering how many stitches she'd need redoing.

The sight of her bloodied T-shirt confused her, and her hands grew warm and slick as Maggie pressed a palm against the hole that had appeared there from nowhere.

"Maggie," Leon's voice called again, closer this time, but still so far away.

Her mind spun as she watched officers run toward her.

They tilted at an angle, and suddenly they were

upside down, running on the grass like it was a ceiling and somehow managing not to fall into the sky.

"Maggie!"

A hand cupped the back of her head, and a voice called out to her.

Somehow, she'd ended up lying down on the grass.

The stars above watched her and twinkled in the night as a familiar face came into view.

"Leon," she said, her voice wrong and slurred to her swimming ears.

"Maggie, stay with me."

She wanted to laugh, but it stuck in her throat. Where was she going to go? Had he forgotten? They were together now. She wasn't going to leave him.

"Maggie, can you hear me?" he asked, his features blurring. "Help is on the way, just please stay with me. Hold on."

Maggie wanted to reply, but she was suddenly so tired. Her eyelids felt heavy, and the stars blurred into one large light.

The light grew and grew, getting brighter and brighter, until everything went black.

Chapter 35

20 July

Beep. Beep. Beep.

"Did you see that?"

"What?"

"Her hand twitched."

"I think she's waking up."

"I'll get the doctor."

"Her eyes are moving. Maggie, can you hear me?"

Beep. Beep. Beep.

Maggie groaned and stirred where she lay. On something soft. Not comfortable, though. She was too sore to be comfortable.

Beep. Beep. Beep.

"Turn that alarm off," she grumbled. "It's too early."

"It's five in the afternoon," replied a deep voice.

"Aye, and you've been asleep for two days."

She covered her face with an arm, the light too bright against her eyelids. "Just a few more minutes."

"Ah, you're awake," said a new voice.

Maggie pried open one eye at the unfamiliar addition. She may not have recognized it at first, but the face filled in the blanks. "Dr. Rajinder. I wish I could say it was great to see you."

"I get that a lot," the doctor said with the same easy smile she always had. She studied the machines Maggie discovered she was hooked up to. "Everything's looking good, as far as these things go. I expect you'll make a full recovery, though you will need to be patient with the healing time. No action out in the field for a while, I'm afraid."

Maggie had seen enough action to last a lifetime. Dr. Rajinder's presence at least answered the question of where Maggie was. The Unit had their own team of doctors, and Rajinder had been tasked with caring for all of them at one point or another in her tenure.

Given the nature of the injuries, the Unit used a private clinic that was as good at being discreet as they were at patching up bullet wounds. Thankfully.

"Don't worry, Doc," Leon said, sitting by her bedside. "I'll make sure she follows your orders to the letter."

"Nothing a few good whiskies can't fix," Ashton

assured at her other side, with all the confidence of someone with a PhD.

"Not for a while, Mr. Price," Dr. Rajinder chided with an amused beam. "She doesn't need your bad influence right now."

"I'll be on my best behavior," he replied, shooting Maggie a conspiratorial wink.

"Good," Rajinder said. "Maggie, I'll swing by to check on you later, and give the boys time to bring you up to speed."

"Thank you, Sabina," Maggie said, her throat aching from lack of use and a nagging thirst.

Leon held a glass to her chapped lips before she even had time to think of asking. He tipped the glass for her to drink her fill.

"You had us all worried," he said, returning the glass to the bedside table and taking her hand. Bags hung under his bloodshot eyes, the wrinkled shirt and length of his beard telling her he hadn't left her side.

"What happened? Other than the obvious," she said, nodding toward her stomach, which would now have two extra scars. Her body was beginning to resemble a patchwork quilt, having had more stitches than one.

Leon kissed her hand before he started. "Ivan shot you."

"Prick," Ashton muttered.

"But not before you managed to return the favor."

"Legend," Ashton chimed in.

"He's dead."

Ashton cheered like his beloved Glasgow Rangers had just scored a goal.

Leon rolled his eyes with long-suffering patience.

"Sorry," Ashton said, holding up his hands. "I'll leave you two be for a while. I've got to check on Tamira."

"Is she okay?" Maggie inquired, instantly feeling dumb for asking. How could she be? At least they'd managed to save her from it all.

"She will be," Ashton said, leaning down to kiss Maggie's forehead. "Immigration was sniffing around and talking about sending her back to Istanbul, or worse, Iran. To no one's surprise, she didn't fancy it, so I made sure she disappeared. She's in the cafeteria now getting something to eat."

Maggie concealed a smile. She'd teased him about it after everything with Bishop had ended, but Ashton really was playing for the right side these days. If she didn't know any better, she would have gone as far as to say he was quite enjoying it, too. Not that she'd ever say that to him. He'd drive straight into one of his "fixing" jobs and scam some drug lord just to prove a point.

"Where will she go?" Maggie asked instead. The needle in her hand feeding her fluids and what she hoped was a strong painkiller itched like crazy.

Ashton shrugged on his jacket. "She's going to stay with me for a while until she gets on her feet."

Despite seeing her in the videos, Tamira amounted to

a complete stranger, and a damaged one at that. Though none of the said damage was her fault, she would need some intense therapy to get over everything that had happened to her, and even then, it might not be enough. Some temporary ordeals left permanent scars, and this wasn't a case of letting a friend crash at his house for a few days. Ashton was taking on a big responsibility, which was about as foreign to him as Tamira would be to his antics and playboy lifestyle.

"That's incredibly generous of you," Maggie said, meaning it, though she suspected his reasons, whatever they may be, extended beyond kindheartedness.

Ashton's cheeks grew red, and he rubbed the back of his neck. He'd never been good at taking a compliment unless it was on his hair or outfit. Any hint that his soft interior was on display was quickly brushed over and covered with a witty joke or scandalous comment.

"Whatever," her best friend said, inching for the door before things got too real. "Right, I'll see you later. Glad you're not dead and all that."

"Thanks," Maggie said, instantly regretting laughing. She'd been shot before, and even the slightest sudden movement made it feel like the bullet was still trapped inside.

"I thought I'd lost you," Leon said once he'd left, sobering her mood.

"You're not getting rid of me that easy," Maggie assured him, her heart swelling in her chest. She'd never loved anyone the way she loved Leon, and his display of emotion made her feel more wanted than she ever had.

"I don't know what I would have done if anything—"

"Well, it didn't," she interrupted, not wanting to see him sad anymore. Not when they had so much to be thankful for. "So, you don't need to think on it. I'll survive, though you might need to be my nurse for a while."

Leon brightened and gave her that carnal look like he wanted to devour her there and then, even in her hospital gown with a mop of unwashed hair. "Only if that includes giving you sponge baths."

Maggie pretended to consider it. "I'll allow it."

"It feels different this time, doesn't it?"

"It does," Maggie said, her eyes welling up. "You're still sure about us being together?"

Leon leaned his forehead gently against hers, so close she could smell the spearmint from the gum he'd been chewing at some point. Her heart fluttered under his intense gaze, eyes so close she could see into his soul. He brushed his lips across hers, then whispered, "I've never been surer of anything in my life."

Maggie pulled him closer and kissed him with everything she had, ignoring the aches the movement caused. None of that mattered. Being so close to dying, she wanted to feel alive. To taste him and show him just how much he meant to her. She put everything she wanted to say to him behind the kiss. Her love. Her trust. Her devotion.

Her hopes and dreams for their future together. A future she never thought possible, and one she would fight for to ensure it came to pass.

Someone cleared their throat, announcing they were no longer alone.

Maggie reluctantly let her lover go, and he straightened once he saw who was paying a visit.

"Ma'am," Leon said, getting up and offering Grace his chair.

"I'd like a word," she said to Maggie, then turned to Leon. "Alone, if you don't mind."

"I won't be far," Leon assured her, kissing her one last time before leaving the women alone.

"He's smitten," Grace commented as she watched him leave, seeming displeased with the fact. "I hope this rekindled romance doesn't impact his work. As you can imagine, we're rather busy at the moment."

"I bet," Maggie said, wincing as she pulled herself into a sitting position, the built-in respect for her superiors having not entirely left her yet.

Grace had recovered well. Other than a few hints of darkened spots under her makeup, she was back to her old self. Her severe bob cut with not a hair out of place. An immaculate royal-blue power suit. She removed her outer jacket and, like always, got straight to the point.

"I want to thank you for everything you've done for

my agents and me. You did what I couldn't, and because of you, my people can sleep easy knowing they and their families are no longer under threat. As can I."

"It was a team effort," Maggie replied. "We each had a role to play in taking Ivan down."

She could never have done it alone. Without Leon, Ashton, Tamira—heck, even Grace herself—Maggie would have failed, and all of them would have suffered the consequences.

"I'm glad he didn't take you down with him," Grace said, in a moment of candor Maggie didn't expect.

"Me, too," she replied, unable to think of anything else to say.

Grace cleared her throat again and looked around the room. Someone had gotten Maggie flowers, and they sat on the television in the corner by the window to soak in the summer sun, which had decided to show its face.

Maggie grinned. The Director General had never been good at small talk. "Spit it out, Grace. What is it?"

True to form, she did. "How would you feel about returning to the fold?"

Maggie frowned. "Why? Do you miss me?"

"You were one of my best assets," Grace said with a glare, never one to dish out compliments when a reprimand was available. "I'd be a fool not to try to recruit you back."

"The agent in me is flattered to hear that from someone like you," Maggie responded, uncomfortable at the swell of pride Grace's words stirred within her. Her old boss's opinion of her shouldn't matter to her anymore.

Grace shrugged. "Facts are facts."

Maggie waited before she spoke, looking for the right words.

"I'd be lying if I said I wasn't tempted, but too much has happened. I'm not the same person I was before. After everything that's happened, I want a new start. I *need* a new start."

Helmsley nodded in understanding, like she'd expected that answer but thought she would try anyway. "If I can't have you back, at least promise me you won't talk Leon into following suit. I can't lose both my best agents in one year. Thanks to Ivan Dalca, I have a severe shortage of staff, and I can't simply ring up a recruitment office for replacements."

"I don't think you need to worry about Leon going anywhere," Maggie said. While she had turned her back on the agent life, she didn't expect Leon to do the same, nor would she ever try to change his mind. He still believed in the good the Unit could do, and she knew he needed to believe that now more than ever.

"Very good." Grace stood and hung her jacket over her arm. "And thanks again, Agent Black. I mean, thanks again, Maggie. I hope this is the last time you and I have to work together."

Maggie laughed again and bit back a cry of pain that

came with it. She understood what Grace meant, even if her choice of words weren't the most tactful.

The Director General said her goodbyes and left, but her words from before stayed with Maggie as she laid there alone.

You never really leave this kind of life once you decide to live it.

While Maggie hated to admit it, Grace was right. The situation with Ivan Dalca only made it clearer for her. Maggie would be wasted if she were to get a nine-to-five job. Not to mention mind-numbingly bored. The idea of gossiping around a watercooler or heading out to teambuilding weekends made her want to vomit.

She wasn't cut out for a normal life. Never had been, even before she chose the life of an agent.

Not many people were capable of doing what she could, and to throw it all away would not only feel like she was tossing aside a huge part of what made her Maggie, but she'd be doing a disservice to those who needed help. To those who couldn't fight back and were desperate for aid. Like Tamira and the other girls she'd saved from the syndicate. There were so many people like them in the world, something she'd witnessed first-hand for most of her life.

There were so many people like Ivan Dalca out there, too. People like Samuel Thomas, and Brice Bishop, people who wielded power like a weapon and used it against those who didn't have any. She had the ability to stop them, just as she had been doing for over a decade now.

The idea had stirred in the back of her head, though Maggie hadn't allowed herself to consider it as anything but a fleeting whim, until now. She needed to check with Ashton and see if he would be interested, but from the changes she'd seen in him over the last year, she thought she'd know his answer.

Maggie may not want to be a part of the Unit anymore, but that didn't mean she couldn't still help people. On her own terms. With her own rules and moral compass. Under her own agency.

Just as Dalca's syndicate had created a hit list of agents, Maggie could create one of her own. A hit list filled with the names of the worst abusers of power she could find, and one by one, she would take them down. There were plenty of them out there, more than enough to keep her busy. More than she could ever take down on her own ...

Maggie grinned. They had no idea what was coming their way.

After she recovered from being shot, that is.

Leon returned, and she eventually managed to talk him into going home for some sleep and to change out of his old clothes. She slept most of the time while he was away, the morphine lulling her into a dreamless slumber and keeping the worst of the pain away.

"Oh, sorry," said a nurse as she entered the room. "I didn't mean to wake you, but these were just delivered for you. Aren't they beautiful?"

The nurse placed the gorgeous bouquet onto the table wheeled across Maggie's bed.

"Thanks," Maggie said, drifting off.

"Aren't you going to see who they're from? I bet it's that handsome man of yours. He's ever so nice."

When it became clear the nurse wasn't leaving without finding out who had sent such an expensive array of white roses and lilies, Maggie forced herself up and picked out the handwritten note.

Dear Maggie,

I heard you killed that idiot Ivan. I should never have entrusted him and his men with the list. You know what they say: "Never use a man to do a woman's job."

I'll see you very soon. Promise.

xoxo Nina

NEVER MISS A RELEASE!

Thank you so much for reading Hit List. I hope you enjoyed it!

I have so much more coming your way. Never miss a release by joining my free VIP club. You'll receive all the latest updates on my upcoming books as well as gain access to exclusive content and giveaways!

To sign up visit

www.jackmcsporran.com/vendettasignup

Thank you for reading HIT LIST! If you enjoyed the book, I would greatly appreciate it if you could consider adding a review on your bookstore of choice.

Reviews make a huge difference to the success or failure of a book, especially for newer writers like myself. The more reviews a book has, the more people are likely to take a shot on picking it up. The review need only be a line or two, and it really would make the world of difference for me if you could spare the three minutes it takes to leave one.

With all my thanks,

Jack McSporran

Made in the USA
San Bernardino, CA
30 March 2019